DEATH OR WORSE

PF LEGGE

First published by Southlands Publishing 2020
Copyright © 2020 by PF Legge
All rights reserved. No part of this publication may be reproduced, stored or transmitted in any form or by any means, electronic, mechanical, photocopying, recording, scanning, or otherwise without written permission from the publisher. It is illegal to copy this book, post it to a website, or distribute it by any other means without permission.
This novel is entirely a work of fiction. The names, characters and incidents portrayed in it are the work of the author's imagination. Any resemblance to actual persons, living or dead, events or localities is entirely coincidental.
PF Legge asserts the moral right to be identified as the author of this work.
Designations used by companies to distinguish their products are often claimed as trademarks. All brand names and product names used in this book and on its cover are trade names, service marks, trademarks and registered trademarks of their respective owners. The publishers and the book are not associated with any product or vendor mentioned in this book. None of the companies referenced within the book have endorsed the book.
First edition

PREFACE

It seems as if this novel has been years in the making as it is the the third of a trilogy that has taken up a great deal of my life over the last four years. The main characters, Conor and Gray, have of course changed over the course of the story but the issue facing them has remained the same; what to do in times of peril. Their previous exploits, chronicled in the first two books, "Almost a Myth" and "Slaughter by Strange Means" are recounted only in part and could be seen as preparation for the conflict portrayed in this book (but not exactly).

This novel, like the others, also explores the themes of friendship, loyalty and the courage to persist in in the face of overwhelming odds. Ultimately, Conor and Gray struggle on, believing in the goodness of life often in the face of convincing evidence that their efforts might mean little in the end.

Unlike many fantasy novels once again the main characters fight almost completely in the dark about the structure of the 'grand plan' or even if there is one for them to follow. So, they rely on each other more than they have ever done. The powers of their opponents befuddle them and other people disappoint as often as they inspire. But they still fight on.

Conor and Gray are hopefully fully drawn, three dimensional beings despite the fantastic setting and their mythical size and strength. They succeed and they fail, like us. Their adventures have been my pleasure to impart. I know I will miss them.

ACKNOWLEDGEMENT

Thank you to those who have helped me, both near and far, Matt R especially. I could not have done this without your measured, eloquent and consistent interest. And my wife Kelly who never stops supporting me, our daughter Amy who designed the cover and helps with the website and social media and our sons Tom and Ben who listen when I want to talk about the work. Thanks CB and Pat and all of my large and caring family. And Cindy my editor. Thank you!

Sharp, the sword and teeth that defend us
Hard, the shield and bone
Strong, the hearts of the Lord and his Hound
For the road they must walk, alone
Traditional Eliti Song

"You think you choose your gods?"
The Other to Conor a few days ago

CONTENTS

CH 1 HUNTERS 1

CH 2 MORE IS BETTER 16

CH 3 WASTED LIFE 26

CH 4 LADY DAREEN 34

CH 5 REFUGEES 60

CH 6 ON THE RUN 72

CH 7 SEE FOR YOURSELF 87

CH 8 D'AEL 101

CH 9 A VOICE OF IRON 114

CH 10 LIKE A GOD 123

CH 11 BIGGER 134

CH 12 WAR 151

CH 13 A MIGHTY FEAT 182

CH 14 NISI 198

CH 15 THE FALL	207
CH 16 WORLD OF STONE	211
CH 17 DEATH OR WORSE	217
CH 18 ENDURE	232
CH 19 LIGHT	246
CH 20 BAD DEAL	251
CH 21 A BETTER STRANGE	256
CH 22 THE STORY	263
CH 23 FALSE FAREWELLS	269
CH 24 LEAVING	282
EPILOGUE	289

CH 1
HUNTERS

Conor rolled restlessly in his sleep. The vivid dreams were with him again. Not like before, when the Other had spoken to him directly, or even as the awful apparition that was the Believer had tried to. Their threats of death and unending chaos were very different from this. It was like he was seeing a murder through shifting dark smoke. He tried to make sense of it, but the movements he could see through the murk were blurry and awkward. The murderers leaned over their victims, unnaturally tall and thin. Their sharp movements didn't seem human, somehow. Something was fundamentally wrong. He felt loss and dislocation. He had the sense that life itself was coming to a grinding, juddering halt.

Conor woke with a jerk in a cold sweat. His head ached and he was sore and tired. He raised himself up and looked around. Gray was a massive furry black bulk beside him. Eromil, the Chan warrior, wasn't too far away from him. On the other side of the fire, Arusin, Pranti and Melnis, the Eliti soldiers, survivors of the hunters' attack, hadn't moved. Conor could see his own breath. He

HUNTERS

pulled the thick Eliti cloak around himself and lay back down. It was cold but not painfully so; winter was coming to an end. The stars flickered through the trees. He slid a hand out from under the cloak and put a log on the embers. The fire flared up, and he saw a flash and felt the heat on his face. Ignoring the memory of the bright blue flame made by the hunters' spears and the pain in his right arm from hacking their strange hard bodies into pieces, he dozed off.

Gray nosed him awake. The sun was up and everyone in his little army was moving. *Let's get going.* Gray was impatient.

Okay. Okay.

They ate, packed, and started walking away from the devastated battlefield and the graves of the men killed by the hunters. And, Conor thought, hopefully towards what was left of the army of the Eliton Empire in the Southlands. If it was still here, it would be marching somewhere along the wide hard road that ran down the middle of the Southlands like the spine of a fish. Built long ago, eerily impervious to weather and time, it was the only path a large force could take before it headed west to the Empire. It was a place to for them to start looking, at least. Gray moved out in front, flitting in and out of the trees, his huge black shadow outlined briefly against the grey bark and the white snow.

Conor was at the rear of the column. The other four soldiers walked slowly, their shoulders hunched against the cold. The destruction of their armies by what could only be described as forces of nature had stupefied

HUNTERS

them. The hunters' attack had silenced them. Yet when they had found them, Conor and Gray had fought and killed the terrifying hunters as other men died like cattle in a slaughterhouse. What Conor and Gray had done was beyond human. So these soldiers followed him and did whatever he asked, despite the fact that they were Chan and Eliti and he was not, and they had not known him until two days ago.

The forest they walked in thinned out two days later. The thaw had begun, and the snow melt made the ground slippery and wet. They were all tired. The afternoon sun shone weakly through thin clouds. The group came to a shallow but swiftly running river, iced over only in places along its edges. The Stoney, Conor thought it was called. *Typical Southlander practicality*, he thought, *the Stoney River*. It was very cold. They speared a few fish there, or at least Eromil did. On the far bank they stopped, made a fire, and ate. Gray had his meal raw and then scouted ahead while the rest of them made camp on the sandy shore.

Later, Conor stood and looked at the rippling water while the others slept. The sound of the river moving over the stones was reassuring—some things stayed true to their nature. Even in his darkest hours, he had come back to the experience of the natural world as being fundamentally true and good. His feet were on this ground. His heart was beating strongly, and he was breathing this air. Nothing could make this wrong. Not the Believer or its successor, the Other, despite their terrible powers. They could alter matter, create monsters out of dirt, snow, and rock, make people their slaves, and bring the hunters—murderers from another world—to kill and burn. Conor sensed that everything he was experiencing right now: air, water, and wood, was under threat. But he was there to defend it. He remembered that the holy book of Eliton said that men like him, and Hounds like Gray, were created, planted somehow, seeds sown by the Lords of Power to arise in the time of need and defend the world and everything in it.

Conor thought, *If that is so, then the Other will reap a bitter harvest.*

How poetic. "Bitter harvest."

Gray had appeared. Conor had not heard him arrive, but their link had been reestablished. Gray's words were cryptic and pointed, as usual.

It just came to me. Bitter harvest.

Next thing you know, you'll be writing it all down. Like a bar scribe at the fights.

Hardly.

Conor looked at his right hand. He could not remember the last time he had written anything. He had been a fighter, a lawman, a soldier, even a general. He did his business with fists, swords, words, and a handshake at best. But writing? No. Not since his days in the war academy as a young man, when he was tasked to compose letters to imaginary kings about how he had won this battle or how he planned to win that one. The military libraries made of white stone, safe and warm, seemed impossibly civilized here in the wet cold wilderness.

HUNTERS

I don't know if I still could write. Conor smiled slightly. *Even if I wanted to.*
Don't know why you would. No need. Really.
Conor sighed. *No.*
The river ran on in front of them, clear and fast. If he remembered correctly, the Stoney ran east to west before it turned south to flow down to the Near Sea. They could walk along its edge and still make their way to the main north-south road. Conor knew he had to be careful with his little army, and it seemed safer to follow the river than wander in the forest. Then again, maybe he just liked the sound. He and Gray walked in circles around the camp for a few moments and then settled in beside the fire and slept like the others.

In the morning, they walked east along wide sandy banks. In the early afternoon the river narrowed and the easy path gave way to steep cliffs. The water cut deep into the rock and earth and they soon ran out of room to walk beside it. The scramble up to the top of the bank was slow and painful. They were all still recovering from the hunters' attack, and the cold and damp made their joints stiff and their hands clumsy.

Gray went up the stones like a mountain goat. He looked down on them and said, *Come on, come on.*

Of course, only Conor heard him. Only he had the link of mind and mission with the great grey-black wolf bear that was Gray. The men from the Empire knew the myth of the Lord and his Hound but no one could know how deep the connection between the two was unless they felt it themselves—which they could not. Conor and Gray were two who lived, thought, and fought as one.

Conor was second to the top of the steep bank. He helped the others, offering a hand to each of them in turn. Eromil glowered at him, but the edge was overhung and she could not lever herself over without something to hold on to. Conor offered his hand and she took it. They found themselves again walking in a sparse forest full of spindly black trees. A path ran alongside the river. Gray sniffed at it, ran forward a few steps and then looked back.

Deer run. Men have used it, but not for many days.

Alright. Lead on.

They moved slowly along the river. They saw no one, although at the end of the second day, close to dusk, they saw bodies float by them in the swift-flowing water. Gray saw them first and told Conor. The column stopped and watched silently as the slick black shapes rolled and slid over the rocks and disappeared downstream.

Eliti or Chan?

Can't tell. Too dark.

Not that it matters. Dead is dead. They can't help us or tell us anything. Gray was very practical.

Knowing how they died might help.

Yeah, maybe. But I'm not going in that river. And Gray was as ruthlessly predisposed to self-preservation as every predator.

I get that.

The river veered north the next day. They crossed in a brief freezing dash and set up camp on the other side. They stripped down and hung their wet clothes to dry.

HUNTERS

The men cast furtive glances at Eromil's luminous pale figure. She had spent years fighting with male soldiers in the army of the Chan Consolidation, so she wasn't shy. She was, in her words, "a war wife of the god, Shenzi." The Eliti, though ruled by the powerful Mothers, had no women warriors. Her ease with her nakedness and her sword had shocked them, at first anyway. But she was strong, just as determined as they were, and had bitched enough about the weather and the food to be considered regular infantry like them.

The hunting had been good, so they weren't hungry. They cooked and ate what Gray brought them and then slept. Gray scouted at dusk like he always did. Conor waited for him at the edge of the circle of light thrown by the flames. When Gray returned, they spoke.

So?

No armies. Although there was a fight not too far from here, probably a week ago. Eliti and Chan dead. No sign of damage to the ground or trees, though.

No Other, then. Conor sighed in relief. *A regular skirmish in a big war.*

Looks like.

How many dead?

Gray did the mental equivalent of a shrug. *Twenty or thirty. Mostly Chan.*

We'll go around. No need to see that.

No.

Did you get to the road?

No.

It can't be far. I'm sure we'll reach it in a day or two.

HUNTERS

Then what?
Look for the Eliti. Maybe they know something.
Maybe. Gray sounded doubtful.
Their holy book...
Yeah, yeah. You read it and we're in there. I'm not disagreeing with you. Let's leave it. In the morning then?
Bright and early... w ell, early anyway. N ot much in the way of bright these days.
No. Does that matter?
No. No it doesn't. I'll take the first watch.
Ok.

Gray wandered towards the fire, took a few steps away from the sleeping group, and settled down. Conor had set watches when they got closer to the road. The Eliti and Chan had fought over control of the road repeatedly. It was the spine of the Southlands and it was bound to attract armies in war. Even with Gray's scouting, he didn't want to be surprised. And the Chan liked to fight after the sun had set.

The night passed. Eromil muttered and rolled around in her sleep (as usual) but none of the men complained. One of them, Melnis, had made an attempt to "soothe" her one night. He lost part of two fingers from a blade she kept tucked underneath her. After that, Eromil mumbled and thrashed in peace.

Gray had the last watch, just before dawn. He awakened just as the sun began to show its pale light above the trees. He usually scouted before the rest got up, and again before they slept. It was his nature and it made them all feel more secure. Gray's massive frame, intelligent golden

HUNTERS

eyes, and sharp teeth helped, as well. The troop knew he was an animal, but with his powerful link to Conor and his size and strength, he seemed more. He seemed invincible.

The sky was grey and low with clouds when they got moving again. Gray led them around the scene of the skirmish. It was an obvious and difficult detour through thick brush but Eromil and the men followed silently, trusting, believing in Conor and Gray. If they wanted to follow this path, then there was a good reason for it. They stopped to eat in the middle of the day and Gray forged ahead. Conor had given his tired troop a little longer than usual to eat and rest. He was starting to get almost comfortable when he felt alarm and a feeling close to panic. He leaped up and his hand went to his sword. Gray did not panic, ever. But this felt close.

Gray! Conor reached out. Their connection needed proximity and Gray was at the limit of their range.

Yes. I'm coming.

Do we need to...?

Yes. Get ready to move. But it's not an attack. Just wait. Almost there.

Fear grew in the expressions of the others as they saw Conor gearing up. The thought of more hunters had them terrified, Lord and his Hound or not. Gray burst into the clearing, breathing hard. Conor was confused. He sensed they were in no immediate danger, but also that Gray was disturbed in a way he hadn't been in a long time.

What is it?

I'm not sure.

HUNTERS

That unnerved Conor. Gray was never unsure. Even when they had seen the Believer's monster made of stone moving slowly in the twilight outside the walls of Dece, Gray had not been conflicted. He had wanted to run then, far and fast. This time though…he waited. Gray was panting, his body an immense black heaving muscular forge blasting steam into the cold air. Conor waited a moment and then said out loud, "Show me."

Gray looked at him closely. Conor felt a strange absence of feeling. Conor tilted his head slightly at the clearly frightened group of soldiers behind him. Then he felt agreement.

Let's go.

And Gray started back through into the forest.

"Wait here," Conor said to the others.

He saw that they were desperate to stay with him but scared to death of what he was going to see. *Strange, how much one look can sometimes tell you,* Conor thought. He put both his hands out, palms down in a gesture to calm them. "I'll be right back," he said, and he turned and went after Gray.

After a brief run down a well-worn path, what Conor saw over Gray's broad back and through the woods that lined the main north-south road confused him at first. It was a large building of some kind. A castle or a fortress. It sat right on the road, though, which made no sense. No one built in the middle of a road ten strides across. It… and then Conor noticed it was moving somehow, up and down and along its surface. It rippled and shimmered in grey and white waves. And it was crushing the road it sat on. They could hear the bricks cracking and groaning.

What the fuck are we looking at?

Look closer. It's the hunters.

Alarm urged through Conor. *Where?*

The hunters were brought to this world by the Other, "from a place with a dark sun"—or so he had said to Conor. Murderous, tall, tubular things that killed with flashing spears and burned men with actinic blue flame.

Where?!

I think the whole thing is hunters.

Then Conor saw. They surrounded the castle but also blended into it. They were coming and going by being shifted in and out of the structure. Like grey logs perpendicular to the ground walking into a walled fortress with no doors. Except once in the building they kept moving, sideways, then upwards, then sideways again, shifting and vibrating until they were impossible to distinguish from each other. Conor was dumbfounded. They stood in silence for a long moment, watching the living castle shiver and move.

How many? How many do you think?

It had taken Conor and Gray to the limit of their strength to kill maybe a dozen or so of these hunters a few days ago.

Thousands. Maybe tens of thousands, if that thing is solid. If there are no rooms inside, I mean. Just them.

The structure was pulsing upward and outward in strange rhythms. Light twisted along its outline and the earth moaned beneath it. Gray's instincts returned.

HUNTERS

Run?

No. Not yet anyway. Conor ran his hand over his face. *Are they coming or going or just…?*

Conor was confused and filled with a sick sense of dread. Gray closed his eyes, shook his massive head vigorously, opened them and tried to re-focus to see what was happening in front of them.

They both saw rows and rows of the almost absurdly tall and tubular hunters. He saw their spears held upright, flashing and sparking as they moved forward, shuffling and sidling into the structure as they did. But others were appearing as some disappeared or were absorbed.

Are there more? Is this army growing?

They were both asking each other the same thing. Closing his eyes, Conor tried to imagine the exact size of the thing in his mind, when he first came upon it. Then he opened his eyes and tried to compare.

It might be bigger. Maybe.

Does it matter? They are here and there are too many of them already.

Yes, but if it's a…a nest, then with the help of the Eliti and the Chan we might be able to deal with them. Conor paused and then made eye contact with Gray. *But if it's an infestation, and they are getting in somehow, more and more of them…then it's too late for us. It's too late for everybody. If the Other has opened a door to one of the other worlds I read about in the Eliti books… and left it open…*

Conor and Gray looked at the terrible scene.

HUNTERS

How could anyone deal with this? This is so much more than monsters made of stone or armies of fanatics. What are we supposed to do?

Run? Gray asked again.

No.

Gray felt Conor's mind turning. He felt that familiar stubborn pull to fight. To confront the hunters. Here. Now.

You can't be serious. There are too many.

Conor's hand went to his sword.

There are never going to be fewer.

Conor felt loose; his head was clearing. It was the siege at Castle White, it was the battle on the road when he had killed the Believer, it was the fight with the snow monsters at Oro. It was his time. Conor was calm and fatalistic. He knew that to fight was to die. But he was ready.

These things have to be...stopped.

Gray moved in front of him, dangerously close to being in full view of the hunters, if they bothered to look.

No, Conor. No. There has to be another way. You can lead us to an Eliti army.

Conor started to go around him.

There may not be an Eliti army at all.

Not in the Southlands, no. But there is still an Empire. There are at least two armies there. The People will fight; you know they will.

The People, as they called themselves, were the tribes warring against the Eliton Empire. They had flocked to

HUNTERS

Conor when he had called for war against the Believer, the Other's cruel and powerful predecessor.

Gray continued, *The Chan, the Consolidation will...*

They threw us out. They threw me out.

Conor and Gray had tried to involve the Chan in their war against the Other, but they wanted only to continue fighting the Empire. Conor was right, but Gray could sense that at least he was listening. Still prepared to fight, but the almost suicidal urge was receding. His sword slid slightly downward into its sheath. Gray kept talking to him.

That was before. Before the Other massacred two armies in the field near Oro. Before the hunters came.

Conor's gaze left the hunters and met Gray's. *So what do we do now?*

Gray spoke calmly and firmly. *We go around. And we keep looking for allies, Eliti and Chan. And any other people we find. We need them.*

Conor's hand left his sword. Gray let out a sigh of relief as it did.

And they need us.

Yes. Yes, they do.

When they got back to the clearing, Eromil was in front of the others. Her sword was out, and she was standing feet apart and chin up right in the middle of the path.

"Is it them?" she asked. "Is it the hunters?"

"Yes," Conor saw no need to lie. "But they are busy, and we can go around."

"Busy? Busy doing what?" Arusin asked.

HUNTERS

He stepped out from behind Eromil. He was the oldest soldier in their little army. His beard was thick and grey. His hands were big, red, and corded with tendons as they gripped his spear.

"Burning men?"

"No…" Conor stopped, unable to describe what he had just seen.

"They are…meeting. They didn't see us. We go around. Get ready."

Gray found a narrow path that led them south, away from the hunters, following the road along its west side, but not too closely. It was hard going at times, but they stayed on it until the sun had begun to set. Then they turned east again, and in a few moments, they scurried across the wide north-south road just as the sun went down.

Conor and Gray had waited on the side of the road until the others crossed. Their footsteps seemed loud in the cold silence. They stopped in the middle and looked north. The sky gave nothing away, but Conor and Gray both felt the bricks underneath their feet shake. They looked at each other.

Can you feel that?

Yes, I can.

Shit.

Yeah. Let's go.

And they ran off the road and caught up with the others.

CH 2
MORE IS BETTER

Early the next morning while out scouting, Gray was surprised by a large group of Northerners, men from the territories beyond the great desert. They saw him first, across a grassy valley that was covered in patchy snow. The wind was blowing hard away from Gray and had masked their smell and sound. When he saw them, they were stopped and staring at him in a line in front of a stand of trees.

What the fuck are they doing here?

The Northerners were a long way from home. Few people who weren't in the uniforms of the Chan or Eliti armies did much travelling in the Southlands since the war with the Bonded. Conor and Gray knew what Northerners were like only through the fights held across the known world. Northern fighters were usually big, hairy men who were very tough, so the promoters in the Southlands and the fighting houses in the Empire valued them. They had long hair tied in back and long beards tied in front. Most, but not all were light skinned and haired.

MORE IS BETTER

They were dressed in leather and armour. They carried swords, shields, and war hammers.

All business.

Gray took a long look to make sure they knew he had seen them.

As he turned to go back to tell Conor what he had seen, Gray noticed movement. He stopped and looked back. One Northerner, a big man in the middle of the line, had his right hand up over his head, palm towards him, his fingers stretched wide.

Curious. But Gray nodded his massive head once and ran back to the camp.

Conor was up and waiting as he had sensed Gray's surprise encounter with the armed men.

Northerners. A group of well-armed Northerners. Not too far up the path.

Northerners? Here? What the fuck are they doing here?

My thoughts exactly.

Did they see you?

Yes. And they tried to, I think, let me know that they weren't a threat.

Conor was puzzled. *How could you tell?*

Well, one of them waved at me.

He waved at you.

Yeah. Like he, I don't know, recognized me.

He recognized you?

Gray rolled his eyes. *Let's go.*

To meet them?

Of course. Let's go.

How many of them are there?

MORE IS BETTER

Probably fifty or so.
We are six.

Conor raised his eyebrows and gestured at the nervous group behind him. They were watching and knew something was up, and if their recent experience was any guide, it wasn't going to be good.

We aren't going to fight. We need them. They are people. Not Eliti or Chan but still people who might fight. You'll talk to them, say something profound and win them over. So let's go.

Right.

Conor turned to Arusin, Eromil, Pranti, and Melnis and told them that there was a group of men up the trail and that he and Gray were going to take a look. The Eliti were panicked at the thought of being alone in the forest again.

Eromil's eyes narrowed. "Why can't we come with you?"

Conor ran his right hand through his hair. "We want to talk to these guys, and we don't want to worry about rescuing you if it goes bad."

Eromil bristled at that. "Rescue me? Me?"

"Yes," Conor said bluntly. "You. And them." He pointed to the Eliti soldiers behind here. "Just stay here. We won't be long."

She muttered something under her breath about being a war wife, but she didn't follow them when they went back up the path towards the Northerners. The others stood silently and watched them go.

Kind of strange how out of it those Eliti are. Gray made the comment as he trotted up the path ahead of Conor.

MORE IS BETTER

They've been through a lot. Maybe more than any soldiers ever.
Except us. We've been through more.
Yes. But we're special. Give them some time.

They soon came out of the forest and on to the edge of the valley that separated them from the Northerners.

We'll wait here. See what they do.

The Northerners were standing around, looking like they were also trying to decide what came next. When one of them noticed Conor and Gray he pointed to them, said something, and the men spread out in a long line. There was a moment of stillness and then the wind came up. The trees rustled and the men stood still. Their braided beards fluttered on their chests. Conor and Gray waited. Then one of them put his right hand up, palm out, fingers spread wide. Conor did the same, and after a moment or two, started across the open ground. Gray followed.

Do you speak…Northern?
Enough. Hopefully one of them speaks Southlander or Eliti.

Four of the Northerners were coming towards them. As they got closer, Conor saw that the man who had signalled to them was deeply scarred down his face. An angry red line crossed one eye and disfigured his mouth. One had an ear missing, another, an obviously broken nose.

Hard looking bunch.
We need hard. Hard is good.
Yeah.

They stopped a few steps apart. The Northerners saw an enormous black wolf bear with intelligent golden eyes and sharp visible teeth beside a very large, intensely muscled, dark- skinned man with brown eyes, a strong jaw line and a straight brow. They moved almost as one, light footed, yet powerful and sure.

The scarred N ortherner spoke first in clear tones. "I am Dvor, son of Dvak. And these are my sister sons."

"Hello. I am Conor. This is my Hound, Gray."

Before Conor could say anything else, the Northerners bowed as one, slightly and from the waist. Their eyes did not leave him, though. Then they waited. One moment stretched out into more.

Weird.

Yeah.

The Northerners stood, waiting for Conor to say something that fit into what was, he was starting to realize, for them a ritual encounter. He probably should introduce his lineage, he thought, then decided it didn't matter.

"What the hell are you guys doing way down here?" Conor asked.

That confused them. They all looked at the leader, who was red-faced and almost embarrassed. He spoke in mannered tones, as if Conor should have known his part and now, he, Dvor, had to cover for him. "We came south, across the great wide. We seek the demon Itax, the Traitor. We have seen evidence of his war. He is here?"

This was something he had said many times, thought Conor.

Does he mean the Believer? The Bonded armies?

MORE IS BETTER

I'm not sure. They started in the north. Maybe that's what they called him up there. Ask him.

"Do you mean the Believer and his Bonded armies?"

Dvor looked puzzled for a moment then his eyes narrowed and widened. "Ah. Yes, yes. The demon Itax, he was called the Believer in this place. We seek him. We are called to war."

They are a little late to that party.

Yes. But they might be here in time for the next one.

Conor said, "Dvor, son of Dvak, I, we, fought and killed the Believer."

"What? Really? Are you sure?" Dvor blurted out, the formalities forgotten.

"Uh, well, yes and no...you see..." Conor hesitated.

Oh, do go on.

"Itax is treacherous and powerful," Dvor said, trying to encourage Conor to continue. "This we know."

"He was...I cut him down," Conor said. "And his armour, silver black and sightless, fell—but he wasn't there."

Another hesitation as he remembered the dreadful scene and then he continued, "And the sky opened, like a crack and light came in colours I have never seen..."

"A formless evil. The Traitor." Dvor nodded and up and down the line, others did the same. "And his slaves fight like madmen. We killed so many and yet they would not stop. How did you...?"

"At great cost," Conor said with a sigh, recalling the fiery death of his friend Tingish and the brutal murder of

MORE IS BETTER

his love Andaine in that last battle on the road. Dvor put his hand on his heart in respect.

They met him and didn't give in. Our kind of people.

Yeah, a different story with the same characters.

They seemed to know me back in the forest, but no talk of Lord and Hound.

Perhaps they have heard of us but we aren't the focus of their legends, or their fight with the Other.

That is alright with me.

Me too.

Conor spoke again. "But he has returned, and he is stronger, more, somehow…"

Conor had fought monsters made of snow and mud and Eromil had described strange sounds and hammers made of thickened air that had destroyed both Chan and Eliti formations. He thought of the carnage they had come across in the forest just a few days ago. Two armies, mashed, burned, attacked by forces beyond human understanding. Then they had witnessed over a hundred surviving Chan warriors killed in one swift, crushing blow. Then the bodies burned with a bright blue flame that came from nowhere.

Gray was thinking of the same scenes. *If we were honest, we would tell these guys to run back up north and hide in their high places.*

There is that. But we need them and they want to fight.

They both thought of the masses of dead soldiers. And the unasked question, what could these guys do?

They are people and we need people. And if anyone can keep them alive in this awful mess, it's us.

MORE IS BETTER

Could be the other way around, you know. We could get them killed a lot quicker.

I'm aware. But more is better. It's going to matter what we do; I know it. And we will need help.

Conor was trying to be hopeful. He remembered that many of the men and women he had led into battle against the Believer—and now the Other or the Traitor or whatever it was—had died. It had saddened and changed him. Some he had liked; one he had loved. But it did not change what he knew was his mission. And Gray's. That was to fight and save whatever was left of the world when it was over.

"I lead a small force of Eliti and Chan warriors," Conor said abruptly. "We fight the Other. We seek the Eliti to help understand our enemy. Many strange things are happening, and their holy book describes some of it."

Dvor looked skeptical. "Our holy ones knew of the Traitor, but that did not help defeat him. Their prayers were thin protection. His power was beyond their understanding. What makes you believe the Eliti can do more?"

Conor answered slowly. "I don't know for sure. But the stories I have read in their holy book…" he paused, "they explain things in a way that fits what we have seen, who we are, and what we have done. There is power in that."

Dvor said nothing. A moment passed. The wind blew and rattled the branches and stiff black leaves in the trees behind him and his hard-faced sister sons.

MORE IS BETTER

Conor spoke again; this time his voice loud and firm. "I have met this Traitor. He tried to frighten me and then sent monsters to kill us. Yet we are here. Will you stand with us?"

Dvor said nothing, he just stood there, looking tough. They all did.

Should we walk them over to the hunters? That might help them make up their minds.

Not a bad idea. But a group this large might get us noticed.

Yeah. Not ready for that.

No.

Dvor turned away from Conor and Gray. The men leaned in and spoke in low tones for a few moments. Then Dvor faced them again. "I, Dvor, son of Dvak, speak for our people. We left the Southlands ages ago to go north, to the mountains. Now we return to face the Traitor again. We will let you walk with us."

Wait, what?

Well, there are fifty of them and six of us. I'd say that invitation is generous. From their point of view.

They don't know you...

No. But they will.

Then Conor spoke. "Agreed. Will you let us lead you to where we think we might find more help in fighting the Traitor? We know where to look in the Southlands."

We do?

Better than them, I meant.

I guess.

Dvor nodded. He seemed satisfied, if not pleased. There was a moment of silence and expectation. A few

MORE IS BETTER

of the sister sons started to shift their weight and fidget. Gray looked at Conor. Conor looked at Gray. Then Conor said loudly, "Let us go."

Dvor nodded, and Conor headed back to his little band. The Northerners fell into line behind them.

CH 3
WASTED LIFE

"What the fuck?" Arusin said as Conor, Gray and the Northerners came into the clearing. The Eliti soldiers and Eromil stood up and shuffled backwards a few steps, eyes wide. They looked at Conor in alarm.

He put his hands up and said, "It's okay. It's alright; the Northerners want the same things as us. They are here to fight."

Eromil rolled her eyes and the Eliti looked at each other and then at Conor. The Northerners kept filing silently into the clearing. When they were all in a big awkward circle, Dvor spoke loudly in his formal tone. "Soldiers of the Empire, Chan…woman. I am Dvor, son of Dvak. These are my sister sons. We came south to fight the Traitor." Then he waited expectantly.

Conor said, "He means the Other, or the Believer."

Eromil shrugged, unimpressed. The others relaxed.

"Right," Conor said. "Anyway, they're with us."

Dvor nodded and his sister sons did the same.

So, did we decide who was in charge?

WASTED LIFE

You know we didn't. But we will lead because we know where the Empire is.

Ah.

So, if you would, find us a path west?

Alright. And I don't know if you thought of it, but my hunting and your foraging can't feed this bunch.

I know. But that's a problem we can't solve right now. And these guys have been on the move for a while and they don't look too hungry.

Conor motioned to Dvor and his men to follow him and he started after Gray. His little army of Eliti and Chan scampered forward in their desire to stay close to him.

The Southlands are fertile and full of game, Conor thought as they walked along. There were farms to steal from and people to kill. He wondered if this hard-looking group of men had murdered, robbed, and raped their way south to their chance meeting. The only Northerners he had met were fighters. And fighters were usually alike across cultures and nationalities. He was a Southlander and knew little of the wider world as a matter of choice—a choice Conor had many reasons to regret. He did not know much about Northern ways. They lived across the great desert, north of the City, the informal capital of the Southlands. The desert was harsh ground and had been a hard barrier to trade and communication for as long as anyone in the Southlands could remember. But the Northerners were people, which meant they were capable of terrible things, and good. And he knew these ones wanted to fight. And right now, although he wished he knew more, that was all he needed.

Conor understood his Eliti followers a little better because he had been to the Empire when he was trying to raise an army to fight the Believer. He had only been partly successful; the country was in the grip of a conflict of its own. There was an ongoing civil war between the Empire and the tribes who lived in the great forests and highlands of that immense nation. From what he had learned, it was a war between cultures and belief systems. And it had come to a head over what was happening in the Southlands. The Mothers, a group of powerful women who ran the Empire, had argued among themselves over whether it was a war for strategic control of a neighbouring nation—or for life itself. The tribes believed Conor and Gray had an important place in the last war described in ancient Eliti mythology as Lord and Hound, yet only some of the leaders of the Empire agreed. It could be, Conor thought, that the Empire would come to the truth of it the hard way.

He looked at Eromil. She was Chan, from south of the Near Sea. The Chan Consolidation was a complete mystery to Conor. He had seen them fight in the ring and in the field and he respected Eromil, who was, after all, a war wife of the god, Shenzi. She had pledged to fight with Conor after he and Gray had defeated the hunters who had attacked them not long ago. But Chan language, culture, and beliefs were completely unfamiliar. Conor felt the familiar flush of shame as he realized how pinched his

WASTED LIFE

view was and how meager his experience of the world had been before the Believer came.

Dvor eased his way to the front and walked next to Conor for a few moments without speaking. It was windy and cool, but the air had no bite and the snow under their feet was wet and heavy. They could see Gray ahead of them occasionally, flitting in and out of the trees as they followed the path made by generations of Southlanders on the way to the north-south road that tied the fractured region together.

"We have heard of you, Conor," Dvor said. "You were a fighter of some renown."

Conor's exploits were well known in the Southlands. He had been undefeated when he left the three rings. He excelled in grappling, striking, and combined weapons—the three types of combat all fighters practiced before the slotted die decreed which would be used on that day. The fighters never knew in advance but for Conor, it did not matter. He was the best anyone had ever seen.

"We are honoured," Dvor said.

"Thanks." Conor smiled briefly. He had tired of the fights years ago. The desperate gambling, the crooked judges and the meaningless encounters with noblewomen had eventually sickened him. That, and the discovery that he really didn't like beating people to a pulp, despite his talent at doing it. He'd drifted into soldiering, and more recently he had been a lawman—until the Believer came. Gray had liked that job. He was happy patrolling the streets. And he had always scoffed at Conor's fighting prowess. Humans did not impress him at all.

WASTED LIFE

They walked in silence for a few more moments.

"It is nice to have you with us," Conor said. "Your sister sons look like strong able men."

"Nice?" Dvor asked, his eyebrows raised. "Nice?"

Conor frowned. "I didn't mean to insult you. Or your men." He searched for words. "It has been a crazy few days. So many dead. So hard to explain why." He looked over at the big northerner. "Relief, then. It's a relief to have warriors with us who want to fight."

Dvor nodded. He looked satisfied with that change. "We will make the Traitor pay for what he has done!" he said as he shook his right fist theatrically.

"I hope so," Conor said.

You know what would be nice? Gray asked. *If one of those morons knew some way to do that.*

The march took the rest of the day. They were about to settle in a damp clearing when Gray ambled towards them. *There's a small castle a ways to the west. I saw and smelled smoke from cooking fires and there are guards on the walls.*

Conor thought for a moment. *How far?*

We could get there before sunset. If we hurried.

Don't think I want to. Better not to surprise them.

Alright.

Any idea who's in there?

Not really. Sun going down made it hard to see. Could be Chan, Eliti, or Southlanders. No way to be sure without having a closer look.

I think we'll sleep here and then go in the morning.

Your call. I think I will go find something to eat.

WASTED LIFE

Gray circled around the group of Northerners straggling into the clearing and headed back into the forest from which they had just emerged. They watched warily and moved away from the massive figure while trying to look like they weren't. Gray ignored them. The only man he respected was Conor.

Later that evening, as the men and Eromil finished their meals and were moving around the slightly aimless way people on their way to bed sometimes do, the ground shifted slightly. They all staggered and looked at each other in alarm. Then it moved again, more. Like a huge rug had been pulled out from under their feet by an impossibly powerful hand. Only Conor stayed up, and him only barely. Those on the ground rolled helplessly and those standing went down hard. Then it stopped. There was a breathless moment.

Conor called out, "Everyone okay?"

Dvor relayed the question.

There were mumbles of agreement and one strangled yell. Conor ran in the direction of the sound. One of the Northerners had fallen on his sword. He had been sharpening it. He looked up at them, his eyes pleading and embarrassed at the same time.

"Help me roll him over," Conor said to Dvor as he knelt beside him. The sword had entered his left side and was stuck in about halfway down its length. "Damn," said Conor softly.

Dvor said something to the stricken man. He took a small flask out of a pocket and held it to the wounded man's lips. He managed a swallow then nodded and

31

closed his eyes. Then Dvor yanked the sword out quickly and broke the weapon over his knee with a snap. Conor jerked at the sound. The stricken man leaped to his feet. He turned away from them and shook his fist at the sky, his back straight and his head thrown back. Dvor looked on, his face shining and his sword out and up into the darkness. They stood this way for a long moment and then the wounded man collapsed. Dvor moved to his side. Dark blood was bubbling out of his mouth and his head lolled back. Dvor held his hand and murmured into his ear. The man was dead in moments.

"Shit," said Conor under his breath. "That was fucking different."

But it was the same, as well. He knew every life was precious—and this one was wasted. The man was young; the beard on his face was patchy and thin. Another casualty in the Other's war.

Some Northerners approached, swords and axes out. They shouted into the cold night air. Their voices were as useless as the white clouds of mist their breath made.

Gray ambled up. *What's the racket?*

One of the Northerners fell on his sword when the earth moved. Conor nodded at the body.

Dead?

Yes.

One less to help us.

Yes. Another life lost to the monster.

Conor and Gray walked away as the Northerners stopped yelling at the sky, lifted the dead man onto their shoulders and strode off into the forest.

WASTED LIFE

What are they going to do with him?
I'm not sure. I think they bury their dead.
Not our deal anyway.
No.
And what was that?
Not sure. It didn't feel the same as when the hunters came. This was more dirt and rock moving, you know?
Yeah. The other time was like the world changed somehow, so that they could come here.
Right. Have you ever heard of the earth moving like that?

Conor thought for a moment as he moved over and sat beside the small fire they had lit. It was warmer there, but not much. *The Chan I met training for the fights spoke of it happening in the Consolidation, but long ago. The earth shaking and moving, buildings coming down.*

But not here? In the Southlands?
No. Never. I had no idea about what they were talking about. Until today.
So, it could be him.
Oh, it's him. Fucker. No doubt in my mind. He's testing his strength.
So what can't he do? He just moved the world.
Well just some of it. And he can't kill me. He's tried.
No. Not yet.

Arusin, Melnis, Pranti, and Eromil had seen them come into the camp. They came over as a group and unfolded their blankets as close to Conor and Gray as they could without getting under their feet. Conor said nothing. The night passed and they slept badly on the cold, hard ground.

CH 4
LADY DAREEN

Gray left before dawn as he always did. Conor had warned the Northern sentries, so they watched in silence as the black bulk slipped into the trees with surprising grace. By the time he returned, Conor was up and getting restless.

See anything?
A pile of stones that used to be a castle.
Shit. Survivors?
Some. I saw smoke from more than a few fires outside the ruins.
Still no idea who they are?
Didn't get close enough. Didn't see the need. We are going that way.
Yeah. If these guys ever get their asses in gear.

Conor jerked his right thumb at the Northerners who seemed to have to exchange involved personal greetings with each of the sister sons before they broke camp every morning.

We need an Eliti in charge. Or you.
Conor just shrugged.

LADY DAREEN

It wasn't too long before they got underway. Dvor gave Conor a wave when his men had arranged themselves in a double column behind him. It stretched back into the trees. Conor's group had been up and ready for a while. Eromil was muttering, her breath steaming in the cold air. The three Eliti were silent.

"Ok," Conor said. "Let's go."

Gray led them out.

Conor let Dvor know what was coming on the march. He didn't want the Northerners charging into a battle with potential allies. They eventually agreed that Conor, Gray, Eromil, Arusin, and Dveel, a Northerner who spoke the southern tongue, would talk to whomever was holding the castle. Each of the peoples involved in the Southlands were to be represented. After a short march, the five of them moved through the snow up to the first of the fires.

"No pickets," said Dveel disapprovingly.

Conor agreed. It looked like an army in disarray. There were several men crowded close to the fire, their backs to Conor and the rest of them. One of the men on the far side finally saw them and jumped to his feet, pulling his spear from the ground and holding it out and up over the flames.

"Hey!" he said in Eliti.

The other men around the fire scrambled out of their chairs, hands grabbing at the weapons they had left lying in the snow.

"Good morning," Conor replied in the same language. "We are glad to see the Eliti army still here in the

Southlands. We need to speak to your commanders. We are not your enemies."

Hearing that startled them. The spectacle of the hugely muscled, dark-skinned man who said it with the imposing figure of the massive black wolf bear beside him shocked them further.

"Hey!" the soldier said again, and he stabbed the air with his spear.

"Stop."

The other soldiers (Conor had counted five of them) said nothing, although their spears were pointing at them as well.

Conor held his hands out, palms up. "We are friends. We fight what you fight." He gestured at Gray and the people behind him. "We have news. Important news. We need to speak to your leadership."

"Of what? The Chan?" The man jabbed his spear at Eromil. "Are you with…the Chan?"

Conor shook his head and Gray rolled his eyes. *What an idiot.*

He's scared.

He's an idiot.

Conor spoke calmly and firmly, "I am Conor. I am a Southlander. This is Gray, my Hound. Dveel is a Northerner." Conor pointed to him. "Arusin is Eliti like you all. And Eromil…she is with us."

"Well, good," the soldier said. He just stood there, spear pointed at one of them, then another. His face was red. He licked his lips, his eyes darting back and forth.

Are all Eliti this stupid? I can't recall. How can he not know who we are?

LADY DAREEN

I don't know.

One of the other soldiers leaned in and spoke quietly to the spear carrier. He whispered back to him and the man ran out of the circle and back towards the largest of the crowds gathered around the largest of the fires.

"You must wait," he said to Conor.

"Alright," Conor said.

There were a few moments of stillness. Then Conor said, "Did you lose many last night?" He gestured at the castle in ruins behind them. "When the earth moved?"

The man shook his head. "Our Mother warned us. We ran out into the night before…" he drew a figure on his chest. "The Other tried to kill us all."

There it is. One of the Mothers of Eliton is here.

The Mothers ruled the Empire. Conor had been a guest of Dareen, one of the capital city Mothers. She was a powerful politician, leader, and literal mother to her clan, the Tormusula. She and the other mothers had the ability to control their followers by inducing powerful feelings of respect, loyalty, love, and admiration. Conor had felt their power and it had very nearly overwhelmed him. But his natural Southlander skepticism had helped, and when Gray was near him, the mothers' power dwindled to nothing. Something about their connection nullified it. Conor was pretty sure that the M others were not aware of this and he had not told them.

The M others got their power from having children with men from other important Eliti families. So they had lots of children. With lots of fathers. They were not forthcoming on exactly how that worked, politically, but it did. These women were a force to behold.

Conor was appalled by the mothers of Eliton in some ways. They competed for power ruthlessly and often abused it. The M others were proud, beautiful, charming, intelligent, self-obsessed and cynical. But they led the largest army in the known world, and one of the most powerful, Dareen, had come to believe Conor when he spoke of the Believer's return as a threat to the entire world. It was she who kept him safe in the Empire and arranged to have him return to the Southlands. Conor hoped it was Dareen who had come.

I don't remember them being able to see future events. I mean, the Mother I was with did not show that talent.

Conor rubbed his right hand over his face.

Mine neither. Although she did get me out of that fighting house before one of the other Mothers could have me killed. That's what she said was going to happen, anyway.

Everywhere you go, that seems to be true though. Someone eventually takes a run at you.

Yeah, yeah…Wait, here comes somebody.

Gray turned his head at the same time as the Eliti soldiers did. A woman was approaching. She was dressed in a dark green cloak with white fur trim. She had a retinue of soldiers and officials behind her. Conor breathed a sigh of relief. It was Dareen. She had listened to him. One of the other Mothers had tried to kill him using an Eliti fighting champion in a staged confrontation. The fight had ended in thirty seconds, with the Eliti unconscious

LADY DAREEN

and Conor untouched. This had enraged that Mother even further.

Dareen walked up to him, swaying and assured, in the way powerful, beautiful, and self-aware women can.

"Conor," she said with a brief smile. "We meet again."

"Lady Dareen," he said. He bowed his head slightly.

"I did not expect to see you here in the Southlands, although I am glad of it. The Mothers decided one of us should see for ourselves what was happening." Her gaze hardened and flickered over the members of his little band. "You have been busy gathering friends."

"Survivors, more like," Conor said. "Do you want to know what is happening, Lady Dareen?" His voice was firm. "Here in the Southlands?"

Her dark eyes narrowed and she stiffened. Dareen was not used to being questioned, especially by a man. Her authority in her clan was absolute. Her guards sensed her anger and they advanced, insulted on her behalf at this sign of disrespect.

Conor did not step back. He had finished bowing to the Mothers long ago. He needed her help, but her power hadn't stopped the Believer, he had. And now the Other, or the Traitor, had killed hundreds, maybe thousands of Eliti soldiers, while back in the Empire the Mothers had argued over whether he was telling them the truth. Conor had seen the bodies, broken and burned.

Gray stood with him so her power to overawe was negated. She was just another person who demanded obedience because of who her mother and father happened to be. There were a lot of people like this in the Southlands before the wars. Men with big mouths and big bellies. Dareen was a woman, intelligent, beautiful, statuesque, and eloquent—but the principle was the same.

Dareen's right hand came up and the men behind her halted. Except one. He wasn't armed and he was dressed in a simple black shift. His face was weathered. He had short white hair, a trim beard and brown eyes. Conor realized with surprise that he recognized him. He was an Eliti holy man, the one who sold him the copy of their sacred book on his way into the capital. The book that explained the myth that Conor thought he was part of. The man nodded to Conor. A thought entered his head. Conor looked at Dareen and pointed to the man.

"Was he waiting for me, Dareen? On the road to Eliton?"

She looked at the ground and then back at him, expressionless.

He persisted. "Did you know that I was coming to Eliton?"

She smiled slightly.

"You wanted me to see myself as part of your mythology," Conor said.

She waved a hand at him. "Recognize, not see. You are part of our story. You needed to know."

She shifted her weight from one perfectly formed hip to the other, and said, "The Eliton Empire did not control the Southlands, but we never lost sight of you. We sent travellers and traders…"

"And fighters," Conor interjected.

LADY DAREEN

"And fighters," Dareen said with a broader smile. "You noticed them, did you?"

Conor felt the familiar sense of embarrassment at Southlander closed-mindedness. His people had turned inward many years ago and had been fragmented and unprepared when the Believer and his Bonded hordes came. And then when Conor had defeated him, the Chan and the Eliti invaded to claim their rights and the Southlands were utterly helpless.

Dareen was reminding him of this. She continued, "We knew of Conor and his Hound, Gray. Word had reached us of your strength and his size," she pointed to Gray.

"Our legends tell us that men and Hounds arise in times of great need and peril. Your war against the Believer and his Bonded armies convinced some of us that those times may have come." She shrugged her shoulders and looked into Conor's eyes, her face suddenly less regal than simply tired. More human. "But I am only one Mother of many. And many did not believe the old stories...I gathered allies and sent people to watch you. You had convinced some of our soldiers to help you. And the savages."

Her face took on a strange aspect when she used that word to describe the people, the tribal inhabitants of the Eliton plains and mountain redoubts. *She doesn't believe they are savages, but her followers do, so she acts the part,* Conor thought. *Strange.*

"But when it looked as if the Bonded would conquer the Southlands, even the skeptical Mothers saw the need to intervene. So, we came."

LADY DAREEN

Conor remembered the massive black and silver squares of the Eliti infantry marching along the north-south road—and the same formations crunching into the rumbling war wagons of the Chan on a dark night not so long ago. Now both armies lay smashed and one of the Mothers of Eliton was here to find out whether it meant the end times had come.

Conor spoke to the white-haired man. "I am Conor, as you know. You are?"

"Thesi," he said. "I am Thesi."

"You are a long way from home, Thesi," said Conor.

"I came because I had to see the awesome works of the Other. And to speak to you."

See the works? What a moron. That takes the fear and death out of it.

Gray stepped forward, baring his fangs. He growled low in his throat. Conor put his hand on th Hound's broad back. The holy man's eyes widened but he didn't step back.

"And to see the Hound," he said. "The greatest and the last."

Dareen looked at the ground when he said this. Her guards gathered around her.

The first part, yeah of course, but last?

Conor felt suddenly queasy. Last?

Dveel stepped forward. He didn't understand Eliti but it was clear that he wanted to speak to Dareen, be noticed by her. Dareen was beautiful and not in an innocent, fresh-faced way. She was a woman in full bloom and the Northerner had been a long time away from that. And her

LADY DAREEN

power to induce feelings of loyalty and love was working on the entire group Conor had brought with him.

Dveel bowed low and said, "Greetings, my lady," like a true Southlander.

Conor did not feel it, her power, but he had in the Empire. He had seen it make men act like puppies tumbling over themselves trying to do the Mother's bidding.

They'll be eating out of her hand before you know it. Can you ask her to turn it off so we can have a real conversation?

I don't know if she can.

"Mother! Mother!"

It was Arusin, edging around Dveel's elbow, trying to get Dareen to notice him.

He's feeling it.

Pranti and Melnis had crept up behind him, their faces showing fear and hope. Conor turned around and saw Eromil. Her face was twisted with confusion. Conor put his hand on her arm.

"What's happening?" she asked.

"I feel it, too," Conor said. "It's the power of the Mothers of Eliton. It works on men and women. Makes them feel for her." Conor did not know why he and Gray were immune, but he was glad of it. Dareen was charismatic enough without it. "When she moves away, it will pass."

He turned to Dareen, interrupting the love-in. "Men are dying here, Dareen. The Other has sent monsters to kill us. How many men have you brought? What are you going to do?"

LADY DAREEN

The men around her looked at him in shock. How dare he talk to their Mother like that? Conor saw shock turn to anger. Arusin wheeled and tried to slap Conor across the face. Conor caught the man's arm at the wrist. Arusin reached for his dagger but Conor's short sword was out and at his throat.

"Easy, big man," he said quietly.

Gray slid in front of them and growled at the knot of angry men. Dareen's hold over them didn't stop them from seeing his bulk and his sharp fangs. They hesitated.

Dareen raised her hands.

"Stop," she called out. "Stop, my friends. We have enemies in the Southlands, but Conor and Gray are not among them."

She looked at Conor and raised an eyebrow. He put his sword in its sheath and let go of Arusin, who stepped back and shook his arm sharply. But his eyes returned to Dareen.

Oh man.

Gray seemed to lose a quarter of his size as his ruff settled and he calmed down.

He's Eliti. He feels like she's his mother.

So weird.

No doubt.

"Conor," Dareen said, "bring the Chan and the Northerner and we will talk."

Do you want to come to this meeting? Or do you want to look around?

Never found talking all that useful. Gray shook himself vigorously. *I'll be close.*

LADY DAREEN

Conor asked Dareen to let her people know that Gray was scouting in the area, and if they tried to spear him, there would be more dead Eliti. The group eventually gathered around the biggest of the fires. Thesi sat beside Dareen. Eromil and Dveel bracketed Conor. With a wave of her hand, Dareen moved her guards to a respectful distance.

Conor leaned forward as soon as they had settled, and repeated his earlier question. "Do you know what is happening here, Dareen?"

"The Other has returned," said Thesi. "That is what is happening."

"No shit," said Conor. "Have you seen the hunters?"

Eromil blanched at the mention of those things that killed men with such ease. Dareen looked at Conor with a question in her eyes, but it was Thesi who spoke.

"Hunters?"

"It is an army that the Other, or the Traitor, as the Northerners call it, has brought to us. They are camped on the road," Conor said as he pointed back towards it.

"Who are they?" Dareen asked.

"More like 'what' are they," Conor said. "When the Other spoke to me it said they came here from a place with a dark sun."

Thesi and Dareen exchanged glances.

"The Other spoke to you?" he asked, his eyes wide.

"Yes, yes," Conor said, and he pressed on. "They aren't men, or women. They are very tall and...they have long bright spears. They are very strong and fast..." Conor trailed off, frustrated by how inadequate his description was. "They are here, they are many, and they have killed Eliti soldiers. That's what matters."

It was Thesi who spoke. "The holy book I gave you…"

"Sold, you mean," Conor snapped, remembering their encounter on the road to Eliton, one arranged by Dareen, apparently. "Yeah, I read it. There is nothing about the hunters, or any of this," Conor waved at the rubble behind them.

"Yes," Thesi said. "It's not the only version…"

"What?" Conor said. "What?"

Dareen looked uncharacteristically uneasy. Thesi looked at her, she nodded, and he continued.

"There are other books. Books only the Mothers have seen. And not just Eliti books," he gestured at Eromil and Dveel. "There is truth everywhere."

Conor was angry now. "What the fuck does that mean? How does that help? The hunters are two days' march up the road. Any ideas on how to deal with them? Thesi? Dareen?"

"The books all tell the same story," Thesi said. He lowered his voice, "The end of this world is here. The doom is upon us."

Dareen looked away.

Eromil leaned close to Conor. "Did he just say…?"

"Yes. He did," said Conor.

"Not if we fight," said Dveel. "Will they fight?"

"Good question," said Conor. He turned to Dareen. "My lady, will you fight? Will the Empire gather its armies and fight?"

LADY DAREEN

Dareen did not look at him. She picked at the sleeve of her green robe. "The Empire is collapsing. The M others do nothing but argue and the army has split. There have been…" she glanced at Thesi, "signs. When our men meet in the streets, even we have trouble restraining them." Dareen put her head in her hands, briefly. "The attacks are brutal…many have died."

I'll bet, Conor thought. Each man feels as if he is fighting for his mother's life. A fucking bloodbath.

"The tribes are running wild in the rural areas." She stared at Conor, her expression bleak. "I have no army to call upon."

Conor sat back. The Empire, gone? Its massive formations. Huge cities. Millions of people, in chaos?

Eromil spoke up. "What of the Chan armies? What do you know of them?"

Dareen waved her hand dismissively. "The Chan have gone. Back to the Consolidation, as far as we can tell. The war is over."

"Back to the homeland, where war will not come," said Eromil quietly.

"Fuck," said Conor savagely. He ran his hands over his face. This was a disaster. Then he had a thought: if the People, as the tribes called themselves, were winning the eternal civil war in the Empire, maybe some would come again to his call.

"Do you have contacts with the people, Dareen?" Conor asked bluntly.

Her face showed her discomfort. "How does one speak to them?" she said. "We tried long ago. The Mothers reached out and we were spurned."

"Nothing?"

Her face hardened. "You know they are true to the old stories. They live closer to the ways of the book than the Eliton. They must know the time has come, with or without the Mothers telling them that it is so."

"Maybe," Conor said. "But they fought the Believer and if…"

"Fight?" Thesi interrupted. "How do you fight the Other? He has power no man can match…he can destroy worlds. There is no way to defeat him."

Conor sat back. Cold sweat broke out on his back and face. Was it over? Was his little army alone? *No. I won't believe it,* he thought.

"So, we should just wait, then?" he said to Dareen. "Until he comes for us?"

"Prayer and acceptance are what we need." Thesi said. "We should pray to the Lords of Power, that they will guard us on the Outside, after we die."

"That's it? That's all we have left?" Conor asked.

Thesi nodded, his face expressionless. Dareen looked away, unable to meet Conor's eyes.

"Is that what you are telling them?" Conor pointed to the guards who waited just out of earshot. "And back in the Empire? Wait and die? And your children, Dareen? What about Dareeni and Nisi? Did you tell them to give up hope?"

LADY DAREEN

Conor had met Dareen's adult children—and slept with one of them. They were both much like their mother.

"Of course not," Thesi said. "They do not need to know. Why make their remaining days full of horror? The end will come soon enough."

Conor ignored him and pressed Dareen. "You hide your despair from them?" he asked. "You make them feel loved and safe? While death stalks them?" His voice showed his contempt. "You treat them like the children they are when they are around you. Worse."

Thesi bristled, "How dare you speak to…"

Conor turned on him. "Shut up, preacher," he said, his voice flat. "I am not talking to you."

Dareen turned to face him but her eyes flickered away from his after only a few seconds. The trim on the cuff of her left sleeve was unravelling in her hand and she continued to pick at it. But she stayed silent.

He tried another tack. "You said there were signs. What kind of signs?"

Dareen looked back at Thesi, who spoke in solemn tones like he was speaking of the dead at a funeral. "The earth shakes. Lightning races across the sky on clear days. Fires burn in the ground that we cannot put out. The armies of the Empire fight each other. The Mothers debate endlessly while their guards shed blood in the capital. It is clear. The end of this world comes."

Thesi paused to let this sink in. He stared at Conor, almost challenging him. But Conor had already seen these things. The Believer's monstrous stone man had thrown lightning across the sky during his war. The hunters' blue flame burned flesh, wood, and stone. And the earth moving was all too fresh. But Conor hadn't given up.

"But the Lord and his Hound are here," Conor said, his voice desperate. "That has to mean something. Your Lords of Power made it so! You showed me, Dareen. We are here to defeat the Other and we can, but we need your help."

Dareen looked at Conor, life suddenly in her eyes.

She does want to fight! he thought. What is holding her back?

Dveel interrupted. "What is happening? When do we fight? Will the Empire come?"

The conversation had slipped into Eliti and Dveel was lost. Conor took a deep breath and turned to him. "I don't know. And as for them," he motioned to the Eliti, "it doesn't sound like it."

Dveel looked angry for a moment. Then his face relaxed and he shrugged. "The Mothers know what is best for them."

Eromil looked worried but she agreed. "They don't want to help. We can't make them. Let's go."

Conor was glad Gray had stayed close enough that their link was negating Dareen's influence over him, at least. He needed to keep a clear head. He wanted to try one more time and he sensed Dareen might be wavering.

"Just give me a moment," Conor said to them and he faced Dareen.

"We are going to fight. The Lord and his Hound and the Northerners and whoever else we can convince to join us. We are not going to ask permission from you. Can I at least get a promise you won't stand in our way? And you'll work to get the M others to let the Tribes cross the Empire unopposed if they choose to fight?"

Thesi shook his head but Dareen ignored him this time. "We here will not oppose you. But I do not speak for the Empire. The Mothers there…do not agree. Our authority is fractured. If the tribes cross the Empire, there may be conflict."

She hesitated, looked away and then back at him, her expression hard to read at first. Was she feeling weak? Vulnerable? Those would be foreign emotions to a Mother of the Empire. She may not remember them. For Conor, it was like looking at the underside of a rock turned over for the first time in many moons. Emotions that had not seen the light of day for years were wriggling out of control on her face.

"Alright," Conor said. "What are you going to do, my lady? You have come all this way." He used the honorific reflexively. Was he feeling sorry for her?

Thesi answered for her. "We will gather those Eliti we can here in the Southlands, and we will head back to the Empire to wait."

For what? Conor thought but he asked, "And pray?"

"Yes, yes," said Thesi sharply. "And pray."

"Is that why you came to the Southlands, my lady?" Conor asked. "To find what's left of your armies and then go home and die?"

She looked pensive. "We suspected something strange was happening here even after you defeated the Believer and his Bonded armies. We knew after the battle at Oro."

LADY DAREEN

Conor remembered the ghostly figures of snow and ice he had fought there. The monsters had attacked both the Eliti and the Chan armies that night.

"Yet still we squabble over what to do," she said. Dareen was starting to sound resigned to her fate. "You remember Samilla?"

"Yes," Conor answered. She was the Mother who had tried to have him killed.

"She, with some of the other Mothers, have made life in the capital impossible for me."

"You left the Empire to avoid war with her?" Conor asked.

"No," she said. "My family is larger, and our history is greater than Samilla's. War with her gives her a status she does not deserve." Her chin came up and her eyes sparked into life. "I am a Mother of Eliton. Our army is here and our people are under threat. I heard many things. I came to see for myself."

Conor sat back. A realization came over him. This woman, the holy man, and their Empire were going to be no help at all. Despite her power, Dareen was here because she didn't know what else to do. And her holy man was even less helpful than she was. Shit. He had hoped for guidance and for allies.

"Would you let me speak to your men?" Conor asked. "Ask them to stay and fight?"

"They will not," she said as she gestured with her palms down. "I don't have the ability to let them go. They are mine and will remain so until one of my daughters rises

LADY DAREEN

to take my place." Dareen smiled sadly. "Mothers cannot abdicate. We serve until we cannot serve any longer."

She shook her head and her dark hair moved gracefully across her face, covering her dark brown eyes briefly. She was powerful, remarkably attractive, and surrounded by fanatically loyal followers. And she was backing out. There was nothing for it.

"Alright. We go," Conor said. He stood up quickly. "Good luck, Lady Dareen."

Gray had appeared to stand beside him, and they turned and walked away. Those who had come with him were stupefied. Dareen's power to create love and loyalty had worked on them. They didn't know her, but they didn't want to leave her, least of all Arusin, the old Eliti. He looked like a lovesick teenager, smitten beyond words to explain. Dveel and Eromil were confused by their feelings but they followed Conor away from the fire.

They had not gotten far when Dareen called out to them, "Conor! Wait!"

"My lady?"

She motioned her guards to step back as she caught up and leaned in to whisper to Conor, "It's Thesi. I don't know if I trust him."

Conor raised his eyebrows.

"He has been a loyal servant and a trusted advisor. And he is a holy man," she lifted her eyes to meet his. "But this…surrender…it feels wrong."

Conor started to speak but then he stopped. Dareen had never been misled or betrayed before—not by one of her followers. It was literally impossible for them to do and just as hard for her to imagine it. She expected only truth, love, and complete loyalty from all those around her. Yet here she was, wondering if it was still so. It was a remarkable admission of weakness from her. There was still a chance that the Empire, or part of it, could help.

Conor tried to shock her into action. "It is wrong. Gag him, or kill him. Then raise the flag of resistance here. Call the Mothers. Call the tribes. Call the Chan. I will stand with you."

She was thinking *No one stands with the Mothers. We stand alone.* Conor could see it in her face. The instinctual arrogance. But then it fell away and Dareen's expression softened.

She needs me and she is starting to understand that.

Dareen smiled sadly at him and even the link between him and Gray could not completely negate her power. It was the power of life itself. For what is life if not mothers giving birth to the new?

"It must be, Dareen," Conor said. "We must fight. For Nisi and all of your children."

"Yes, it will be as you say, Conor, Lord of the Hound," she said. "Even if we die in battle, it is better that way."

Dareen turned and signalled to her guards. One walked around the fire and approached, his head bowed. She said something to him quietly. He bowed lower, turned, walked up to Thesi, and speared him through the chest. The holy man's eyes bulged, blood spurted from his mouth, and his hands grasped the shaft of the sword. He looked to Dareen, took his hands off the spear and held them out, imploring her.

LADY DAREEN

Her face was hard as stone.

His face contorted into a snarl and he rasped, "All of you will die and I will eat your souls…"

Another guard came from behind him, and Thesi's words were strangled on the spear that punched through his spine and out through his throat. More blood flowed and Thesi's body went limp and he fell into the fire, sparks flaring.

As the Eliti soldiers pulled their spears from his body, Dareen said, "Let him burn." Her words were harsh and loud.

Conor was startled by the quick and brutal execution of a man he was just beginning to distrust.

Gray had come back to the circle of people around the fire. *Was it something he said?*

In a way, yes. It seems as if the Other was doing the talking for him. Through him. He counselled surrender; Dareen disagreed.

Hmm. Might be kind of a good sign if the Other is trying to get the Eliti to stay out of it.

How?

It means they matter. The Other believes they are a threat. And if he was going to burn this world to a cinder like you said he has done to others, what difference would the Eliti army make, no matter how big?

Maybe. Maybe.

Was she getting advice?

I put in a word or two, yes.

To kill him? I'm shocked.

I suggested silence or kill. Dareen is a mother of the Eliton Empire. She chose to kill.

LADY DAREEN

Did you know he was of the Other? Did she?
I just wanted him out of the way. Dareen thought he might not be trusted. A big leap for her.
I'll bet. No one lies to the Mothers.
No. it's impossible when they have you.
He did.
And now he's dead.
You can. Lie to her.
Yep. If I need to. Helps when you are around. Otherwise, I'm almost as helpless as everyone else.
Almost.
Yes. Almost.
What now?
Well we gather up these Eliti, send for more, and call the tribes.
And the Chan?
We'll have to speak to Eromil about that.
It's a long way to the Consolidation.

The Chan Consolidation was as far south as the Southlands went and then farther. Weeks of marching, and then there was the Near Sea to cross.

Maybe we can catch them before they leave the Southlands. Some, anyway. And send others to call for help.
We need them all. And it still may not be enough.
I know. But we have to—
Fight. Yes.

Conor and Gray's private conversation was interrupted by Dareen. She called out to Eromil, "Eromil, war wife of the god, Shenzi, you must get to the Consolidation." Dareen motioned to Eromil as she spoke. "Talk to your people. Tell them what you have seen here. Tell them we need their help."

Eromil looked back and nodded, her expression a mixture of fascination and shock. Dareen had focused on her and she felt the full force of a mother's power.

"Yes, of course, my lady," she said as she bowed. "But…"

She had promised her sword to Conor when he had defeated a group of hunters and saved her life. She looked at him, imploring him to release her and end her agony.

"It's alright, Eromil," he said. "We are all on the same side here. Dareen is right. We need the Chan and you can speak for us."

"I will leave immediately, my lady," Eromil was relieved that she no longer had to resist Dareen's power. "Would that be…?"

Dareen interrupted her, "Yes, yes," she said. "And take this with you."

She signalled to her guards to bring her a satchel that had been at Thesi's feet. She searched it for a moment and brought out a small bundle. It was a leather-bound bag, similar to the one the Eliti officers had given Conor when he had tried to recruit the Chan to fight the Other, not that long ago. Dareen had suspected that he would try that, and had sent the package with the army he had travelled with. Conor raised his eyebrows when he saw it, and then looked at Dareen.

"It's a text," she said. "A holy…a history book that the Mothers have kept for themselves. It helps to explain the struggle, the eternal war of the Lords of Power against the Other, or the Traitor, or the Believer, or whatever name he has taken in this time, in this place."

She put her hand on Conor's arm, leaned in, and spoke to him like he was her child. "It may help them decide."

"It didn't last time," he said.

"True," she smiled briefly. "But much has happened since then. Has it not?"

"Yes," Conor admitted. "And I hope you are right, Dareen. I really do."

"You are the Lord of the Hound and he is here. It is true."

Conor saw belief in her eyes.

"We will defeat the Other or this Hound will cover the world in darkness so the Other cannot consume it, and us as well."

I'd prefer to defeat him.
Yeah.

"I'm going to bring the Northerners we met here." Conor said to Dareen.

"Can I stay?" Arusin asked. The old soldier looked back and forth between Conor and Dareen like a child looking for his parents to decide whether he could stay up late.

Doesn't she get sick of that?
I don't think so. She thinks she deserves it. All the Mothers do.

"Of course," Dareen said and smiled briefly at the man, who staggered under her gaze.

"Arusin," Conor said, "thank you."

"Yes," he said. His eyes never left Dareen.

Shit.

LADY DAREEN

Yeah.

"Dveel!" Conor called.

The Northerner blinked and shook his head once. He turned to Conor, shaking off his need to stay close to Dareen.

"We're going back to get your people. Come with us. Eromil, you come too. We'll gear you up as best we can and get you on your way."

She swallowed hard but said nothing. Conor looked at Gray and then they started the walk back to the waiting Northerners.

CH 5
REFUGEES

They had a couple hundred men between them. Warriors. Humans. Victims. All and none. Conor and Dvor sent six of the fittest and fastest sister sons with Eromil, much to her dismay. Dvor swore they would not slow her down or "do anything untoward." He promised the runners that he would geld them personally if they did.

Conor warned them to stay off the road and avoid the hunters' "fortress." They gave him puzzled looks. He shrugged and said, "You'll know it when you see it. Believe me."

After they had packed food and water and tied down everything that rattled, they ran off into the forest along the path they had just come up. Eromil did not look back.

I'm not going to miss her.
I will.
Do you think we'll ever see her, or any of them, again?
I don't know. Conor scratched his chin. *I really don't.*
It's right that she is trying.
Yes. She's very brave. And she's just one more sword here. She could bring thousands.

REFUGEES

Hopefully.
Yes.

Later that day, Dareen, Conor, and Dvor decided to strike north, away from the hunters' "fortress" to try and connect with any Eliti units still wandering leaderless in the Southlands. The two major cities of the Southlands, Dece and the Desert City, were up there as well. More recruits for the war to come.

Before they set out, Dareen sent runners back to the Empire to try once again to convince those Mothers who had been her allies in the past to come to her aid. The tribes of the People of Eliton were also to be sought out and told of the end of times and the war to decide the fate of this world.

The march north started poorly. Dareen's military leader, Commander Tanerosi, was a young man. Competent, but young. The Northerners did not like him; he had short hair and was beardless. It didn't help that he also yelled at them—a lot. The warriors refused to stay in column and took frequent breaks to talk with their brothers. It didn't take long for Conor to suggest that they lead the march with Conor and Gray scouting in front of them. That pride of place kept them moving and away from the strict discipline of the Eliti formation.

They stayed on the north-south road. It made marching easier. After a couple of hours, they came across a group of bedraggled Southerners shambling along in the same direction. Most of them were women and children. They were tired, cold, and wet. And fearful. The Northerners

REFUGEES

frightened them and the few men among them drew their weapons and forced their way to the front.

Gray had been scouting off the road to the west of the column, so the meeting was abrupt. Conor tried but it was mostly Dareen's presence that calmed them after a few moments filled with shouts and panic. Their leader was a sharp-eyed woman with red hair and a piercing voice. Alees, she called herself. They had been walking for many days, she said, because early in the Chan invasion, their armies had commandeered their entire town and kicked them all out. Not killed, though, Conor thought. Kicked out.

Edgeroad, Alees said it was called, and it was far south of where they were. The little band had wandered throughout the Southlands, picking up stragglers from other broken villages and foraging as they went. Now they were heading to Dece.

Dece was, Conor recalled, a city built on gambling, the fights, and whoring, where the crime patrons held the power. Conor had seen it fall to the Believer and his hordes. He assumed it had fallen hard and not much of what passed for society there would still be standing. But it was right on the road and they would find out soon enough.

Dareen decreed that the Eliti forces would escort these people to Dece. Dvor was appalled and protested despite Dareen's powers. Conor backed Dareen; he figured these people had as much a stake in what happened in this war as anyone. Thus, their little band grew by fifty or so.

REFUGEES

Older, younger, and more female. Gray had said when he returned. *They'll get in the way and die easily if we have to fight.*
Some women can fight.
Some.
We couldn't just leave them.
Yes, we could.
You know what I mean.
I do. And you may regret it.

They picked up more stragglers as they marched. The road attracted them, as it was the backbone of the Southlands. All commerce and travel led to it, so the people who had been dispossessed got on it and started walking. Some went north and some went south, and the road accepted them all the same. And so did Conor and Dareen.

Dece posed a different problem. They came upon its low walls late one afternoon. The sun was still up, shining weakly, bu t it still got cold when it went down. Most of the army, if it could be called that, were anxious to spend a night indoors.

"Dece!" some cried out. "There'll be food there. And beds!"

Others were uneasy. They had heard of the city's fall and seen the mindless brutality of the Bonded. Then they had been shoved aside by the Chan and Eliti armies, vast impersonal forces beyond the experience or the memory of most Southlanders. They wanted to keep walking. They used the old saying but with a new meaning, "Nothing good ever came out of Dece!"

REFUGEES

They are going to be frightened of anything. And everything. Gray moved around to get a better look at the looming city. *For a long time. A long time.*

The walls were deserted. No guards in armour peered around the crenellations at them. The main gate was slightly ajar, as if the owner had left in a hurry and had forgotten to close it all the way. There were a few people with them who knew the place well. Conor and Dvor convinced Dareen to send patrols into the streets led by these guides before they took the whole group in.

Conor and Gray explored on their own.

Where to?

They were walking down a silent street. Gaping black windows stared down at them.

Conor pointed. *The patrons ran this city out of a central location. Massive houses. Just up a ways, right on this street.*

Lead on.

The streets were narrow and treacherous. There was none of the usual traffic and the desultory snow removal had not happened. The snow was melting and then refreezing at night on the cobbled surface and it was slippery. Gray was sure-footed but even he was struggling to stay upright at times.

Fuck. Conor nearly went down. His right hand splashed in the wet snow.

Are you sure we want to stay here?

Conor grimaced and wiped his hand on his pants.

There are buildings with roofs here, anyway. If it's deserted, we'll be alright. There might even be food in a warehouse or something.

Right. Food. In a warehouse.

REFUGEES

Conor heard the skepticism in Gray's voice.

A few moments later they heard a commotion to their right, down a narrow lane. Conor turned and led them towards it. The shadows of the buildings had prevented the sun from melting the snow here, and the footing was good. Conor broke into a run. He soon saw struggling soldiers framed in the slim opening ahead. An Eliti patrol had run into trouble. Conor's right hand went to his sword and he drew it tight across his body. Gray was right behind him. Conor could feel his excitement—no, anticipation. Gray didn't love fighting, but he loved doing what needed to be done.

Conor didn't slow down as he left the alley. He piled into a knot of men and women, knocking them all back and some of them to the ground. Gray leapt into the space he had cleared, and roared. They had barged into a significant street brawl. There were forty or fifty Eliti and civilians, broken by their charge into two groups. Conor could see the fever of the fight was on them and despite his size and Gray's noise, the groups in front of them were gathering themselves to attack again.

"Wait!" Conor yelled. "We—"

He dodged a short spear and it thunked into an Eliti shield behind him. Gray immediately dashed into the crowd, grabbed the man who had thrown it by the ankle, and snapped the man sideways with a jerk of his massive head. The man's arms flew up and he crashed into the building on their right. Conor moved smoothly and quickly into the group and punched the largest man he could see in the face with the pommel of his sword. The

REFUGEES

man went down like a falling tree. Then he gripped the front of another man's shirt with his left hand and threw him at the same spot Gray's victim had hit. The man piled into the wall and slumped on top of the first man, who had not moved. Gray jumped up on another man's chest and forced him to the ground with a thump. He pressed his muzzle into the man's face and bared his long white fangs. The man dropped a long knife and whimpered.

"Wait! Wait!" Conor called out. "We do not want to hurt you!"

Both the Eliti and the others stood in stunned silence. Conor and Gray's assault had taken only an instant, but their speed and power were shocking.

"It's them. It's Conor and Gray."

"They're here."

"Conor, help us." A woman's voice. "We have nothing."

"Conor…"

The babble of voices grew louder until it was impossible to understand what was being said to him. Conor sheathed his sword. Gray stepped off the man he was threatening, almost daintily.

"Stop!" he yelled. They did. He turned to the Eliti, who had remained in formation with shields and spears up, at the ready.

"It's alright," he said, and he motioned to them to lower their weapons. "We' re good."

The officer in charge of the men stepped forward, nodded to Conor, and then barked out an order. The shields crashed to the ground and the spears came up to point at the sky.

REFUGEES

Over the next few hours, they found out that the city was occupied by desperate, hungry people, most of whom had also been driven from their homes throughout the Southlands. There were now more people to protect and feed, which somehow made Conor feel better. He had spent enough time wandering in isolation with Gray—and without him. And he felt less hopeless when he was in a crowd. The people were what he was fighting for, after all. He used to think that he was happiest out in the wilds with Gray, hunting, searching, or just wandering. But now, with the threat of annihilation by the Other, he was discovering that he liked being around people after all.

Dareen was satisfied by the decision to take them in and Dvor was confused. She had used her power to calm the refugees and they returned the favour by feeling the gratitude she seemed to need. Dvor wanted to fight somebody, something. And gathering non-combatants and setting pickets and searching for food was not fighting. He and his men could not understand why Dareen and Conor were so enthusiastic about saving old men, women, and children, essentially tying themselves to them. Dvor was always pointing this out.

"If the Traitor desires it, these people," he said two nights later, waving dismissively at a bunch of them clustered around an open fire, "these people will tear us to pieces. Or die trying."

"True," Conor said. "But could not the same thing be said about your sister sons?"

REFUGEES

Dvor's scarred face went red. "We fought him in the north," he said. "When the others turned, we did not. We will fight!"

He struck a heroic pose, one hand on his heart, the other clenched in a fist in front of him. Conor said nothing. Dvor strutted away, muttering.

So theatrical.

That might just be their way.

Maybe. And maybe he just has a rod up his ass. But he's right, these people can't help us.

Before he answered Gray, Conor blew into his hands, trying to warm them. *I know. But we can help them.*

Really? Can we?

Gray cast these thoughts over his broad back as he ambled away from the conversation as easily as he had joined it. Conor did not answer. Whatever he said, Gray would not understand it. The Hound did not, could not, fully comprehend the depth and nature of this conflict. His mind was too focused on what was right in front of them, what was happening today. The underlying motivation, the point to which it was about life in this world—especially about the lives of men, women, and children—was not something Gray thought about. The Other or the Traitor had an unearthly desire for death and the idea that it waited for them even after death gave Conor the belief that he must try to save them all.

Conor had been a lawman, a fighter, and a soldier. He had seen men at their best—and their worst. Berserk soldiers in the field felt and thought little. Rage and bloodlust overcame them. But when the bodies cooled,

REFUGEES

so did they. The Other's rage burned hot always and the death of entire worlds had not lessened his hate. He, and his goals, were the same—despair, chaos, death—and his thirst for these was never slaked. He was not a person. Not even a he. It was a monstrous eternal enemy.

Conor felt that only he really knew this. Only he had spoken with it, seen its dark visions, felt its madness and malevolence. Only he had been thrust into the void, the space between the stars, so cold, so vast, so desolate that the Other had expected him to go mad. But he had survived. And he had fought the monsters and the hunters that he knew still squatted on his world like a growing pustule, awful and real.

In the face of that, Conor knew that every life was precious. So he would go on collecting people, all kinds of people, and giving them refuge and hope and fighting to keep them alive, whether Gray or Dvor wanted to or not.

They stayed in the city for a few days, scavenging and absorbing the people they found into their growing community. Dareen was invaluable. Her emotive power calmed the refugees. She couldn't entirely erase the Northerners' desire to fight, but she lessened it. Conor and Dvor had them train as hard as they dared. They couldn't afford accidents. Some of the men and women they encountered wanted to fight as well, and they folded them into their small fighting force. Conor and Gray searched the city for weapons and food. They scouted outside the city looking for signs of the hunters. And each night they stood watch on the low walls, looking south down the road towards the place where the hunters gathered.

REFUGEES

One cool evening they stood together, watching. It was clear and there was a quarter moon. A mist covered the fields surrounding Dece. Abandoned farm buildings dotted the milky white expanses like even black rocks in a tidal pool.

This isn't a very big wall.

No.

I could almost jump over it.

Yes.

There were a few moments of stillness.

How long are we going to stay here?

I thought that question was coming.

And?

I'm not sure.

I don't like it here. We aren't the law. We aren't soldiers in an army. We aren't doing anything.

"*Worth doing*" was what Gray had left unsaid, but Conor understood who and what he was.

Could they leave? Conor thought of his little army. Pranti, Melnis and Arusin had happily joined Dareen's Eliti guard. Eromil was fascinated by Dareen's power. A woman in charge of so many. But now she was far away.

We need to scout further. Go on a real foraging trip. See what's out there.

Maybe.

Conor knew Gray wanted out of the city but also that he might have a point. *Dareen wants to stay here, and wait to see if the Eliti come.*

Even the people?

REFUGEES

Yes. Even them. You know Dvor and his boys will want to come with us. The Northerners were as restless as Gray.

They might be useful.

Yes. Where do we go?

Back down the road? Gray let out a long, deep breath and tried to sound nonchalant. *See what the hunters are up to?*

Seems like the only place.

Conor and Gray looked in the same direction, still as statues, out over the sea of flowing mist and the dark shadows of houses and trees.

Tomorrow, then?

Tomorrow.

CH 6
ON THE RUN

The next morning, Conor informed Dareen that he and Gray would be taking the Northerners down the road to forage and look to see what the hunters were doing. She was surprised by his straightforward statement that wasn't a request, but she acquiesced without argument. The Northerners were getting harder to handle despite her powers, and she knew as well as Conor and Gray did that they needed a task beyond training civilians. She had her guards— and her wants and their desires were the same.

Arusin, Melnis, and Pranti wanted to stay with Dareen *and* go with Conor. The men had a primal trust in Conor and yet Dareen was their mother. They looked back and forth at them, agonizing like children of a marriage that was falling apart, until Conor spoke to them. He reassured them that it was alright with him if they stayed and Dareen smiled and said she would be honoured by their service.

Oh, come on.
I know, I know. Almost done.

ON THE RUN

That is still so weird.
Yeah. Although it fits this fucked up place.

Dvor and his sister sons were ready faster than usual. Conor had told them of their mission the night before and they were through their formal greetings and salutations and in formation before Conor had finished talking to Dareen.

It was always easier marching on hard surfaces, so they used the road. Gray scouted ahead so they could get out of the open and hide in a stand of trees or an abandoned house if trouble came up the road to meet them.

Which it did, later that afternoon. They had warning this time, thanks to Gray.

Hunters. I'm coming in on the west side.

Conor yelled a warning and they got off the road, scurrying like rats, and took shelter behind a barn with half a roof. Conor stood at the corner of the barn wall, peering around it. The weather was almost pleasant. A steady mild wind pushed full white clouds, sending them scudding overhead. Conor saw Gray running hard, a black streak through thin forest towards them.

You being chased?
No.
What exactly did you see? How many?
Hunters. And does it matter?
Can you be a little more specific?
What do you need to know? They are coming.

Conor could almost hear the strain in Gray as he ran. It didn't really make sense, but he could. *How many? How long till they get here? Do they...?*

ON THE RUN

Lots. All of them maybe...not too long. And you are not going to like what you see.

What?

I'm almost there.

Gray burst from a stand of trees not far from the barn. He settled into a trot, his red tongue lolling out, massive chest heaving as he panted loudly. He moved in behind Conor and said, *Look. Listen.*

Conor stared down the road. He heard a faint sound, a keening warble over a noise like wind over dry grass. The road he looked down was absolutely flat. It was made at a time when men could do things they no longer could. It did not crumble along its edges. Weeds did not force their way through the tightly packed bricks. It did not buckle when winter came and went. It was as constant as the light of the sun for Southlanders, and had been for as long as anyone could remember. And now it was moving, vibrating, almost shivering. Conor felt a deep uneasiness. And then as they waited, the hunters came into view. The hissing had changed into a buzzing drone. They came in a shimmering, moving wall of tall grey bodies with sparking, shining spears held out in front of them.

Shit. What is that?

Some of the spears seemed to have torn or twisted flags or banners of some kind. They were held up and away from the column, at the end of the spears.

Are those...?

Men. Yes.

ON THE RUN

The hunters had impaled them on their spears. Some twisted and writhed, still alive somehow. Eliti, Chan, Southlander, it was impossible to tell. It was a sickening and threatening sight—a grisly march of agony and death.

How many?

Not sure. All down the column.

As they watched, the hunter army disgorged individual hunters who swayed and lurched off the road, gibbering and hooting. They struck buildings and trees with their weapons, sparking fierce blue fires that flared and burned both wood and stone.

Dvor edged forward. "What are these...things?" His eyes were wide with disbelief.

"Those are the hunters. That is what we call them." Conor said grimly. "Killers from a place with a dark sun."

Dvor's features hardened. "The Traitor. He has brought them."

"Yes," Conor said.

"They do not...belong here."

Conor nodded. He had fought them before, and knew they were not of this world. Alive but not flesh, bone, and blood. They were immensely strong, hard to kill, and their spears were like lightning. He had seen just a few rout a strong force of disciplined Eliti regulars in an instant, turning a battlefield into a scene more like a group of hungry men with spears chasing poultry in a barnyard.

Dvor barked an order in his northern tongue and his men drew their weapons with a soft clatter.

They can't be serious.

ON THE RUN

Conor reflexively reached out a hand and put it on Dvor's right arm. Despite his desire to join them, he shook his head.

"No. Not unless you want to see your sister sons on spears like those poor souls."

Dvor looked back and forth between the hunters and Conor.

"We have come a long way. And lost much." Dvor's eyes flashed. "And now we are to watch as these things burn our world?"

Conor glanced at Gray, who rolled his eyes. The predator knew the mismatch between their force and the hunters. He wanted to run—and quickly.

Tell them we can't attack.

Conor hesitated. It didn't make sense, but he wanted to fight as well. Here. Now.

Conor! We will all die here. For what? Think!

Reluctantly, Conor spoke. "We, too, have lost much. Friends. Family. Love. My heart cries out for vengeance." He shook his head again. "But to die here, unremembered, in a senseless fight against overwhelming odds? No, Dvor. No."

Dvor frowned, grimaced, and then sheathed his sword. His sister sons did the same. Conor smiled briefly. They turned back to the road and watched the hunter's column continue to ooze along, their scouts burning anything close.

What if they burn this barn?
It'll take a while. If they don't notice us, we stay put.

ON THE RUN

After a few moments Gray, who was slightly behind Conor along the wall, asked, *Any end in sight?*

You saw more of this army than I did. Just a second...yeah. Might be thinning out. Yes, there are definitely fewer toward the back.

The little band waited. Squatting in the snow and mud, the Northerners made no complaint. The barn was far enough from the road that none of the hunters came to fire it. When the last of the hunters had wobbled and hooted past, Conor and Gray led the others out onto the road. They stood in a group looking after them. The taciturn Northerners were visibly shocked.

Was that all of them, do you think?

I don't know.

Then Gray nosed the road. *Take a look at this.*

Conor knelt down and put a hand on the tightly packed bricks.

What am I supposed to be noticing?

Look closer.

Then Conor saw. Tiny striations had formed in the bricks and were spreading out. Thin, jagged black lines were working their way through each stone as he watched. Conor pushed his finger into the edge of one. It gave like a loose tooth. The north-south road, legendary symbol and heart of the Southlands, was crumbling.

Well, that's terrible, Conor said as he stood and wiped his finger on his tunic.

Yeah. I know. And interesting.

What?

ON THE RUN

Think about it. Why send the hunters here? Except to torture us? Make us feel like it's all falling apart.
It is.
Gray bared his teeth, obviously irate. *But remember what you said before. The Other can burn entire worlds. He has shown you that.*
Yeah...
Then why send these things, with abilities just beyond everybody except us?
Maybe he can't destroy this world. Conor waved his hand over the road and the surrounding fields.
Because we are on it. Maybe it is about us.
And maybe he's just a bastard.
Yeah.
Conor looked at Dvor and the expectant faces of the rest of his men.
Not sure what to do about it right now. All-powerful god, or bastard, he's put us in a bind.
Right. Confront them with what we have and die. Or stand aside and watch them burn everything and kill everyone they can touch.
"Conor?" It was Dvor. "Should we get back? The hunters will fall upon Lady Dareen and the others if we don't warn them."
Shit. He's right. Conor gritted his teeth. *And they might do something stupid like stand and fight.*
If Dareen is threatened, they will.
"Let's go," Conor said out loud to Gray, Dvor, and all the Northerners, and he started to run off the crumbling road toward the closest clump of trees. Conor

ON THE RUN

and Gray ran across the wet grass, breathing easily. The Northerners scrambled to keep up. This was when Gray felt best, running powerfully in the wild with a purpose. Conor usually felt the same way, but he was not as good at not worrying about the reasons that started them moving and what might be waiting for them when they had to stop. But they set a punishing pace and did not wait for the Northerners strung out along the path behind them.

Their focus narrowed to the path Gray took them on. He sniffed out the game trails quickly and kept them hidden from the road as best he could. They leaped streams and fallen trees, ducked branches and splashed through mud and water. Gray could hear the heaving breaths of Dvor and his men. But none complained. Every few moments, through the tree cover, they would glimpse the eerie sight of the hunters on the road on their left. Tall, grey, and packed tightly together, they could burn men with a blue fire so bright it was hard to look at. The hunters did not notice or did not care about Conor and Gray's small force as it raced by them through the forest not far away.

Eventually, they left the hunters behind them. When they did, Gray veered closer and then on to the road.

Flatter is easier.

Right.

They kept running, Conor and his massive, fierce black furred companion. The pickets on the walls of Dece did not challenge them when they approached. The men looked relieved to see them back so soon. They were powerful figures out of the old stories which now fit into

79

the chaotic events that had brought them to this place so far from the Empire.

Conor and Gray raced through the streets towards the building that Dareen had taken as her headquarters. They rounded a corner and ran right into a clump of men and women surrounding Dareen. Something had happened which had stirred up the people they had found in the city. Voices were raised and hands were pointing and gesticulating. Even Dareen's powers couldn't calm them down.

What the hell...

"Lady Dareen!" Conor called, trying to push through the excited crowd and get her attention. "Lady Dareen! We have urgent news!"

She saw Conor and looked alarmed at his expression. Sh e spoke quickly to the official beside her, who yelled out a curt order. Her guard moved into the crowd, pushing them away from her roughly.

Dareen's hands came up and she spread her arms wide. "Friends," she said, "I will hear all your petitions! The food we found will be distributed. Please, friends! But now I must speak to Conor."

Even with Gray close, Conor felt the pulse of emotion wash over them all. *How kind and good she is. How fine it is to be here with her, a Mother of Eliton! She will take care of us. It will be alright.*

Gray broke into his thoughts. *I thought that crap didn't work on you when I'm around. You should see the look on your face. You look like a lovesick boy.*

She must be using all her strength.

ON THE RUN

Dareen approached, her guards lining the street. They were staring at Conor and Gray and they gripped their spears tightly.

And what exactly are you going to say to her? What...
The road leads right to the gates of Dece. We have to go.
Where?

But Conor had turned his attention to Dareen.

"Conor," she said, her dark brown eyes fixed on him. "You have news? What have you seen?"

"Hunters," he said. "Many hunters are coming up the main road. They will be here today."

She looked at him warily. "Can we stop them? This city has walls and we have fighting men."

Conor shook his head. "No. No, we cannot. They are too strong and their spears...They are burning everything in their path. We must—" he paused as Dvor and some of the Northerners clattered into the square. Dvor jogged up to them. Conor continued, "I was telling Dareen that we must leave Dece."

She looked at Dvor, who nodded in agreement, so out of breath he could not speak.

"And where are we to go?" Dareen asked sharply.

See?

"Anywhere but here. Dece is right on the road. The army of hunters have not wandered far from it, as far as we have seen. We go west, cross-country."

"What if they follow us?" Dareen asked. "What then?"

"We run," said Conor. "We set a rear guard if we must, but we run towards the only help we can hope for. From your Empire."

ON THE RUN

Conor pointed at Dareen as he said this. A few of her guards muttered and grunted at this but it did not bother her.

She smiled, but her eyes did not. "Agreed. If we run, we must hope for help." She turned her head and picked at her sleeve absentmindedly. "How long until the Chan come? If Eromil is successful."

Admitting that the Empire needed help was difficult for her. She looked off into the distance as she spoke, unable or unwilling to let Conor see her expression.

"Weeks. Maybe more," Conor said. "If the army of the Consolidation hasn't left the Southlands. And if she finds them and if she hasn't been killed by the hunters along the way." Conor hesitated. "There are more of them. Many more. And they may be going south."

Conor looked at Gray, who stared back blankly.

"Ah, yes. Well…" Dareen said.

"We will stay, Lady Dareen," Dvor blurted. "We will make sure you can get away safely." He looked at her admiringly. "You, and the rest, of course." He had noticed how his offer might have sounded to the men around them. His face went slightly red.

What an idiot. He is going to get killed. And his men along with him.

Dareen is powerful. He is just trying to please her. But Conor was once again made uneasy by Dareen's ability to influence those around her.

"Pointless death does not help us," Conor said. "We need all the warriors we have."

ON THE RUN

Dvor bristled at Conor's suggestion that his offer was a stupid one. "Someone has to fight. We have come a long way—"

"We know, but—"

Dvor interrupted him. "We do not know you, Conor. We do not know your mother or your father. We have heard of your skill as a fighter but we do not know what kind of man you are." Dvor pointed at his own heart. "The worst of us can fight. And we will fight." His diatribe ended with his finger in Conor's broad chest.

Conor thought for a moment, then said, "I honour your journey, Dvor. And your courage. But you will die. You and all of your sister sons." He was matter-of-fact. "And you won't hold up the hunters for more than a few moments. It's senseless."

He turned to Dareen, "My lady, please, tell him to…"

Dareen spoke curtly. "If Dvor desires to help us all escape I do not see why I should stop him."

Oh, she's loving this.

She hasn't seen the hunters. She doesn't know.

Are you defending her? I thought when we were together you didn't feel her power?

I don't. But I'm trying to understand them both. I'm not in charge here. We need to convince, not command.

Well get convincing, because we have to go.

"Dvor, my lady," Conor said softly, "the Northerners don't have to stay here. There may be a time coming when a stand is needed. But now, we need to go. Everyone. Please."

ON THE RUN

"And if they leave the road and come after us? When we leave?" Dareen asked again.

"Dvor and his sister sons will be our rear guard," Conor said. "Of course. That honour will be theirs."

Dareen seemed satisfied that she and the refugees would be protected. Conor turned to Dvor. He nodded but kept his hand on the pommel of his sword.

"That honour will be theirs?" You sound like the Northerners. If they need to hear it, I'll give it to them.

Runners were sent to the refugees scattered throughout the city to let them know they were going to move. Conor didn't know exactly how many people they had with them. He figured around a hundred Eliti soldiers and guards for Dareen, forty or fifty northern warriors, and perhaps three hundred refugees, mostly old men, women, and children. Dareen was everywhere, soothing and persuading. Even the most cantankerous of them calmed when she spoke. But even with her powers, it took time to get them all moving.

Conor and Gray stood on the walls and looked down the road, straining to see the first sign of the hunters. They would be the last to leave, along with Dvor's Northerners, of course, who lined the parapet beside them. Dece's short walls were a deliberate choice made by the city patrons who wanted their city to be open to all who wanted to trade, gamble, whore, and fight, no matter where in the world they were from.

These walls wouldn't have held up the hunters. They could step right over them.

Yes.

ON THE RUN

There. Conor pointed south.

In a few moments, Gray could see a faint shimmering low on the horizon, like the first star on a hot summer night.

"Where?" Dvor asked.

Then one of his men said something in Northern and his finger followed the same path as Conor's. Others joined in pointing and talking excitedly.

"Dvor, can you send one of your men to see how the rest of them are doing?"

Dvor didn't react. He stared down the road, transfixed by the now-visible sheen of the spears of the approaching hunter army.

"Dvor!" Conor said, louder.

He pulled his gaze away from the road slowly, looked at Conor blankly just for a second, and said something to the man beside him. The man bowed slightly and took off down the stairs and into the city.

How long do you think?

Hard to say with those things. Hour, maybe two.

Shit. If they come after us, we won't be able to get away.

We will.

You know what I mean. All of us.

It would be wrong to die with these people. With a world to save.

Gray felt Conor's stubbornness.

We could start with them.

Gray started to argue but stopped. They had to run but Conor was not going to budge until he had to. He had spent much of the last few moons running. First from the Believer's army through the Southlands, then

ON THE RUN

to the Eliton Empire and back again with an army of their own. Then Conor had gone back to the Empire again to find Gray, who had run free after the Believer's death. Now Conor and Gray were back together in the Southlands, facing the awful army of the hunters, this time with nowhere safe to run and no real force of their own.

But maybe we'll fall off that bridge when we get to it.
Maybe.

The Northern messenger scrambled back up the stairs and said something to Dvor. He nodded and barked out an order. The Northerners turned as one and started filing down the stairs and back into the city.

"The evacuation is almost complete," Dvor said to Conor. He waited until the last of his sister sons had gone.

"Thanks," Conor said. He put his hand on Dvor's shoulder. "We'll be right behind you. I don't know how well those things see. And I don't really want to find out."

After Dvor left, Conor and Gray crouched down behind the parapet.

What are you waiting for?

Conor did not reply right away. His head was down; his hands hung between his knees.

I'm getting tired of running.
But you see the need, right? We can't stay here. You said.
Yes. Still.

Conor's expression was bleak.

Yeah.

Their heads still down, they moved off the wall and ran after the Northerners into the streets of Dece towards the western gate of the city.

CH 7
SEE FOR YOURSELF

The hunters burned Dece; Conor saw the blue fires reflected in the clouds behind them as they stopped to camp. He stood with Gray, Dvor, and Dareen watching the flickering light along the horizon, like lightning strikes that wouldn't end. The people from the city murmured and the Eliti soldiers and Northern warriors stared, but no one said much as they watched the terrible spectacle.

Dvor sent his men out in pairs to watch for hunters coming in the night. The Eliti set up in their organized way, with straight lines of white tents, palisades, and timed watches along the perimeter. Dareen's tent was precisely in the middle, as usual. Eventually, Conor slept while Gray patrolled even further into the forest than the Northerners, not trusting them or the Eliti guards. He came into their tent in the predawn darkness and bumped hard enough into Conor's cot to wake him.

Your turn.

Conor rolled out of his blanket and then the tent, eyes bleary but his head clearing rapidly. He always woke up fast.

SEE FOR YOURSELF

It was misting slightly. He pulled up the hood, wrapped the waterproof Eliti cloak tighter, and walked to the edge of the camp. He nodded to the Eliti sentries, who stood a little taller when they saw him, figure out of myth that he was.

When one called him "M'lord," he corrected him. "Just Conor, my friend. And what is your name?"

"Arrusden."

Conor walked with him in the darkness and they spoke of the cold, the mist, and the day. It was simple, direct, unaffected, and personal. It was what soldiers did and what they wanted from men who led them. Conor moved on after a few moments.

The night passed and the hunters did not come. In the early morning light, the Northern sentries came back into camp while the Eliti were breaking it down. The group ate and then moved after Dvor and his sister sons had exchanged their elaborate greetings.

It was slow going cross-country through patchy forest in the early spring. Even in the clearings it was hard work just to walk and the children and the elderly slowed them even further. Some paths they followed simply ended and the column would have to unwind, reverse, and wait until a new one was found. They walked into a bog late on the third day, soaking most of them and causing no end of confusion. Conor and Gray, who had been at the rear watching for hunters, were called up. Dareen was waiting for them, surrounded by her guards. The edge of her fur-lined cloak was splattered with mud and she looked tired and sweaty.

SEE FOR YOURSELF

Not what she is used to.
Obviously.

"Conor, you must lead," she said. "Your Hound must scout for a clearer path forward. We can't go on like this."

Conor looked at Gray.

There is no path that I can find that will be wide enough for this many.

The plains can't be far.

The plains west of them between the Southlands and the Empire stretched out wide and flat for a long way. When they reached them, it would be easier for this group to move.

No. But a four-day walk is turning into ten. Maybe more. And if the weather breaks at all, this bunch will be in real trouble.

Yeah.

Yeah. We didn't think this through.

If we were going to stay with them, we didn't have much choice. But we have to stop. At least for a few days.

Agreed. I'll...

"Conor!" Dareen said sharply.

"Yes, m'lady. I was just thinking." Conor ran his hands through his hair.

"Yes?"

"Perhaps we should find a spot and make camp?"

"What? Just for tonight?"

"No. A more permanent camp."

"What? I thought we decided..."

"Well, the hunters don't seem to be following us." Conor gestured at her guards. "And your people can build a solid camp in a day or two. There is a lot of lumber around."

"And how will we find help?"

Conor looked at Gray.

Use the base as a focal point. Send scouts in all directions except east. Might work.

Yeah.

"We will still look. Send out scouts. But without dragging these people with us."

Dareen said nothing at first. She picked at her sleeve.

Conor waited. He knew her men would do anything to please her, including building a comfortable place to hole up. The refugees would be happy to stop walking through the snow and mud. He could use the Northerners as the scouts. His plan made sense and would be accepted. Conor also knew that she felt what was happening to her was undignified. Beneath her. She was a Mother of Eliton and she was on the run, tired, dirty, and wet. It was impossible, and yet it was true. The world had changed. She had to, as well. Dareen would agree with him.

"Fine. Find a place on higher ground and we'll build there."

"Thank you, Lady Dareen."

"We passed a place that would work this morning; it was not too far back."

"Yes, I remember," said Conor, recalling a rise like a bump on a flat log topped with a stand of trees.

Dareen said, "I will tell the Eliti and the refugees."

She noticed that hill.

Smart and full of surprises.

SEE FOR YOURSELF

Maybe she knew we were going to have to do this. And she let us think it was our idea.

Yeah. Maybe.

She has been in charge of men her entire adult life. And some men need more than love and loyalty.

Like the feeling they are in charge.

Yeah.

Dareen interrupted them. "And you will press on. Keep going west, with the Northerners?"

Conor could feel the emotional power coming from her, compelling him to do just that, if that was what pleased her. He shook his head and grinned at her. This time, it was what he wanted to do, as well.

"Yes, Lady Dareen. We will."

Dareen smiled in return, yet hers was a little unsure. Her uncertainty was so genuine it surprised and attracted him. When they made eye contact, he realized his smile had pleased her as well—and that had unnerved her. Conor's face went slightly red and he bowed awkwardly.

They went to Dvor and he agreed that it was time to leave the refugees. He reminded Conor he hadn't wanted them along at all. "Not fighters. Not warriors. Just mouths to feed."

He sounds like you, Gray.

That's because he's right.

Some of them would fight alright.

Yeah, with another six moons of training. We're better off without them and you know it.

Maybe. The Eliti we leave behind can protect them from anything other than the hunters anyway.

SEE FOR YOURSELF

Right.

Facing west away from the road they split into squads of eight to ten men. Each took a point on the horizon. They promised to send any refugees they found back to the fort the Eliti were building in the forest. If they robbed, raped, and killed in the Southlands before, they were ordered not to now. The Northerners showed no expression when given this order. Conor did not know what to think about that.

What's done is done. Let's go.

Five groups set out. Conor and Gray went straight west, alone. The most direct route to the Empire.

They hadn't been walking for a full day before Gray heard someone tracking them.

Someone is behind us.

Conor was instantly exasperated. *Probably one of the Northerners. Lost.*

I'm not sure. I'll circle around and see. Want to wait?

Yeah.

Conor moved off the trail and squatted behind a fallen tree. He used to be very good at waiting; it was part of a soldier's and a lawman's life. And he was born calm, he had been told. But as he shifted his weight from his right to his left foot and felt a cold drip of water down the back of his neck, he was deeply irritated. Lately it seemed like his emotions were making calm harder and harder to find. His encounter with the Other, his monster, and now the hunters, was doing something to him. He was quicker to anger, to draw his sword, to rush in. And that realization bothered him as well, which made him even less calm.

SEE FOR YOURSELF

Shit. Where the fuck are you, Gray?

Conor wondered whether he was in full control of himself anymore. The incident at the road when they first encountered the mass of hunters disturbed him now, in retrospect. He really had wanted to attack the huge aggregation, which was utter madness. The endless war between and Other and the Lords of Power (as described in the Eliti holy book) was happening here and now. But was he Conor the man or the Lord—just a weapon? He hated the idea that he wasn't in charge of his actions. *I'm going to make sure I am, from now on.* Conor took a few deep breaths and peered through the tree trunks back along the trail.

Conor saw the Eliti soldiers at the same time Gray got close enough to talk to him. They looked winded, red-faced, and frightened. When Conor stepped out onto the trail, he could see the relief on their faces.

"Melnis? Pranti? What are you doing out here?"

Good question. Gray trotted up behind them.

"Conor. Thank the Mothers we found you."

"Yes. You did. Now what are you doing here?"

"Lady Dareen sent us," gasped out Melnis, the younger and taller of the two men. "She said to tell you that the Chan have come. Eromil brought them."

That was quick.

Yeah. They must have been looking for the Eliti when she went looking for them.

How did they find Dareen?

No idea.

SEE FOR YOURSELF

Melnis interrupted, "Lady Dareen says you are to return. She needs you to help talk to the Chan."

Conor was skeptical. Dareen rarely needed help from anyone. And after his exchange with the Chan a few moons ago, Conor knew the Eliti and the Chan had informal relations and that language wasn't an issue.

She needs you to tell them about the hunters. They have to know about the Other; they met him at Oro. And on that battlefield.

Right.

"Lady Dareen needs you now, Conor," Pranti added. "We cannot wait. We must go back."

Gray rolled his eyes. *She works these guys hard.*

Conor thought about the Northerners, and dismissed them from his mind. There was no point worrying about them. They could still look for help, no harm there. He had questions for the Chan and wondered whether he could talk them into helping…and they were now only a few hours away.

"Alright. We go back."

Gray had already started east along the trail.

There were a lot of Chan warriors at the camp when they arrived. From the vantage point at the top of the hill, Conor could see the path they had bludgeoned through the forests and fields from the southeast. The wide wheels of their war wagons had helped them cross muddy ground and they had cut down the trees they could not avoid. The powerfully built, long-necked beasts who pulled the wagons had stomped and huffed in their harnesses as they passed them. The pale skinned, leather armoured Chan milled about silently, eyes wide at the sight of Conor and

SEE FOR YOURSELF

Gray, who was pleased—if that word could be used to describe his feelings.

Many warriors. Many.

Yeah.

It took them more than a few moments to find Dareen in the confusion. When they did, she was seated in an impressive wooden chair that looked like it had just been made. Several Chan were standing in front of her, while her guards lurked behind. Pranti and Melnis faltered at the edge of the gathering. They looked at Conor for guidance.

He patted Melnis on the back and said, "Thanks boys. We've got it from here."

The two Eliti stood around a bit hoping Dareen would notice them but she didn't, and they wandered off. She did see Conor and Gray, though, and she stood up and gestured for them to join her. The Chan moved aside, not quite as impressed as the Eliti regulars.

They expected us, though.

Right.

Conor immediately recognized the Chan leader who had dismissed him and his appeal to fight with the Eliti against the Other not so long ago. Eromil stood close to him. She nodded to Conor.

Things have changed since then.

Perhaps. Yes.

The rest of the Chan looked at him blankly.

"My lords, this is Conor and his hound, Gray," Dareen said, a satisfied smile on her face. "The Southerner I told you of. He is a fighter, a soldier, a lawman. He raised an army to fight the Bonded fanatics. He was imprisoned by us, and yet when freed, he came back to fight the monsters at Oro."

The Chan exchanged glances. The Other's creations had killed Eliti and Chan that night.

"He will speak to you now."

The men who faced him were expressionless, neither impressed nor dismissive. Conor hesitated. He did not know where to begin. He did not want to thank or welcome them. They hadn't come to the Southlands to help anyone but themselves. They had ignored him in the past. He started getting angry.

Forget all that. They are here now. Convince them.

Perhaps this is me as a weapon, angry at not being used. But maybe I'm just sick of trying to convince people of something that we know to be true.

Just tell them. Like you do.

Alright. Alright.

Conor spoke plainly. "There is a new enemy in the Southlands. We have seen them. Fought them."

Conor saw that Eromil was tense. She swallowed hard. Her hand was on her sword hilt.

"They are on the road east of us. An army of living things, unlike us, and with a hatred for all life. Eromil has seen them, too."

Conor pointed to her. She stepped away from her commander and bowed deeply to Conor and then to the rest of the group.

"Conor and the Torit," she said, "fought and killed many of these things. They are very tall, with bright spears

SEE FOR YOURSELF

that..." She struggled to put her experiences into words, the same way he did when he tried to describe them. She looked at Conor, her eyes pleading for help.

He carried on for her. "They are called hunters. At least, that is what the Other called them when he spoke to me." Conor tried to make eye contact with everyone in the circle. To convince them. "He, *it*, brought them to this world. To kill, burn, and break us. We must stop them. It is the only thing that matters now."

"And the Eliti?" one of the Chan spoke. "Where are the Eliti?" The other Chan grunted in approval.

"I am here, a Mother of Eliton," Dareen said as she stood up. "And I am ready to fight with you."

Her guards looked at her adoringly. They were ready to die right then. But the Chan Conor had met while he was a fighter were much like the men he saw here. Taciturn and stolid. They had to be feeling what Dareen was putting out, but they didn't show it.

"Yes, but where is your army, Lady Dareen? You have no more than a cohort here."

She smiled weakly and looked almost embarrassed.

Another of the Chan spoke. "You are indeed formidable, Lady," he said with a hint of a smile, "and we hear you. But if these hunters are as Conor says, we need warriors, not words."

"I have sent messengers to the Empire. They will come." Dareen sounded like she was sure of it, but the Chan were not ready to accept her proclamations.

"When, Lady Dareen? When?" one said. "Do you know?"

SEE FOR YOURSELF

Dareen hesitated, then shook her head. Only slightly, but still a no.

"So do we fight these things without the Eliti? And if our army is broken by our victory?" The Chan said it like it was a foregone conclusion. "Then will the Eliti begin the war over the Southlands again?"

Dareen shook her head more vigorously this time, "No. No, that is over."

"So you say, Lady Dareen."

Another Chan jumped in. "Do you speak for the Empire?"

He has to know she doesn't, thought Conor. No one did, as far as he could tell.

Dareen responded, "The Empire is not what it was. It may never be again." She took a deep breath. "But what is happening here is something more, greater than any war ever fought. It is the end times and we must do our duty." She looked at the Chan, imploring them, "We must fight, for all of us, Chan, Eliti, Southlander and northerner. We are people and our differences are not as many as what we share."

Conor could almost see the waves of emotional power coming off Dareen. He felt it, even with Gray next to him. But her words were truth. He had made the same speech many times.

I hope she has more luck than you did.

It worked sometimes. Sort of.

Yeah. And you didn't have her powers. Or her tits.

Conor looked at the Chan. *I don't think her tits matter all that much to those guys.*

SEE FOR YOURSELF

You never know. You people are strange about that.

Dareen was, in fact, almost eerily attractive. Her ability to induce loyalty, love, and respect in those around her was astonishing to Conor. And she was obviously intelligent. But Conor had also seen the Mothers at each other's throats back in the Empire. They were all like Dareen, beautiful, smart and powerful—but people, nonetheless. And if he read the Chan leaders properly, that was exactly what they were thinking as well.

He decided to speak. "But you know what happened at Oro? And to your forces east of the road?"

The Chan exchanged looks but did not say anything.

Conor continued, "Eromil has told you what she has seen? What we have done? What has come to our world?"

"We have heard," one of the Chan said.

"None of you saw the monsters and the fires? None of you saw the bodies of your warriors smashed and burned?"

The Chan started talking among themselves. Conor did not speak their language but he knew what they were talking about. He waited. Dareen moved towards him and put her hand on his right arm, a thank you. Then one of the Chan stepped forwards.

"We will see these hunters for ourselves. You," he pointed to Conor, "will show us the way."

Conor nodded.

"The army will stay here until we see."

"Thank you…" Dareen hesitated. The Chan had not introduced themselves. One spoke,

"Gettil. I am Gettil. I speak for the Consolidation."

SEE FOR YOURSELF

"Ah. Thank you, Gettil," Dareen said and she smiled at him. He smiled briefly in return. Then he turned and walked away, followed by the others. They began barking orders as they did.

Well that's done. When do we leave?

CH 8
D'AEL

After they arrived, the Chan had set up in a wide perimeter around the hilltop encampment. They dug ditches and set stakes. Their huge round tents went up and their bright, heavily scented orange fires started burning. They tethered their war beasts in groups of three to long tree trunks set atop their stumps. The beasts stood calmly, watching the camp being constructed with huge black eyes, chewing at the bales of hay the Chan had pulled out of their wagons for them. They must have gotten used to the smell of the Hound, as they just stepped aside almost daintily as Conor and Gray passed by them.

The Eliti soldiers busied themselves with their own duties and the civilians tried not to get in the way. The Southlanders were mostly just wide eyed and silent in the face of the imposing military organization and sheer number of foreign faces.

Conor and Gray drifted through the camp at dusk, Conor nodding and smiling when recognized. The Eliti soldiers liked talking to their living legends and the Chan who spoke Southlander were curious. They saw Arusin,

Melnis, and Pranti, who had been assigned to Dareen's protection unit. They looked conflicted but said they were happy to be back with their own people. Eromil was at Gettil's shoulder, half translator, half bodyguard, it seemed. Her fascination with Dareen was still evident. Her face shone as she listened to Gettil and Dareen discuss something. Conor and Gray walked by and she ignored them.

I'd like to know how she found the Chan so fast.
Yeah. Almost like they were looking for us too.
Seems like it.

Conor and Gray had a tent the Eliti had provided and they ate what the Eliti cooks made for them while sitting outside of it, just nodding to those who passed by, mouths full. Then they went in and slept.

They left when the sun peeked over the horizon, wan and white through the mist. It was cold. Gettil, Eromil, an Eliti officer they didn't know, and twenty Chan soldiers went with them. Their leather armour had been stripped of most of its bulk and their swords were tied behind their backs. Gray had scouted a path, so he led them into the forest that surrounded the camp. Conor knew they had a few hours at least before they had to worry about being detected so he settled in to the march behind Gray. They skirted wide meadows full of tufts of tan grass and snaked along game trails Gray had discovered. The pace was brisk but not punishing. All Conor could see was forest and all he could hear were the faint creaks of leather armour and sodden footsteps of the men behind him.

D'AEL

Gray forged far ahead of them as the sun rose to its apex in the sky. They halted when Conor heard Gray telling him, *I can see the road ahead. No sign of the hunters.*

Do we stop here? Or come up to you?

Wait.

Conor turned and put his right hand up in a universal stop sign, or so he hoped. It worked, and the column halted when Gettil repeated the gesture. They had travelled southeast, hoping to be able to take a hidden position to observe the hunters moving along the road.

They are coming. Stay there.

Conor crouched and the others did the same.

Gray approached them not long after. *Many hunters. New bodies out front, it looks like. Fresh. Alive.*

Conor grimaced. *Wait here a bit and catch the train?*

Yeah. Better chance to stay hidden.

Conor turned to Gettil. "Tell your men we are close. Stay quiet and move when I say."

Gettil nodded and whispered to the man behind him, who gestured to the others to wait, his right hand out, palm up. They squatted in the cold, tension growing. Conor saw Eromil's face, pale and strained. He breathed slowly, feeling the urge to fight rising inside him. He struggled to prevent his caution from being overthrown.

Be Conor. Not the weapon. He said it to himself over and over. He could sense Gray's questions about this forming.

Let's talk about it later.

Alright.

D'AEL

Gray immediately accepted any suggestion not to talk about something. They waited a good long while.

Gray finally stirred. *I'll go see.*

He moved away. The column shifted and regripped their weapons but no one said anything. Conor found he could not wait so he crept along the path behind Gray. He sensed no warning so he didn't stop until he saw him. There was a ditch behind a stand of trees that overlooked the road ahead of him. Gray was crouched there. Conor crawled up beside him and then got into a squat, his hand on his friend's broad back.

The hunters moved along the road. Their tall grey bodies swayed, their spears shone brightly, sparking at times. They hooted and gobbled when one of their number weaved away to stab a tree or a house along the roadside, immediately setting it afire with bright blue flame. Gray growled deep in his throat and Conor felt the absurd but expected powerful urge to pull out his sword and charge the hunters. The column stretched out in front of them, but to their left they saw it coming to and.

Time to get Gettil up here?

As good as any.

Right.

Conor scurried back. "Just you," he pointed to Gettil. "We have to make sure we aren't seen."

As he got up and turned to go, he saw Eromil start up after them. Conor held his hand up. "No."

"I've seen them already," she hissed at him.

"Yeah," he said. "I know. You sure you want to come?"

D'AEL

She said "no" under her breath but she followed it with, "I'm a war wife of Shenzi. I will go where Gettil goes."

Gettil's eyes widened at the sight of the hunters. Conor could hear Eromil taking rapid shallow breaths. After a few moments, Gettil turned and slumped into a sitting position, his back to the road. Conor moved around to face him while Gray kept watching the horrible parade.

"So?" Conor asked.

Gettil rubbed his hairless chin with his right hand. He looked at Conor with his pale blue eyes. "Can they be killed? Do they die like men?"

"Yes. I—we—killed many."

Tell him.

"But," Conor said, "They are very strong and fast. And their spears burn flesh, wood, and stone."

Gettil grimaced, almost in pain. Conor sensed he was thinking of how many of his warriors would die if they confronted those things.

"We don't have a choice, Gettil. They must…"

"Yes. We do," Gettil said quietly and firmly. "We can go back to the homeland."

"And Mori will protect you?"

Conor remembered Eromil's recounting of how the homeland of the Chan was protected by their god, Mori. War had never come to the Consolidation and they believed this god made it so.

"That column of monsters will move south eventually. You must know the days of men fighting men are over. You must." Conor gripped Gettil's arm. "The world…"

D'AEL

"Is coming to an end?" Gettil scoffed.

"No...well, we don't know that. But we must fight."

At that moment, the strange noises coming from the hunters grew louder. The clamour increased, its discordant sounds grating and harsh. Eromil clapped her hands over her ears and looked at Conor in desperation. She was afraid and trying not to show it.

Something's got them riled up. And it's not us.

Conor crawled back up the embankment and peered out. The end of the hunter column was disintegrating. Heavy-headed arrows were sleeting into it from the forest somewhere on Conor's right. Hunters were falling and careening side to side down the road. They screamed and gibbered and hooted and shook their bright spears.

Conor felt anger. He whirled on Gettil. "Did you order an attack?"

Gettil looked confused. "Attack? No, of course not."

"Well someone is fucking doing it."

He knew the Empire did not rely on archers. He spun and tried to look down the road without getting too far into the clearing.

So who is it?

No fucking idea. But they are getting some work done.

The arrows continued to thud into the hunters. Conor remembered the shock up his arm when his sword cut into them. He recalled it was like hitting a bag of gravel. There were many arrows. They flew fast and they were sticking. Armour-piercing heads, he thought. Must be. From a longbow. They were hard to handle and took a

D'AEL

lot of training. Then his heart jumped. The tribes! The people of Eliton are here!

Good.

As Conor watched, some of the hunters formed up into a compact group just off the road. As they did, the arrows stopped. The hunters hesitated and then charged into the woods, spears held out front, hooting as they ran out of Conor's sight. The column continued on, oblivious or unconcerned. The fallen hunters' arms and legs flailed wildly as they lay on the ground, abandoned.

"What is happening?" Gettil asked from over Conor's shoulder.

"Someone has attacked the hunters with heavy arrows. Now they are running, I think."

Gettil craned his neck to see. "Hmmm." Then he looked at the wounded hunters, rolling spasmodically on the ground. "What about them?"

Conor thought for a moment. "We wait and then we kill."

It was not long until the army of hunters faded from view. The group that had left the road to chase the archers were crashing through the underbrush far to their left. The sounds coming from the wounded hunters on the road had not lessened. Conor drew his sword.

The first hunter he came upon had an arrow stuck into one of its bulbous dark eyes. The wound had leaked black fluid and the hunter was drumming the ground with his arms and legs and screaming long discordant notes into the cold air. Conor's sword smashed into its body just below the mouth opening. It died with a gurgle.

D'AEL

Another hunter had pulled itself half upright, leaning on one long arm and slashing at the air with its sparking spear. Conor approached and feigned an attack. Gray had circled around while he did, now he dashed in and seized the supporting arm in his teeth and pulled. The hunter went flat, his spear flew up, and Conor impaled it with his sword, gritting his teeth as he pushed down into its hard, lumpy body.

Conor looked up to see Eromil, Gettil, and his guards hacking away at the other wounded hunters, like a pack of wild dogs savaging wounded beasts. Except these beasts had long arms and bright sharp spears. Conor tried to cry out when a Chan warrior got too close, but he died burning on the end of a hunter's spear. These were hurt and weakened hunters, and it still took four or five warriors dashing in and out, slashing with their long flat blades, to kill each one.

When it was over, the Chan and the one Eliti officer gathered around Conor and Gray. They were sweating despite the cold, breathing heavily and wide-eyed. There were four dead hunters. Six of their own number had been injured, two killed. Stabbed and burned. Over twenty hardened Chan warriors and Conor and Gray to kill four wounded hunters.

"It was like cutting something made out of rocks," one Chan blurted out in heavily accented Southlander.

"What are they?"

"Where do they come from?"

Conor spoke. "They are hunters. Brought from another world to kill us. "

D'AEL

"They aren't..." the warrior hesitated, unsure what to say.

"No. They aren't like us. They are not life as we know it in the Southlands, the Consolidation, the Empire—or anywhere else, for that matter."

"But they can be killed. They die, like us," Gettil said, examining his notched sword as he did.

"Eventually, yes," Conor said. "They do."

The group stood in silence for a few moments. A couple of the Chan dragged their dead away from the hunters, whose bodies were beginning to fall apart as they watched. Their spears were now a dull flat black.

Gettil said, "Take their swords. Leave them."

A couple of Chan walked over to the bodies and stripped them of their weapons.

"I think I may know who shot those arrows and wounded those things." Conor pointed at the crumbling bodies on the road. "It must be the tribes of Eliton. They fought...well, some of them fought with us against the Believer and his army." Conor put his hand on Gray's broad back. "We hoped they would come and fight with us again."

"Why?" asked Gettil. "Why would they come?"

"Dareen has sent word to the Empire, as you know. She has also contacted the tribes, telling them what we are facing here." Conor shrugged. "And it looks like they came."

"The tribes, they are Eliti?" Gettil asked.

"Yes, but they are different. They are at war with the Empire."

D'AEL

"I like them already." Gettil said this with a humourless smile.

"Me too," said Conor. "Let's go find them and maybe kill some more hunters."

The Chan left their dead without looking back. They paired up to help the wounded. Gray led them back into the forest and they tracked northward, parallel to the road. They had seen the hunters charge in but after that, nothing.

It shouldn't be far.

What?

The, uh…fight.

You think the tribes would stand toe to toe with the hunters? They aren't that stupid. Gray left out the obvious implication that Conor was thinking that everyone was like him. He dodged a low hanging branch.

Yeah. You're right.

They'll stay just out of reach. And have traps set.

That would be their way.

Maybe, if they are D'ael. And if they had time.

When at war, the tribes' different clans took on specific roles. Ambushes were the job of the D'ael. They were hulking men who moved silently and killed efficiently. Conor had fought with them against the Believer and he had been impressed by their skill and bravery.

As they struggled up a greasy incline, Gettil said, "I wonder how many came to the Southlands this time."

"All of them, I hope."

"There are many of these tribes?"

D'AEL

Conor had not seen the great forests and the hidden mountain redoubts of the tribes of Eliton. Gray had, but he wasn't one for being impressed by human civilizations. Conor had been in the huge Eliton capital and seen their massive infantry formations in battle. If the tribes hadn't been conquered, that was enough.

"As many as there are stars in the summer sky."

"We will take any that come, with thanks." Gettil said grimly, obviously affected by the fight with the wounded hunters.

"Yes."

Gray froze. *Wait.*

Conor crouched and threw up his right hand. The column halted quickly with only the slightest of creaks and snaps of the lacquered leather armour of the Chan. Within a few moments, they heard and then saw the hunters moving back onto the road. Following no path, they moved through the trees awkwardly yet without slowing, swinging their arms and tilting strangely, spears held upright. The wild hooting and groaning had ceased. Tall, silent, and sinister, the grey monsters passed out of their sight.

How many?

I wasn't counting, were you?

No, dammit. I wonder if...

Not likely. Not enough time. They chased and the D'ael ran.

They'll go back to the column and the whole thing will be repeated somewhere down the road.

It's not enough to stop them. It will just piss them off.

We have to stop them.

D'AEL

I know. Let's go.

Gray led them down the path as they looked for the D'ael.

But it was the D'ael who found them, appearing late that afternoon at the head and the rear of the column simultaneously. Gray had been scouting ahead and they had moved in behind him. The big, bearded men were clad in mottled grey and white clothing. They had blended into the late winter forest so perfectly that Conor had nearly impaled himself on the long knife the lead D'ael held out in front of him.

He didn't expect Conor's broad smile and hearty Eliti. "Hello!"

"Who are you?" the man asked. "Why do you hunt us?"

Get back here.

On my way.

"I am Conor." He turned and gestured behind him at a wary Gettil. "This is Gettil, a commander of the Chan Consolidation, and these are his men."

Swords were out all along the column. D'ael were appearing out of the trees on both sides of them. They could throw short knives with devastating accuracy, Conor recalled, and they had all seen the arrows. The Chan were nervous. This had the makings of a disaster.

Conor put out both hands. "Easy, boys. We're all on the same side here." He said it in Eliti.

Gettil translated, but the swords stayed out.

Conor continued, "We were watching the hunters. Gettil had not seen them before."

D'AEL

The D'ael in front of him frowned. "And he did not believe. That, I understand."

Gray burst into the clearing. The D'aels' eyes went wide. Loud calls echoed into the forest, "The Lord and his Hound are here!"

"It's true!"

"It is the end of days!"

"So it is true," the leader said. "I am sad to have seen it. So comes the end of days."

Conor had heard this phrase before from a warrior of the people, in an Eliti prison camp many moons ago, but she had used almost exactly the same words. The People believed that the coming of the Lord and his Hound was an old story come to life which told of the end of all things. The citizens of the Empire were conflicted about that, and that was one of the reasons they were at war with each other.

"Maybe," Conor said grimly, "if we don't stop those things on the road."

The D'ael eventually agreed to go back to the compound with them and meet Dareen. Conor knew they weren't the biggest clan but they were influential. He was eager to know if the rest of the tribes were coming, especially the assault clans, where the real numbers lay. *If they did*, Conor thought, *if they came, we have the beginnings of a chance.*

Even Gray was glad to see them. *It's strangely comforting to see those guys.*

Agreed.

CH 9
A VOICE OF IRON

Conor nodded in the direction of the big D'ael seated across from him at a huge round table in the Eliti command tent. It was their turn to host the meeting of the leaders. Dareen was on Conor's right, her eyes alert, looking regal. She had two guards standing behind her chair. One was Arusin, a nice gesture. He was too old to be much use on the battlefield but he was so obviously and hugely proud to be one of Dareen's personal guards that Conor smiled when he saw him. The man tried not to grin in return but as his eyes flicked over at him Conor saw one come and go.

Dvor was there, with Dvak. The Chan had found him and he had returned to be part of this parley. Some of his sister sons were still scattered all over the western half of the Southlands looking for the Eliti or the clans or anyone who could help.

Gettil and his Chan commanders came in last. He nodded to each of the representatives and then Dareen asked each to introduce themselves. They did. Dvor immediately stood up and tried to tell the story of his

A VOICE OF IRON

family from the beginning but after two sentences Dareen cut him off with a wan smile. "You can speak of this later. Now we will move on to more pressing matters."

Dvor coughed and turned a little red in the face, but he sat down. He leaned back and whispered a few words to Dvak and they both shook their heads. The D'ael leader introduced himself as Baragara. His gaze lingered on Dareen, flat black eyes staring at her like a challenge. But she did not rise to it. She simply nodded, smiled, and looked away.

"We are here to speak of those things on the main road," Gettil said when the introductions were over. "Something new has come here. We need to know what you can do to help us against these...things, these hunters."

Conor nodded when he used that word to describe them, the word the Other had used.

An odd way to put it. Us helping them. Isn't it the other way around?

Not really.

Why?

Well the Empire's army is in the wind, according to Dareen. It may never come. It might not even exist. There are only 40 Northerners in the Southlands. We are the army of the Southlands, us two. Impressive, but two. And the D'ael haven't said the tribes are coming. At least not yet. That means Gettil and his people will pay the highest price.

Ah. Isn't this your time to say something noble and inspiring?

Nope. Not yet. We go where the big boys and girls decide to go.

If they do. The Chan may bolt. You've heard Eromil. Back to the homeland.

A VOICE OF IRON

True. But Gettil has seen the hunters. And when they are done here, they could march south.
With no one to stop them.
Right.

Dvor stood up first, again. Conor was not surprised. The Northerner was sure of his importance and that of his little band. He swore to fight the demon Itax and all his manifestations. He described this intention loudly in florid language. This time, Dareen allowed it. Dvak tugged his tunic when he started in on the history of his people again and he sat down abruptly.

Dareen was next. She was gracious, thanking the Chan and all who were present. Then she spoke of the Empire, first taking a deep breath. "The Mothers are in conflict. The unity of the Empire cannot be assumed. What has become of the army at home, I cannot say. It is fractured, at best."

She looked at Baragara, who stared right back. She asked him, "The war between the Empire and the clans? It continues?"

Baragara answered in a low voice. "Your forces no longer test us on the forests' edges. Or in the mountains. Of your cities, we know and care little."

"Ah. As I suspected. It has gotten worse since I came here."

"Worse for you, perhaps," Baragara said.

Gettil interrupted. "Eliti problems are not the issue here."

Dareen bowed her head slightly. "Agreed. I am sorry. I was just looking for information." She put both hands on the table and leaned forward. Then she looked at each of the people at the table in turn. Conor could feel power pulsing out from her and he could see it in their faces. All had heard of the Mothers of Eliton, but hearing and experiencing were different things. Conor remembered his shock at the feelings of love and loyalty he had experienced against his will. The tent was completely silent save for the strange low hiss from the white Eliti globes that lit the space.

"Our holy books speak of this," Dareen waved at those gathered around her. "All people in the known world uniting to fight the Other who is attempting to destroy us all." She turned to Conor and Gray, who sat behind him. "It speaks of the Lord and his Hound, created for the very purpose of opposing him."

Conor stared straight ahead. The Northerners and the Chan craned their necks to look at him. Her Eliti guards nodded in agreement and Baragara and the D'ael looked on with narrowed eyes.

Conor knew their presence was a double-edged blade to the Eliti and the D'ael. To some, they were harbingers of a dark fate. That was another piece of the myth she did not mention to the gathering. In it, Gray somehow covers the world in darkness rather than let the Other prevail. The tribes' version of the story seemed to be that once the Lord and his Hound were announced, that end was near. In the past, Conor had convinced some of them to fight anyway.

There were those in the Empire who believed in the old stories, and those who thought they were nonsense.

Dareen had come to his side thinking the end was near. Other Mothers had not. As a result, the Empire was collapsing in on itself as the hunters advanced.

"We must fight," Dareen said, her eyes bright with conviction. "The hunters, or whatever the Other brings against us."

Dvor thumped the table in agreement. Dareen's guards glared at everyone, daring them to oppose her. Baragara nodded slightly, but the Chan were impassive.

Dareen turned to Baragara. "Will the tribes come? Will they fight?"

He shrugged. "We are of the people. We are here. We fight."

I can see why you like these guys.

"And we thank you," Dareen said. "But you know what I am asking."

Baragara stood up. He was a big man. His mottled tunic stretched across his chest. He was heavily bearded and his long black hair was tied in a single strand down his back. Even white teeth shone out in the semi-darkness as he spoke. "My people have seen the signs. Lightning on clear days, shaking earth, and the blue flames of the hunters. The Empire retreats from our forever war. Is it truly the end of days, we wonder? Some said they had seen the Lord and his Hound, and fought for him against madmen and monsters. Others said he had died in an Eliti prison. We had a Hound with us, but of his Lord we had no sign. We came to see and we still do not know."

Baragara looked at Conor when he spoke the last sentence.

A VOICE OF IRON

"Prophecies are untidy things," Gettil said.

"Until now," Dareen interrupted. "The Lord and his Hound are here. They sit beside you."

"So you say," Baragara said as he squinted at Conor, tilting his head slightly.

You might have to get involved here.

Yeah.

Conor started to rise when he noticed Arusin furtively gesturing to someone across the table. Eromil stepped forward. She had been at Gettil's elbow and Conor had not seen her.

She cleared her throat. "I am Eromil," she said, "war wife of the god Shenzi, and I will speak for those who cannot." She turned and looked at Gettil, who nodded curtly.

As she began, Conor sat back down.

"Not long ago, I was with another unit of our army. We had located a large Eliti force. Our seekers had led us to them and under the light of the stars and our sacred fires, we fought."

This could be awkward.

Wait...

"Then, it came." Eromil swallowed and her voice became almost a whisper. "We saw blue flashes in the sky, like lightning, but it would not stop and then the wind...it..." she slashed the air with her right hand, "cut us down. It smashed us, it..." she struggled to continue her face twisted in pain.

"Burned," said Arusin loudly. "We burned. I was there. I was at that battle. I saw. The air killed us."

A VOICE OF IRON

There was silence.

"We heard...reports," said Gettil quietly.

"As did we," said Dareen.

"Believe them," Eromil said. "We ran. Those of us that could. But in the forest, we met Conor and Gray. They gathered those that survived together, Chan and Eliti. We went back to the battlefield. He wanted to see. To understand. There, the wind attacked us again, killing us, and then Conor..." She looked at him, imploring him to explain the unexplainable.

He got up and started speaking. "The Other—or Itax, or whatever name you want to give it—tried to kill me. It drew me into the void and threatened me with oblivion. It showed me entire worlds on fire, and stranded me in the endless distances between the stars."

The faces around the table were skeptical, some grim and some merely curious. Eromil and Arusin were afraid.

Conor continued, "It had spoken to me before, in my dreams and awake. Murderous thoughts and words. It started at the battle of Oro, when I fought its creations."

"We had reports from Oro as well," said Gettil.

Dareen nodded in agreement.

"But it could not kill me then. Or when I was with Eromil and Arusin on the battlefield. Or even in the void. But it promised to make me feel the pain of watching my world be destroyed by the hunters, beings it sent from a dark and twisted world."

"They are horrible, the hunters," Eromil said, too loudly. "They kill men like we kill birds or rodents. But Conor," she pointed at him, "he is not just a man. He moves like water and hits like the hardest war hammer. And Gray, the Torit, he savaged them and then his breath put out the fires that burned us. They, the two of them, they killed them all."

She stopped, breathless and a little embarrassed by the rush of words. Arusin's head was pumping up and down in affirmation, looking around the table, challenging any to disagree.

Gray started to encourage Conor to speak, but he stopped. He did not have to. The Conor he felt in his mind was changing. He had noticed it first in his irrational desire to confront the hunters when to do so was to die. Conor was sure. He no longer doubted his place in this war. It was not like the blinkered fanaticism of the Bonded. He was sure like the forests of the Southlands were a hundred shades of green, like clear water ran its streams and the wheat grew in its fields.

"And now there are more, thousands more, spreading like a disease on our land. We will fight." Conor put his hand on Gray's back. "Will the Chan? The Empire? The tribes?" Conor stood straighter and stronger than any man in the tent. Perhaps any man they had ever known. He looked down at them, his face scornful. His voice cracked like a whip. "You saw them, Gettil, on the road. And you, Baragara, and Dvor. You know what hunts us. What will you do?"

Conor felt a surge of conviction and power. Dareen looked shocked and then her hands covered her face. Arusin bowed. Dvor was on his feet, his sword out. Baragara stood as well. Gettil frowned but his hand was

A VOICE OF IRON

on his sword hilt, and Eromil looked at Conor, her face shining. No one spoke. They waited for him.

Shit, Conor. What was that?

"I am tired of talking," Conor said, his voice like iron. "Fight or run; do as you will. We will face them tomorrow." With that, Conor stalked out of the tent, Gray at his side.

CH 10
LIKE A GOD

Dareen came to him later that evening, alone. Conor was sitting outside his tent, wrapped in a cloak, staring into a fire. Gray was inside, asleep. He stood up when he saw her.

"Lady Dareen."

"Conor."

He pulled another camp stool out of the tent and she sat. She rearranged the folds of her dress. He looked at her and then back at the fire.

"Has Gettil come to talk to you?" she asked.

"No, he has not."

"Baragara?"

"No. I had to send Dvor to bed, though," Conor said with a grin. "He wanted to attack the hunters tonight."

Dareen smiled. "Baragara came to see me."

Conor looked up in surprise.

"The tribes will come. Like wind over the grass they will come, he said. He has sent word. They are two days away, maybe three."

"Ah."

LIKE A GOD

"They had come across the plains, just in case." She stared into the fire for a few moments. "You are surprised?"

"Well, to hear of it this way, yes. I am happy. We need them but the People and the Empire have been fighting for so long..."

"And we are Eliti all the same, in some ways." Dareen smiled at him. "In this strange place, in these strange times, we see our similarities are more than our differences."

Dareen shifted forward in her seat, elbows on her knees. Not a leader of the Empire now, not powerful and remote. Just a woman carrying a heavy burden.

"Conor, Baragara is afraid of you. So is Gettil."

"What? Why?"

"You showed them something in my tent, tonight. Something they have never seen. Do you remember the holy books of Eliton? Do you remember I said that there were books only the Mothers had?"

"Yes."

"Well, there is something in them you need to know."

"I will read them."

"Oh no, no," Dareen said, shaking her head. "These books will never leave the libraries of the Mothers. Never. They are under our seal."

"Ah," Conor said. The fire snapped, embers flew and then settled. Dareen looked at him over the flames.

He looked back at her.

"Well?"

"Conor, you are more than you know." She looked at him with dark brown intelligent eyes. Her smile was wistful, almost sad.

LIKE A GOD

Gray had come out of the tent. He sat beside Conor, his golden eyes fixed on Dareen.

She smiled at him in the same way. "And you, Gray. I know you understand me. You are more."

Gray did not stir. Now Conor leaned towards the fire and kept his eyes on it.

Dareen continued. "The Lord and his Hound. Here to fight the Other and protect this world." She chuckled quietly. "Simple, yes?"

"It has not always seemed so. Now it does."

"But do you know who you are? What you have become?"

Conor was surprised to hear these questions from her. He had been asking them of himself since his days as a lawman and the rise of the Bonded. Had they not been answered? The sense of personal responsibility and desire to fight had been growing over time. He did not question his righteous anger anymore. "I am Conor, Lord of the Hound, Gray. And I am not alone. Allies and friends have fought with me as well."

"But you led armies did you not? Of Eliti and the tribes?"

"Yes."

"And fought stone men at Castle White, burning men in the battle of the road, and snow creatures at Oro?"

"Yes. So?"

Dareen leaned back and folded her arms. The fire outlined her perfect features in black shadows. She spoke softly. "You lost your parents as a child?"

LIKE A GOD

"Yes," he was abrupt. "They were Bonded. They left me as the Bonded left their children all over the Southlands."

"I am sorry."

Conor shrugged, "It was long ago."

"And your only true love, Andaine? She died on the road?"

Conor sat back and eyed her warily. He did not like to talk about her. "Yes," he said flatly. "The Believer killed her before I killed him."

"Did you?"

"Him? Yes. But then the Other came and it is worse."

"Yes."

Dareen brushed her thighs with both hands, then picked imaginary lint off her dress. "You never lost a fight, Conor?"

"No."

"Wounded in battle?"

"Twice. Once by one of your Hirashu and then by the snow monsters at Oro."

"Seriously?"

"No, not really."

"And the Other has spoken to you in a voice only you can hear? As the Believer did before it?"

"Yes."

"Ah…Conor, does any of this seem more than odd to you?"

It did. He had often wondered where his "gifts" had come from. His parents were unassuming as far as he could remember and was told. He had been in so many fights, melees and battles and had always emerged almost

LIKE A GOD

untouched. In battle, he had "second sight," some had called it. He saw what was coming in a way that others could not. And he was big, unbelievably fast, smooth, and stronger than any man he had ever met. It wasn't even close.

"Losing your parents must have been hard. And Andaine."

Conor knew both of those events had nearly broken him. He had barely survived the second. Perhaps Dareen knew that somehow.

"Of course," he said, irritably, wondering what she was getting at.

"Yes. Either could have stopped you from becoming, you. And they came from the hand of the Believer, not a man or even a person."

Conor was sickened by her statement. He had not ever, ever, thought of those events in that way. Was she saying it was part of a plan to stop him from…?

"All those people? My parents? Andaine? Because of me?"

"That is one way of seeing it."

Conor put his head in his hands and shook it.

But Dareen pressed on. "Another way would be to say that the Other doesn't want you to become who you will be. Strong enough to defeat him. It has tried to break your spirit. It has tried to kill you. It tried to take this world. But it could not, at least not yet."

"My parents? Andaine? Tingish, my friend? The people of the Southlands?" Conor was aghast. "And Myra, her sister? Just to get to me?"

LIKE A GOD

Dareen looked at him calmly, her mouth a thin line. Conor got up and walked around the fire, in a daze.

She continued, "Would those friends and Andaine have chosen any differently if they were told who you were? If they knew how important you would come to be?"

"They wouldn't have believed it. I didn't."

"I think some of them probably did." Dareen continued, her voice firm and sure. "Conor, we are talking about the entire world. Our world. The eternal war between order and chaos is here. The Believer was the first test; you triumphed. You defeated its human armies. Then the Other brought the hunters. You were born to be our champion and you must be, no matter what the cost. Your people would have known this. They fought for you, with you. As will we. And do not doubt there will be more of this hell to pay."

Conor stared into the black sky above them. "I will fight. That I know."

Dareen spoke again, more softly now. "Conor, there is something else I think you should know."

"Yes?"

"You are not just the Lord of the Hound, Gray."

Conor tilted his head back down and looked at her with his eyebrows raised. "No?"

"No. Not just that." Dareen squared her shoulders and sat up very straight. "You are an incarnation," she hesitated, searching for the right words, "an iteration, of the two Lords of Power themselves."

LIKE A GOD

"What? What does that mean?" Conor almost squeaked when he spoke.

"It is clear." Dareen stood up. "Your voice in the tent was that of a god. Even I almost knelt to you then. I , a Mother of Eliton, who bows to no man." She shook her head and smiled a rueful smile. "You lost your love, your friends. We imprisoned you. Cast you aside. Ignored your warnings. You survived. You grew stronger, stronger than the stone man at Castle White, the snow monsters at Oro, stronger even than the hunters. The Other spoke to you. Tried to kill you. Yet you did not run. You show no fear. You command us by your example, yet you only ask us to fight with you."

Dareen spread her hands out in front of her, imploring him to believe her.

"That is why you frighten the men around us. They are hard men, Conor, but they feel you are different from them. From everyone. You are…more. A god." She shook her head again and looked at him from under her dark, even brow. "I should be kneeling now."

"Please don't. And I don't believe it," Conor stood and paced around the fire. "I've never, I'm not…I can't do what it can. I can't move the earth or create monsters or control minds. I just fight, and talk."

"So far, yes. And you inspire others to fight as well."

"I've had a lot of practice at that."

Dareen smiled a little. "Yes, you have. And even I, a Mother of Eliton, with all my power and an Empire behind me, am inspired. But we are weakening, Conor.

LIKE A GOD

The mothers are fighting each other and the Empire is divided."

Dareen's composure slipped and Conor saw flashes of uncertainty and fear.

"We shrink in your shadow, Lord."

"Bullshit," said Conor.

Dareen laughed out loud. "How dare you speak that way to me!" she said, mocking herself.

"My lady," Conor bowed.

She smiled at him. He sat down. They looked at the fire together in silence for a few moments.

"Our power comes from our children," Dareen said suddenly. "We reflect the power of life itself. That is what we believe. But you…"

Conor changed the subject; he did not want to talk about himself anymore.

"What of the women of the Consolidation? The Southlands? Why don't they have your abilities?"

Dareen's face showed her old impatience and arrogance. She straightened up and said, "We are Mothers of Eliton. We are different."

"That's not much of an answer."

She shrugged, "Why are you a Lord? Why are you stronger and faster than any man? Why can't anyone kill you?"

Conor looked up into the sky, speckled thick with bright stars.

"I don't know. I…the Believer was wrong; his creations were wrong; the Other is wrong; the hunters don't belong here. We need to make them leave, or kill them all. And

LIKE A GOD

we, Gray and I, we can't do it alone. These things, I am sure of."

"Ah, Conor, you are a blunt instrument, a true Lord of power."

"A weapon."

"That is one way of seeing it. We will help you win this war. The only war that matters. Because if we don't," she pointed at Gray, sitting beside Conor's chair, "he, your Hound Gray, will cover the world in a darkness that will never lift."

The Lords of Power had decreed that, or so it said in the Eliti holy book. The Hound was this world's final line of defence, but his power was only there to deny the Other victory. No one knew what followed the Hound's last act of defiance.

Dareen stood up. She was almost unnaturally vital. She was smart, powerful, beautiful, and she thought he was a god. She had said it. Her body was curves, angles and flat planes. He caught himself staring at her.

She arched an eyebrow. "Conor?"

"Dareen, I…" he stuttered and looked away, not knowing what to say.

"You have been on a lonely road, Lord Conor. And you have seen and done terrible things." She looked at him with an appraising stare. "You could take me. Men do this. I have seen Mothers do it, as well. A lord such as you could not be stopped."

Conor grimaced.

Dareen responded to his expression in a tone that was almost resigned. "You would not need to strike or threaten me. If you commanded it, with the voice of a god, I do not know if I could refuse."

Conor cut her off. "What other men will do does not concern me; I will not. I do not want this power. Do not speak of it to me again."

"As you say, Lord."

Conor shook his head again, looking away, and then back at Dareen. She was so much like her daughter, Nisi. Conor had befriended her while in the Empire. Nisi had come to him the night before he left. She wanted to be a Mother of the Empire as well. She was as ambitious and strong willed as her mother was. If only she was here.

Dareen spoke. "I have sent for her." She had read him, and not for the first time. "Better for her to be here than waiting behind our walls for…ah…"

"The end of all things? Is that what you were going to say?"

Dareen smiled. "No. For you to save the world, Lord Conor."

She wanted to keep the focus on him. Conor changed the subject again.

"But the journey for Nisi, is it safe?"

Dareen scoffed. "She will be a Mother of Eliton. She has guards. She is ready to see the world outside the Empire, dangers or no."

Nisi had shown her ambition. Conor knew she wanted the power and the responsibility of helping to run the huge Empire of Eliton. And if the Southlands were where things were to be decided, then the Southlands are where she would want to be.

LIKE A GOD

And she might want to see me again.
I heard that, Conor. Romance will be the last thing on her mind.
Yeah. Well, maybe not last.

For the Mothers, it was all about bloodlines and family ties. They were blatantly mercenary regarding prospective fathers of their many children. Dareen had found him suitable for her daughter and Nisi was more than willing. But before that had been decided, they had spent some time together. Real affection had grown between them. It was arranged, their tryst, but it was more than that.

"She will be happy to see you, Conor. Trust me."

Conor smiled briefly. She saw through him. He looked back at the fire, unwilling for some reason to let her see his eyes.

"I am going to bed," she said as she came around the fire and patted him lightly on his right shoulder. "Perhaps our Lord should rest?"

Conor nodded dumbly. Dareen said goodnight to Conor and then Gray, then turned and walked away in the cool night.

O Lord, what are your commands? Gray's mocking had returned.

Conor gave as good as he got. *Get bent. I'm going to sleep. Try not to cover the world in darkness until tomorrow morning at least, will you?*

Conor opened the flap of his tent, went in and slept.

CH 11
BIGGER

The next morning, it was decided that the Chan army would wait as long as they could for the tribes before confronting the hunters. Dareen said nothing to Gettil or Baragara about the conversation she'd had with Conor the night before. The D'ael were tasked with shadowing the hunter army. They left the camp early in a tight single file. Conor and Gray went with them.

The D'ael were quiet, efficient, and supremely confident. They had quickly gotten over the sight and power of Conor and Gray. There was no staring, no obvious signs of deference as with many of the Eliti. Conor was relieved and Gray did not care.

"No attacks, then?" Baragara asked as they strode across an open valley. It was clearing; the wind blew almost warm. The footing was sloppy but firming up in some places.

"No," said Conor. "Not yet. We don't want to turn them against us before we are ready."

"What about taking one? Alive. We haven't tried that yet."

BIGGER

"What for? There is no evidence that they speak anything like a language. Or that they even know or care why they are here."

Baragara shrugged. "Knowing more about your enemy is the first step to defeating him."

"Yes. But...those things aren't like us."

"Still, no surprises is best."

What could be more surprising than the fact that those things are here at all?

Right.

Just at that moment, a jagged bright light arced across the sky, followed by a resounding and enormous cracking sound. Everyone in the column flinched into a crouch, faces up. A blue slashing remnant remained in their vision. They could not tell at first if it was still in the sky or seared into their eyeballs.

I cannot get used to that.

Me either. Shit.

Conor shook his head to clear his vision and then stood up. They had seen lightning bolts across clear skies before. The Believer and the Other had created them. A shared talent. Conor assumed they were a means of communication or intimidation. Nothing else made sense.

"It is the Other," Baragara whispered. "He speaks."

"Yeah," Conor replied, "and he's saying 'fuck you.' Let's keep moving."

Baragara made a signal with his right hand. The D'ael rose as one, hitched their packs, and followed Conor and Gray as they walked ahead.

BIGGER

They caught sight of the hunters as darkness fell. The column had silently crept up the road. It was full of them as far as they could see, standing close together, spears sparking blue, shifting and vibrating, the air filled with their strange hoots and calls.

"Not moving," observed Baragara.

"Doesn't look like it," said Conor.

"Resting maybe?"

Conor shrugged, "Who knows? Maybe they are waiting for us."

Yeah, and maybe they are having second thoughts.

"We just sit tight and see what they do next. Baragara, we need eyes on the entire force. Spread your men out?"

Conor asked because he wasn't the commander of anything or anyone, despite what Dareen had said to him. But Baragara nodded, held up his right hand and made several quick, distinct gestures. Immediately, the D'ael split up and started to move south through the trees parallel to the road and the heaving mass of hunters.

They sat for most of the night. The D'ael sometimes changed positions down the line. Conor and Gray stayed at the head of the column. They had done this kind of thing many times before. Conor was better at it. It wasn't long until Gray decided to "scout" the entire area. The moon rose and the air was just cool, almost refreshing. The D'ael weren't talkers; Baragara was constantly on the move so Conor watched and breathed and was just there. In the stillness of the first shimmer of dawn, the hunters started to get louder. The shivering and shaking increased in intensity. Spears started to wobble and wave.

"Something's happening," said Conor to no one in particular.
It's happening here, too.
They getting ready to move, you think?
Maybe.
We should, too.
Conor stood up and looked for Baragara. After a few moments he saw him coming up the path. The D'ael around him started to fade into the forest away from the road.
"What do you think?"
"I am not sure. Something has got them worked up."
"Yeah. We are getting ready to move out."
Conor peered through the branches and saw that the hunters were reversing. The spears now slanted south, down the road, away from the general direction of the camp.
That's good, right?
Yeah, for us. Not so much for whoever is south of here.
Should we go see?
We were told to keep an eye on them, so, yeah.
They were screaming now, distinct individuals showing at the sides and front of the column as the hunters disengaged from the masses of their kin. Tall, tubular, dark grey, and murderous.
They moved south with the hunters the entire morning, the strange army becoming more and more agitated as it went. The D'ael melted in and out of the forests in front and behind them, keeping pace.
Are they going faster?

BIGGER

Conor stopped walking for a moment and looked carefully. They were. The long strides of the hunters were speeding up.
Yep. And getting louder.
What's up?
I have no idea.
Then Conor heard a sound he did not expect. A faint, peeling thin call. It was an Eliti battle horn! An army from the Empire had come! He felt a chill, punched the air and almost leaped with exultation. They were coming up the road and would meet the hunters right in front of them.
And how is that good?
Conor's elation was replaced by a familiar sick sense of dread. *Shit.*
The Eliti would be slaughtered. This was wrong, this coming collision. The Chan were back at their camp, the tribes were who kne w how far away, and the Eliti coming north could not know what awaited them. The rough plan he had in his mind for a gathering of forces and a battle on their terms at a place of their choosing was at risk.
Shit.
We have to warn them. Stop the battle from happening. We're not ready.
Yeah.
"Baragara?"
The D'ael leader, who had joined them when they had halted, didn't answer at first. He was staring open- mouthed at the hunters, his usual dead- eyed calm overcome by the

BIGGER

sheer strangeness of the sights and sounds coming from the terrible army on the road.

"Baragara!" Conor grunted, louder this time.

He turned, his mouth now closed, his eyes narrowed.

"We are going to try and warn them."

Baragara nodded curtly. "We'll stay out of sight."

Conor nodded back and said, "We'll be back as soon as we can."

"And if you can't? Stop them?"

Conor had no answer to that. He shrugged and shook his head, his face grim.

Let's go.

Gray hurtled south down the path beside the road, his huge black frame disappearing quickly. Conor ran after him.

Gray, sensing Conor's need, pushed the pace. Here, Gray was at his best. Running towards danger in a good cause with Conor in tow. Gray saw the path racing underneath his paws, felt the branches slap at him, smelled the wet grass and wet soil every time he took a breath.

After running at a full sprint for a long stretch, Gray began to feel his legs stiffening and his heart pounding, yet Conor stayed hard on his heels. Gray surged ahead in a desperate burst of energy, branches whipping his broad face. Conor kept up. Gray twisted and dodged around trees and brush as the trail thinned out. The sounds of the Eliti horns increased and they could now hear the tramping of thousands of marching feet. Gray was struggling to catch his breath, panting hard. On and on they ran, Conor keeping up an impossible pace. Once

BIGGER

Gray nearly stumbled on a log that lay across the path. He began to slow, despite himself. Conor ran by him, tireless.

Not far up the path, Conor finally stopped. *There they are.*

Gray jogged up to him. In the distance, they could see the solid black and silver mass of men that was an army of the Empire of Eliton.

Hirashu?

These were the horse-sized lizards full of claws and fangs that the Eliti used against cavalry and on guard duty.

Not that I can see.

Keep looking.

Conor remembered the pain he had felt when one of them had sunk its claws into his shoulder. *How are we going to do this?*

Only one way.

You and I in the middle of the road.

Yep.

This was something they had done before but for Gray it felt different somehow. Gray's chest was still heaving from the impossibly fast run down the path. He saw that Conor wasn't even breathing hard. He was becoming someone— something— that Gray was almost afraid of.

Gray eyed Conor. He had always been single-minded, but the certainty, the conviction that what Conor wanted he was going to get was hardening in his mind. Gray could feel it like a wall, blocking any attempt to dissuade him. Conor believed he could stop an entire army single-handedly by simply standing in front of it. He was absolutely sure. Gray wasn't.

I don't know. Not all Eliti see us as their saviours. Or even their allies.

These ones will. They're here, aren't they? In the Southlands, getting ready to attack the hunters? We only need them to wait until we are ready.

Conor felt Gray's hesitation. It was only partly his natural predator's aversion to risk without almost certain reward. *I'll need you with me. The Lord and his Hound and all that.*

I am aware.

So let's go.

After what he had seen and what he felt in Conor's mind, Gray saw no way of convincing him to stop and think about what he was doing.

Yes. My Lord.

Don't be like that. And he was already moving out of the forest and i nto the clearing beside the road.

Gray waited until he stopped at the road's edge and turned to see if he was coming. Then he joined him and they moved into the path of the approaching army.

Not what we usually do, Gray said as they walked, his claws clicking on the brick.

What?

I mean, usually we are trying to get people TO fight.

You're right. Come to think of it.

They walked on.

It's going to be a nice day.

Yeah, not so cold.

Conor squinted up at the sky, clear now, then back at the Eliti.

They aren't stopping yet.

No. Not yet.

Then Conor hesitated, stumbled, and stopped. He put his head down and his hands on his knees.

Gray felt his confusion. *What's wrong?*

I feel strange.

Gray looked at him in alarm. Maybe that lung-busting sprint was catching up to him. He could not recall the last time Conor had been sick. Tired, angry, enraged, indecisive, and even emotional, but not sick.

What is it?

It's going. I just felt light-headed. Weird. Conor stood up. He blinked a few times and ran his hands over his face and through his thick black hair. He made eye contact with Gray.

The Hound's golden eyes were wide and his fangs were bared.

What? What's wrong?

Gray stepped away from Conor warily. Gray was shocked. It seemed to him as if Conor was bigger. Taller. Wider. Bigger.

Do you feel alright?

I'm getting there. Why? Conor put his hands on his chest, his arms, his thighs. *What are you staring at?*

Are you sure you feel alright?

Yeah, I already said that. It's passing. Why are you looking at me like that?

BIGGER

You, Conor, you've changed. Something is different. I think you're taller. Bigger than you were. You have...grown.

Wait. What?

I have eyes and I have been beside you for the better part of 20 summers. I watched you grow into a man. And now you're growing again.

I just felt strange. Alright? I don't feel bigger.

Well, you wouldn't.

You're not bigger.

I didn't say I was.

But you've always been the biggest Hound anyone has ever seen.

True.

Maybe I'm just catching up?

Maybe. Gray did not come closer. *In one day?*

I don't fucking know.

It's the Lords of Power, maybe.

Am I a weapon?

The thought had come into their minds instantaneously. They both thought about what Dareen had said about Conor, and how he had changed over the last few weeks. Especially when they had encountered the hunters. Ever practical, Gray shook himself all over and started walking again.

If it's coming to an all-out war, bigger is better, I guess.

I guess.

Can you walk?

I told you, I'm fine.

Gray eyed him skeptically.

Are you sure?

Now Conor was exasperated. *Of course.*

BIGGER

When they got close enough to be obvious to the Eliti, they heard shouts. A unit detached itself and began marching towards them. It was a solid black and silver mass of spears and shields running towards them in precise unison.
About time.
Yes.
The two groups kept closing.
Do you notice anything different about those guys?
Gray peered at them, his head slightly forward.
Yeah. Maybe.
Their shields are much larger. Their spears are longer and the blades at the end are different.
You might be right.
I am. Like they know what's waiting for them up the road. Not that it will matter.
No.
Gray eyed Conor.
You really are bigger.
Conor took his sword out and looked at it. He held it out, trying to get some sense of proportion. He realized it felt like it was like a training weapon. For boys.
Gray's eyes went wider. Then he snorted. *You've split your pants. And your shirt.*
What? Ah shit! Conor's face went red for a moment as he looked for the evidence.
Gray walked around behind him. *It's mostly in the back. And under your arms. They won't be able to see it, really.*
Conor raised his sword arm to look and his shirt tore audibly. *Fuck.*

BIGGER

Just don't move much. You don't want to be naked by the time we start talking.

Fuck!

The Eliti soldiers slowed after a curt order from an unseen officer, then they stopped a spear's throw away. Their shields were black, tall, and wide. Their spears were more than twice the length of a man. The front two rows of the unit lowered them, the wicked silver blades wavering slightly.

"Who are you?" a loud voice called out.

Here we go again.

Shut up.

"I am Conor, Lord of the Hound, and this is Gray."

Silence.

"We must speak to your commander. You must stop your advance."

Silence again. Conor continued, more agitated. "Death awaits you on the road."

"We know what waits for us. We have seen them."

It was a woman's voice. The closed ranks of the Eliti split and a dark-haired, visibly pregnant woman dressed in black furs stepped out through the shields and spears. It was evident from the way she carried herself that she was another of the Mothers of Eliton. Conor recognized her from his time in Eliton. He did not know her name. She had not been friendly. She was shorter than Dareen but she had the same confidence and presence.

"Conor," her expression was guarded. "I thought you wanted us to fight. And now you stand in our way."

"My lady...?"

BIGGER

"Telikonta," she said.

Conor's words spilled out quickly. "My lady Telikonta, the hunters are gathered in force within a few hours' march. Dareen and a Chan army are camped north of here. The tribes are coming in great numbers to fight. We must gather our forces before we can confront them. Please listen to me."

"Hunters? Is that what you call them?"

"It is what the Other called them when he spoke to me," Conor said.

Telikonta grimaced, then tried to hide it.

"He sent them here," Conor said. "Opened a pathway for them to travel from another world."

Telikonta pursed her lips. "Really." Then she changed the subject. "You have befriended the Chan? And the savages?"

Still? Doesn't she realize all that shit is over?

Yeah, yeah. Give her a minute.

She looked up at him, her head cocked to one side. "So, what would you have us do?"

Stop, Conor thought. But he hadn't thought beyond that. He rubbed his face. "How many soldiers did you bring?"

She was obviously offended that he didn't add her title and her name, but she replied, "Twenty-six cohorts."

"Hirashu?"

"One hundred."

Conor looked surprised.

BIGGER

"They are at the rear of the column," Telikonta said. "They do not do well around the...hunters. Not yet. We are training them."

"Right." Conor decidedly quickly. "Stay right here, please, Lady Telikonta. We will contact you when the tribes get here. Then we will decide our strategy."

"And the hunters?"

"Are coming towards you. At least, they were."

"Perhaps we should withdraw? Move a few hours south?"

"Even better, Lady Telikonta," Conor said, and smiled. "Thank you. We will send Eliti runners from our camp when the tribes come."

Telikonta nodded. Then she looked Conor up and down. "You need a new shirt," she said with a sniff. "And pants."

He flushed. "Yes, I'm sorry."

"No need to apologize," she said with a wave. "Yet."

Conor bowed awkwardly.

"You are not what I expected, Conor Lord of the Hound."

"My lady?"

"You are less, and more," she said, her eyes hard. "But the Hound, here in the wild," she looked at Gray, "He is magnificent."

Thanks. I think.

Gray bumped into Conor's hip hard enough to put him off balance.

Let's go.

"He thanks you, my lady. Till we meet again."

BIGGER

Conor and Gray set off down the road, found an exit through the trees, and ran off towards their camp.

Gray's usual ability to see or hear danger approaching did not help against the hunters, and they confronted one not long after. It loomed in front of them suddenly as they came around a bend in the path. Its spear flashed forward and singed the fur on Gray's back. He ducked low, his ears flat, and bared his teeth. Conor leaped over him and crashed into the hunter with his shoulder. It reeled backward and to the side and Conor ricocheted off it into the brush.

Gray exploded out of his crouch, leaping up onto the creature, trying to bite down on one of the long arms. Conor scrambled up as he did and hacked into its back, both hands on his sword, using it like an axe. The hunter screamed, an ululating sound. The blow jarred Conor. When Conor levered the sword out of the body and pulled it back to take another swing, he saw that it was cracked and bent.

Shit.

He dropped it. Gray had one of the creature's arms firmly in his jaws, but he was now hanging on the wildly thrashing monster while it tried to stab him with the long sparking spear it held in its other hand.

Little help here.

Conor grabbed the other arm and swung around in front of the hunter. It looked at him with round black eyes like balls stuck on a tree trunk. It opened its wide mouth and howled at him, shaking and vibrating as Conor and Gray, now on the ground, held its arms tight. Then, with an audible snap, Conor broke off the arm he had been holding, grasped the spear and ripped it out of the hand that held it. He shoved it up into the roof of the hunter's mouth to where he hoped the brain was. Its screams rose to a crescendo, and then ceased with a crunch as its legs collapsed and it fell back onto the path.

There were a few moments of silence as Conor and Gray caught their breath and looked at each other.

What the fuck was that?

If they've left the road, we are in trouble.

And this one was alone.

Also bad.

Do you think they saw us go and sent that one to kill us?

Conor grimaced. *I fucking hope not. That would mean they are thinking, not just killing.*

Gray looked at Conor more closely.

What?

Now you are naked.

Shit. Conor looked down. He was barely covered in strips of clothing hanging from his shoulders and legs.

And what was that? You tore its arm off.

Had to do something. Conor bent down and picked up the hunter's ruined weapon. He held it up to Gray. It drooped like a dead flower. He tossed it aside. *We need to let them know what's happening. Back at the camp.*

Right. Let's ...

They heard Eliti horns hooting in the distance. And faintly, the eerie trilling of the hunters.

Fuck. Are they attacking?

BIGGER

Conor was bewildered. *Where did they come from? How long were we off the road?*
I don't know. And I hope it's not all of them.
Maybe they split up?
I don't know if that's better or worse.
One or many, those fucking things are hard to kill.
Which way?
Conor hesitated. The pull to fight was overpowering, but he needed to tell Dareen and Baragara about the Eliti army that had come to fight with them. He stood there, agonizing.

Gray decided for him. *We need reinforcements. Let's go.*

CH 12
WAR

The camp was calm, almost sleepy, when Conor and Gray arrived. Thin columns of grey smoke arose from cooking fires. The white tents of the Eliti were scattered among the Chan huts in an attempt to break down the animosity between the armies that had been so recently at war.

The Chan pickets were startled by the pair as they raced by them, Gray a black streak and Conor, glistening with sweat and barely clothed.

"Hey," the younger one of them said. He was a Chan soldier who had never actually seen Conor or Gray.

The man beside him swatted him on the shoulder, "That's them, you idiot."

"Oh, right."

"Bigger than I thought," one said.

"That's because you're an idiot."

The Chan and Eliti guards at the tent moved in front of them as they skidded to a halt. These were elite troops and not as intimidated as the pickets.

"What is this about, then?" One of the Eliti stepped forward. "The command council is meeting and is not to be disturbed."

"Perfect," said Conor as he started towards the door. The soldiers moved in front of him, hands went to swords and spears came up.

"Conor, you cannot enter without my Lady Dareen…"

Gray snarled and his hackles rose. The guards stepped back but then recovered.

"It's alright, it's alright," Conor said, motioning to Gray and then the guards, his palms down. "Tell them, please, that Conor and Gray have returned. There is an Eliti army in the Southlands not far from here and the hunters are on the move against them." He swallowed and then said, "We must help."

One of the guards grimaced, wheeled around and pushed his way through the men behind him and into the tent. They waited. The tension eased. Some of the guards started to grin and poke each other.

What a bunch of morons. But, then again, you are naked.

Conor looked down. Whatever scraps of clothing had covered him before he started running had disappeared. His body steamed in the cool air.

Ah.

His hands moved to cover himself.

"The Mother!" The guards were suddenly mortified by the thought that she would see Conor this way. One whipped off his cloak and handed it to Conor. He took it with a nod of thanks and slung it over his shoulders. It barely reached his waist.

WAR

Not quite.

No.

He shrugged off the cape, wrapped it around his waist, and held it there. The soldiers tittered, Gray rolled his eyes, and Conor went red in the face. Then the tent flap opened and the Eliti officer gestured to them to come inside.

I'm going to get something to eat while you talk.

Don't go far. I want to be clear-headed when I am talking to Dareen.

Alright.

Gray sauntered off into the camp as Conor went into the tent.

Conor walked to a space filled with Eliti and Chan officers. Since there were more of them, it was a Chan tent. It was dark, pungent, and lit by bright orange fires. The Chan met standing up and in a circle.

Dareen was facing him and as she started to greet him, her eyes narrowed and she cocked her head slightly.

"My lady, and everyone."

The Chan were again impassive and the Eliti were obviously insulted at his appearance on their Mother's behalf.

"What happened to you?" Dareen asked.

Conor thought about telling her that he had grown but instead he said, "An Eliti army is here. Lady Telikonta has brought ten thousand men. They are on the road south of here. She agreed to join forces, but I believe the hunters have attacked them. Or some have. We heard the sounds of battle and we ran here to get help. We must march."

His demand was met with silence.

"What happened to you?" Dareen repeated. "Where are your clothes?"

Conor felt the urge to fight rising in him. He was getting angrier by the moment. He snapped, "I don't know and it doesn't matter. The Eliti need our help. Now. We must go."

His voice was very loud, almost rumbling in the enclosed space.

"Where are the D'ael?" Gettil asked.

"We left them in a forest beside the road watching what we thought was the main body of hunters. But now I am not so sure. One of them attacked us on the trail. It was alone; we have not seen that before. They may be splitting up and spreading out. We must join forces with the Eliti and force them all to fight. We must."

"Agreed," said Gettil abruptly. "More will be better against those things. Lady Dareen," he turned to her and asked quietly, "will you stay here with your force and protect the civilians?"

"Of course," she said quickly with a shallow bow. "Of course."

Gettil bowed in return and strode out of the tent, followed by his staff. Conor watched him go and then stood in front of Dareen and her officers and guards.

"You need clothes," she said to him. "And weapons."

"Right."

"Stay here. They will be brought to you." Dareen said this with a faint smile. She inclined her head and then she, too, left the tent. Her men followed.

WAR

Conor was alone in the strange orange light of the torches. He realized he was cold so he stood closer to the fires, slowly rotating to warm one side of his body, then the other. Eliti soldiers brought clothes that barely fit him. The sword was too small but he took it anyway. He asked for a spear. It was long and heavy in his hand. The helmet would not fit on his head. While he dressed, Dareen came back in the tent, by herself. He did not stop.

"Conor, my god, are you taller?"

"Yeah. And heavier. Gray thinks so."

She looked at him, eyes wide. "What...?"

"I don't know. Isn't it in one of your secret books?"

"No. Nothing like this. The voice, yes, but..."

Conor tightened up his sword belt. "Yeah, well, it doesn't change anything. I need to go with the Chan and help them link up with Telikonta."

"And kill hunters."

"Yes, that above all."

Dareen held her hands out to the fire, warming them. "Telikonta is very strong-willed. And smart. Her men will fight until she tells them not to." She turned to him, her dark eyes warm, and said, "I would tell you to be careful, that the armies of this world need you, but—"

Conor cut her off. "I have to go."

"Yes. Good luck, Lord Conor."

"Shit," he muttered under his breath as he pushed aside the flap of the tent and walked out into the cool air. Gray was waiting for him.

Run?

WAR

They found Gettil standing at the edge of the encampment. His army was forming up behind him. Huge wagons filled with archers and spearmen were pulled by the now armoured long-necked beasts, and rumbled and creaked as they came up. Long lines of infantry were shifting and coalescing into columns while their officers yelled orders. It was an impressive sight.

Conor nodded to Gettil. "How long, do you think, before you get underway?"

"We will be moving within the hour," Gettil said, glancing back at the moving mass behind him.

"Alright. We will go ahead, try to get to the Eliti."

"We'll have to use the road if we want to move fast."

They both knew that might mean contact with the hunters before the armies could reinforce each other.

"The wagons," Gettil gestured at them. The large wheels were sunk into the soft wet ground. "We can't go cross-country all that way. We can't." He shook his head.

They heard harsh cries, the cracking of whips, and the ominous clinking hum of a disciplined army on the move.

Conor nodded. "We think they moved south to attack the Eliti. Maybe we can catch them between the two armies and—" Conor smashed a fist into an open palm.

Gettil grinned without humour. "Maybe."

"I will send back word, if I can," Conor said.

Gettil nodded. "Go."

Conor and Gray turned as one and ran off over the brown and white fields and into the forest. Conor ran tirelessly and Gray hung grimly on his heels. This time he knew Conor would set a heart-bursting pace, and he

WAR

was ready. After a long afternoon of running along a slick narrow trail, they came upon the D'ael squatting in the bush a distance from the road. One of them looked back and signalled for them to get down. They crept up to his position and looked through the trees. The hunters were still visible. Jammed together. Vibrating and softly hooting in long rows as they slowly eased down the road..

"Are there more, or less?"

The man shrugged. "I'd say less, but I can't see the end of the column to the south of us."

"Where is Baragara?"

The ma n poked his thumb southward. "Down the road somewhere. If you wait, he'll be along."

"Thanks," Conor said, "we'll go look."

They hadn't gone far when they heard shouts and the wild ululations of the hunters.

Here we go.

Yep.

Conor increased his pace, which Gray had thought impossible. He could not keep up.

Conor!

Through a gap in the trees, he could see hunters moving off the road with their long awkward strides, shaking their bright white spears. Arrows flickered out of the trees. Most missed, but some struck the hunters with solid thumps. Gray saw Conor even further ahead of him, sprinting through the forest and with a roar, launching himself into a group of hunters who had broken through the brush and were chasing the D'ael away from the road.

WAR

Damn. Are you trying to get yourself killed?

But as desperate as he was, as insane as the attack appeared, Gray knew that no hunter could kill what Conor had become. It would take more than a few of those spindly monsters. Conor hacked, speared, spun, and danced death on them. Gray strained to join the melee and be by his side. Four or five of the D'ael were visible. When Conor appeared, they threw their short knives into the eyes and mouths of the hunters, drew their long blades, and closed in.

Gray saw a man die as a blazing spear transfixed him. Another D'ael sparked into flame when one of the hunters, holding him at arm's length, thrust a spear into him lengthwise from shoulder to hip. That hunter died when Conor broke it in half with his bare hands, one foot planted on its body as a lever. Gray fastened his fangs on a hunter's arm, which was extended into a spear thrust, and then sank and spun, pulling it off balance. It thumped into the snow and Conor leaped upon it, stabbing out both its eyes with quick punching movements. They left it, thrashing and screaming in the wet grass. Conor thrust his spear into another, twisted, and lifted it off the ground, then he threw it like a farmer throws a bale of hay. The hunter flew over their heads and landed in the trees with a crunch. The D'ael stopped for an instant and stared. Then they roared as one and plunged back into the fight.

The hunters who remained upright began to move back towards their column until they were running, their long strides taking them out of range with surprising speed. Arrows followed them, knocking one down. It crawled into the forest, bleating and screaming in pain. Baragara, one arm pressed into his side, blood flowing from it, ran in front of his men and called for a halt. Conor stood, body steaming in the cold air, glaring at the retreating hunters with Gray beside him.

The D'ael gathered around Conor. They were in awe. Conor was still furious. Gray was somewhere in between. He felt the singularity of Conor's purpose clearer than ever before. He had known Conor in a way no one had ever known him, and Conor was becoming something strange and almost frightening. But Gray was nothing if not practical. If Conor needed to be angrier, stronger, and larger to defeat the hunters, then he was alright with that. Gray had seen the awful power of the Believer and the Other. It did not bother him that some previously unknown abilities had started showing up on their side of this war, whether they were Conor's or someone else's.

"That's the first time I've seen them run," Conor said, gasping for breath.

"Yeah," Baragara replied, unable to say anything else.

The D'ael and Conor and Gray stood for a few moments, breathing hard in the cool air. The dying hunter thrashed. The wind blew and rattled the branches of the trees around them.

Baragara broke the silence. "We can't stay here. Another foray off the road without you two with us and we'll be.... Which way, do you think?"

Conor shook his arms and stomped his feet a few times. He wanted to fight, to destroy the hunters, but now he had to think. The hunters were starting to show a semblance of planning, putting individuals on the path, mounting an attack on the D'ael and then returning to their army.

"We're going south. You could head back to the Chan or follow us to the Eliti. We will be moving fast."

Conor could see that Baragara was conflicted. He wanted to stay with Conor because of what Conor could do, but his unit was too small to help in an all-out battle.

"We're coming."

"Alright then. That's good," Conor said. "Let's go."

And they set off, Conor in front setting an impossible pace through the trees.

They heard the battle long before they could see it. The distinctive and eerie hoots, warbles, and screams of the hunters were still unnerving. Conor ran faster, leaving even Gray behind. The D'ael were strung out behind them, silently running as hard as they could.

The black and silver lines of Eliti were drowning in the stick figures of the hunters. Like ants, they swarmed. The long spears of the Eliti waved and stabbed, but the hunters were climbing over each other to get at the Eliti, breaking their disciplined ranks into panicked individuals. It was as if a brush fire of bright blue flame was moving along the front line, grabbing, spearing, killing, and burning. The hunters did not attack a certain point or hold troops in reserve. It was an all-out assault without order or sense.

Conor hesitated. What could one man do in the face of this madness? A door between the stars had opened on his world and it had brought waves of shrieking hunters who were rolling over the Eliti army. Perhaps he should wait for Gray and the D'ael, create a force that could punch through the roiling mass and reach the Eliti leadership. Form some kind of plan. He held the long Eliti spear like a toy in his hand. Then he felt again the righteous, uncontrollable anger. It boiled up inside him. He saw people dying, writhing and burning, afraid, crying but still fighting, trying desperately to save their own lives and those of their kin.

This is wrong. It shouldn't be happening. They don't belong here. They are like the dead in a dream. Wrong. No!

Conor ran into the maelstrom.

Gray came up to the rear of the battle and waited for the D'ael while he searched for Conor. He could not see him. For a moment his heart sank but then he felt the savage anger of his Lord, and Gray sensed the direction he should look. Off to his left there was a disturbance, noticeable even in the chaos. There was a different sound coming from that direction, perhaps only a Hound could hear it in a battle of this size. The hunters, usually mad with rage, were making unusual squawks and squeals there. And they were rearing up, scrambling to get away as arms and legs and pieces of their bodies were flying into the air. Above the cacophony, these hunters were screaming—Gray could now hear it clearly—in fear.

But Gray was different than what Conor had become. He would not rush in to almost certain death. He still had to be cornered into that and he wasn't. He ran along the edge of the battle, snapping and biting at any that stabbed at him. But not many did. They were fully engaged with the Eliti or trying to get away from Conor. He reached the point where he was as close to the disturbance Conor had caused in their packed ranks as he could get.

Conor!

Gray! To me!

For the first time since Gray had chosen Conor to be his Lord so many seasons ago, he hesitated, unsure if going to him would mean certain death. Gray had fought with Conor for many years and risked his life beside him in battle many times. But he was a predator and had run from danger as well. To plunge into the mass of hunters meant certain death. It was madness. Getting to Conor would be impossible. Gray could not see him. All he could see were bobbing, weaving, hooting, and screaming hunters. Their arms flailed wildly; white and blue light streamed from their spears. The noises they made were almost a physical barrier.

The D'ael ran up to him. Wild-eyed, knives out, breathing hard. Gray turned to look at them. They hesitated, as he had. The scene was beyond anything they had experienced, no matter how many raids they had been on or how many times they had fought the Empire. They were looking at the chaos the Other believed was at the root of all creation. It had been brought to their world and their minds rebelled.

Fuck.

Gray! To me!

This time Conor was not asking. Gray had never heard an order from Conor before. He was changed. Now Conor commanded him, a Lord to his Hound.

WAR

The D'ael were not part of the assault tribes, masses of armoured men and women who were on their way. The D'ael were born and bred for night actions, kidnappings, assassinations and targeted assaults. They had no place in this huge slaughter. They turned their backs and ran.

Damn. Gray said, surprised, and he leaped into the battle.

Gray bounced off a hunter, whose stabbing spear singed the fur on his broad back. Gray snarled but did not stop. The packed bodies of the hunters didn't leave much space for Gray's desperate dash. They were hard and spindly, and their long, stick-like arms and legs scratched and poked and bruised him as he worked his way past them. But their spears moved like living things. Bright, sharp, and burning hot. Gray was scarred more than once in his rush to get to Conor.

He was fortunate that the hunters were creatures of one mind. They were so intent on getting at the Eliti that it took time for them to notice him, and then he was gone. Gray pressed through what was for him an almost impenetrable forest of tubular shafts, grasping hands, and bright, hard lights. For a moment he was lifted off the ground entirely, jammed between so many alien bodies that he lost his footing. He started to panic and lashed out at the nearest one, teeth grinding on the tough, granular skin of a hunter. It howled and reached down for him with one hand and tried to bring its spear down through the tangle of arms and legs with the other. Gray bit down harder, tasted his own blood and saw the spear rise above him. He clawed for footing but three of his paws were off the ground. He thrashed but he could not move. He crunched the long arm in his teeth but he could not get away. It was his end, and he closed his eyes, but then there was a shift, an opening, and light streamed in all around. The hunter who threatened him suddenly had no arm, and then the top of his head disappeared as well. He let it go and it fell away from him.

Gray.
Conor.

They were in a small clearing Conor had made. It was ringed with dead hunters, and parts of dead hunters, and wounded hunters who screamed and thrashed. The other hunters they could see pressed up against each other, backing away. Their spears were a ring of light and fire but they did not attack.

Conor. If they all came at once…
They tried that.
Ah.

The battle raged. They could hear the clashing of arms, the breaking of shields, and Eliti screams and cries as well as the strange warbling and hoots of the hunters.

This is horrible.
Yeah.

Conor's chest was heaving. His body glistened with sweat. His sword was notched and his spear was half its original length. He was covered in the black fluid that was hunter blood.

How far is it to the front lines? Where are the Eliti?
That way. Conor pointed to his right. *Somewhere. I'm not sure how far.*

WAR

Alright. Is that where we want to be? The front lines? Where else?

Gray sensed again that Conor's anger and resolve to fight and kill had hardened in his mind. It was not going to be easy to discuss tactics or strategy.

Alright.

Right. Shall we…?

Lead on, Lord.

Gray had called Conor "Lord" many times, usually when he had done something stupid and always with a hint of mockery. But this time…was different. It was an acknowledgement. A recognition. But Conor had become so focused on killing that he did not notice. He turned and with a roar crashed into the wall of hunters, Gray right on his heels.

After the initial rush, the hunters simply parted like a flowing river on a rock when Conor and Gray approached. Their immense strength was negated by the refusal of the hunters to engage with them. The only advantage was that they got to the crumbling front lines of the Eliti formations quickly.

The Eliti cried out when they saw him. "The Lord and his Hound are here! The Lord!"

Conor stalked in front of their lines like the god they'd read about in their holy books: massive, covered in hunter blood, fearless, and enraged. But the hunters retreated wherever he went and attacked everywhere else. The long spears of the Eliti were not that effective against the hard, heavy bodies of the hunters. They simply advanced into the gaps, lit the heavy shields on fire with their spears and then reached over the blue flames and grabbed struggling Eliti, lifting them up to be skewered. Then the bodies were held aloft, burning banners of flesh and flame. When he could, Conor cut these poor victims down and killed those hunters who held them with vicious strokes but everywhere he stopped an assault, another started behind him. The hunters feared Conor and Gray only when they were within reach. They seemed to have no memory of what happened to the others, and there were so many that it did not really matter. There were always more.

Gray grew more desperate. *This isn't working.*

What?

Conor, we aren't winning here.

Conor looked at Gray, almost surprised. *We are killing them. And they can't stop us.*

Yes, but we aren't winning. Look around you.

Conor did. Again, there was an oasis of strange calm on the narrow front of the line they protected, broken only by writhing and dead hunters on the ground.

They aren't learning that when I reach them, I kill them. They need to be taught.

Conor, they aren't. They won't. Look. There are too many.

Conor's mind did not register what Gray was saying for a long moment. He was just there and smashing and killing hunters and there was nothing else. It was as if that was his breath, the beating of his heart. But he had to admit, he had killed fewer in the last few moments than the ones before. His breathing had slowed, as had the number of killing strokes. Was his anger not enough? He looked at his sword. It was notched and bent. Was it taking him longer to kill each hunter? His spear was cracked and the blade was broken. He turned to Gray. His Hound was scarred. Conor could smell burnt fur, see Gray's bloody mouth, his intelligent golden eyes questioning him. Conor shook his head. It was if he was being asked to come down from a great height. The air was clearer up there, the horizon easier to see, the actions he had to take simple and direct.

And from far below he could hear Gray. *Conor. You must think. Be more than a weapon. You must.*

The raucous sounds and sights of the battlefield intruded. Human and hunter voices. The blue flames of the burning shields, white sparkling spears. Conor was still enraged. He still wanted to kill them all. But he could not do it alone. Gray was reminding him.

Telikonta. We need to get to Telikonta. And they need to drop those shields. Conor pointed to the soldiers in front of them. *Tighten those ranks. Keep the hunters at spears' length away.*

Right. Tell them, and let's go.

"Drop your shields!" roared Conor, waving at them, his hands down.

"Tighten your ranks, bring more men up!"

Conor ran up and down the Eliti lines, hunters fleeing from him as he did. The Eliti followed his advice. Some units had already done it. The shields were just a hindrance and a weapon for the enemy.

Soon, the struggle took on a different tone. The hunters still attacked, still killed and burned, but the rate slowed. These actions had bought them some time, at least. Conor and Gray shouldered their way through the lines, with Eliti soldiers yelling, "Make way. Make way for the Lord and the Hound. Lady Telikonta!"

When they broke through the front lines Conor realized they were inside an enormous square. The hunters pressed in on all sides. The Eliti had pushed out the sides of their army beyond the road. Black-clad relief formations stood waiting to be ordered into the line. The men were grim and white-faced. Despite Gray's proximity, Conor could feel Telikonta's power supporting them, giving them courage.

Keeping them from running, you mean.

Same thing.

They approached a knot of Eliti soldiers surrounding Lady Telikonta. They stepped aside as Conor and Gray grew near.

"Lady Telikonta."

"Conor. You again. Did you bring aid?"

"No...yes. Well, they are coming."

"When?" Her voice cracked out in the still air, rising even above the din of the battle. "We can't, we won't be able to…"

She looked at her officers and they looked away. Admitting her army was being destroyed was beyond her. Even now, a Mother of Eliton was not able to admit that the world had changed.

Conor saw her discomfort and jumped in. "The Chan are coming. The army is moving and will be here by the end of the day. And the tribes are coming to fight."

"But—"

WAR

Conor cut her off. "My lady, tell your officers to order your men to drop their shields. They are worse than useless. Bring more soldiers up, create an impenetrable wall of steel."

The usual response of the Eliti to this kind of thing would be to threaten Conor with death for daring to speak to their Mother that way. But they saw the army being degraded and heard the screams. They were glad to have something helpful to say to their men that might help them survive, if only for a while longer. Telikonta looked around, her officers nodded, she returned it and one of them scurried off.

In moments, they could see shields dropping all over, the men shuffling in closer like ripples in a dark, armoured pond. The square contracted around them.

Now what?

Around them, the battle raged. All around them, hunters still attacked and Eliti soldiers died. Conor looked in all directions.

How long, do you think?

Telikonta will keep them fighting, Two hours, maybe three.

If she wasn't here, it would be over already.

I don't know. There's nowhere to run. And the hunters don't take prisoners.

What can we do?

You aren't feeling like you did...?

Conor looked at Gray, eyebrows raised. Gray had vomited huge amounts of thick, black smoke at crucial times in the fight against the Believer and the Other. It

169

had protected them from the Believer's powers and put out the blue fires of the hunters.
No. Nothing.
We could sally.
Yes. We could.
Gray felt the huge mountain of anger inside Conor rising again. He had talked to him, convinced him to speak to Telikonta. But it hadn't changed the facts. Should he now try to stop him from trying to single-handedly defeat the hunters? Dying senselessly was not in Gray's nature. But was it time? Was there no other choice?
When do you think the Chan will get here?
It doesn't matter. It will be too late. It's not going to change what is happening.
Telikonta said, "Conor!"
Loudly. They both realized it wasn't the first time she had said it.
"What can we do now?"
Conor shrugged, "Keep fighting, my lady. Help your men."
She nodded grimly. "And what will you do?"
Gray bumped his hip.
Sally?
"Give me one hundred men," Conor said. "A full spear. We will lead them out and try to relieve the pressure on the east side of your formation. It looks the weakest."
Telikonta looked at her officers. They conferred quickly and then sent a runner to one of the reserve units standing near them. He bawled orders in Eliti and a group

of them peeled off from the larger unit, then marched over to the command group.

"Will these men do?"

The Eliti infantry looked young and scared. But they were bathing in the waves of emotion from Telikonta. They would die for her. They would do anything for her.

"Yes." He walked in front of the unit and spoke to them. "Men. I am Conor and this is my Hound, Gray. We are going to relieve the pressure on the eastern side. We will lead you out. Stay close to us and each other. We will create a path. You must sweep it clean."

He signalled to their officers and they came forward. He told them they needed to form the unit into a three-rank square. Then Conor spoke to the unit again. "No one wants to go where we are going. Many of you will not return. But the battle to clean our world of these things has begun. We must and we will do our part."

"For Eliton!" one of the officers cried.

"For our Mother!" yelled another.

"For Conor and the Hound!"

The Elitons' horns blew. The ranks parted. Conor and Gray led the Eliti unit out of the deceptive calm of the enormous square and into the heaving mass of hunters.

Conor and Gray's sortie was only a part of the enormous battle. When they eased back into the square, the unit they had led was half its previous size. The Eliti who fought with them were full of their Mother's love and inspired by Conor's strength and Gray's courage, but many fell to the hunters all the same. There were only survivors at all because Gray reminded Conor that he should bring at least some of them back to Telikonta. Conor had ceased his personal war long enough to look back at his tattered band. He had merely grunted and aimed his attacks in support of the Eliti lines. It did relieve the pressure but the flow of hunters away from their assault only increased the pressure elsewhere.

Conor could see that Telikonta and her entourage were growing increasingly desperate. They were close to panic.

If she goes, they go.

Yeah. Fuck.

You need to calm her down. Give her hope.

But Conor's mind was on fighting and killing hunters. He did not want to convince or inspire. Gray could sense an implacable conviction that it was past time to talk.

We need them to hold out. And I can't do it.

Conor turned and looked at Gray. *Can't you?* Conor's eyes were oddly intense.

What do you mean?

You can help.

How much can I do?

You can cover this part of the world in darkness, Gray. The hunter part.

Gray took a step back. That was a command. Again. But the smoke came from him unbidden and he had no sense it was about to return. It left him wracked with pain and the uncomfortable memory of being totally out of control. The Eliti and the tribes said he was to cover the entire world with it if the Other was about to triumph. What was supposed to happen after that, they had never found out.

WAR

Conor, you know I can't just cough it up.
Can't you?
No.
You must.
Well, I can't.

Conor loomed over Gray. Despite his frantic dash up and down the road and the wild battles, Conor was not tired, not afraid. He was not only larger. His muscles strained at his skin. Striated and bulging, he looked as if he was about to explode.

Conor, what is happening to you?
I am becoming what I need to be. And so must you.

The voice in Gray's head was hard and without emotion. A god's voice.

I can't.
Do it.
I cannot.
You must.

Those last two words felt like they were pressing on Gray's mind like a huge hand, forcing it to bend to Conor's will. Gray's eyes began to water; his throat twitched and burned. He looked at Conor for an instant. Surprised.

Damn.

Gray hacked. He coughed. His back spasmed and he bucked and jumped. He had never felt anything like this. Smoke leaked out between his clenched teeth and out his nostrils; it hung in the air as if waiting. Then Gray roared. It was a bellow of pain and power, of threat and promise, of rage and retribution.

WAR

And then the smoke poured out of his mouth, flowing almost liquid, a black avalanche flecked with red flame. Telikonta and her guards stood awestruck, their faces frozen in shock and fear. Conor folded his arms, his face grim. Gray puked up the black fume with increasing intensity.

"It's the end!" One of the Eliti yelled out as he fell to the ground, covering his face with his hands. Others went to their knees, signing across their chests over and over again.

"Conor!" Telikonta ran to him. "What's happening?"

"What must."

She stood pale and still beside him, her eyes wide, but she did not cry out.

Gray writhed and twisted. More and more of the black smoke issued from his mouth. It started to coalesce and move in a circle around him. It became a swiftly moving cloud, denser than the thickest fog and blacker than the darkest night. Then, with a loud bark and snap, Gray's jaws closed and bit off the end of the smoke, which was almost solid. Gray fell to the ground. He lay on his side, his body wracked with coughs and then he was still.

The thing that issued from him could no longer be described as smoke, or fog, or anything anyone on this world had ever seen. It rose above them, maintaining its circular shape. It whirled in the sky while the battle raged.

Conor could see the Eliti were faltering. The hunters were close to breaking the square in two places. Burning bodies were hoisted on bright spears. Men lay crushed and broken on the ground. The noise the hunters made was a physical presence. Conor looked at Gray. His eyes were closed and he did not move. The thing he had created spun above them, getting thicker and denser. Telikonta sidled closer to Conor. Her guards and officers stared at the sky and then at their crumbling army, unable to understand the madness that surrounded them.

Suddenly, the black thing above them began to spool off into thinner and thinner lines, spreading out as it did like an uncoiling snake, ready to strike. It separated into finer and finer filaments, moving above them like an enormous net. The sky began to darken. It was harder to see if it was still spinning, the lines were so thin. As they watched it began to solidify, like a cap, a dome over them that was widening and blocking out the sun.

"He will cover the world in darkness," breathed Telikonta. "It is the end of our days."

Conor's satisfaction at forcing Gray to act began to turn inside him. All at once he had the horrible sense that he had gone too far. He had been so sure of himself that he had forced Gray to act, something he had never done before. Had he started it? The beginning of the end? Was that possible? He had only wanted Gray to help defeat the hunters. He had never seen so much of the smoke before and it had never behaved in this way. Had he triggered the end of the world when all he wanted was a victory at this place, at this time?

Maybe there is no difference, he thought. Maybe the hunters could not be defeated by the people alone. Perhaps it is the end.

Conor ran over to Gray, who had not moved. He knelt beside him. The Hound was warm. Conor felt his breath rising, shallow and halting, thin streams of silver and grey saliva dripping from his muzzle. His golden eyes stayed closed. Conor reached out for him with his mind.

Gray!

He sensed nothing. Not a sleeping consciousness, not a wall of incoherence, nothing.

Gray!

The conviction Conor had of the righteousness of his cause and the confidence he had in his newfound abilities filled him. He commanded Gray, *Gray! Wake up!*

He still felt nothing. Above them, the black dome was growing. It covered the entire square and was spreading out over the battlefield. The sun was a dim circle of light. It was darker and getting colder. Conor felt another spasm of unease. He did not know what to do. Gray's breath was slowing. His eyes did not open. Conor spoke to him again.

Gray!

Nothing.

Telikonta touched his shoulder. He turned to her, feeling her emotional power unfiltered as the link between him and Gray was completely severed. He wanted so much to please her, protect her, make her proud of him. Her perfectly proportioned and exquisitely female face was strained, her eyes almost pleading with him for help. But she had not panicked and her power was keeping her entire army in the fight, which continued unabated. They were dying for her and she was loving them for it. But it was crushing her, as well.

Conor understood for the first time that the love and loyalty the Mothers engendered in their followers was reflected in her. She loved them like the children they had once been, innocent and vulnerable, when they were men and women and neither of those things. He could not believe that she was strong enough to endure this pain. He felt it and it was overwhelming him. Conor had not experienced the Mothers in defeat. The sacrifice she asked them for was breaking her heart and her sadness was so overwhelming that if it spread to her army it would doom them all, no matter what happened to the darkness that Gray had brought to the world.

Tears came to Conor's eyes and the hardness in him cracked with a short, deep sob.

"Telikonta," Conor said to her, "you are so strong. Stronger than any Mother has ever had to be. You know your men need you."

Conor said this and realized he was doing what Gray told him he should. She nodded and with the faintest smile, went back to her officers. Conor hung his head, remembering his callousness, his disdain for frailty and that his commands had laid low his Hound Gray, his best and truest friend.

The darkness deepened, the black dome covered more and more of the sky. Conor only faintly sensed this as he again knelt beside Gray, his hands in his thick fur, calling to him.

Gray. Come back, my friend.

WAR

He felt nothing. The part of him that was Gray was empty.

Don't go.

In the background he heard a strange trilling sound, growing louder and louder. It was not made by human voices. He glanced up but he could see nothing; his eyes blurred with sudden tears. He dug his hands deeper into Gray's fur and leaned close to his silent companion.

Gray. Come back.

Memories came to him of Gray by his bed in the academy. The only warm thing in his hard, lonely life as a boy. Gray running by his side on a hunting path in sunshine and open country, a training track or a street in the city, chasing a lawbreaker. Gray mocking him when he acted like a lovesick child, comforting him when Andaine died and fighting with him against criminals, fanatics, and terrible creatures from another world. He recalled Gray's golden eyes looking at him for purpose. And laughing at his mistakes. They hadn't always agreed, but Gray was as loyal a friend as could be imagined and he had risked his life for Conor time and again.

And now Conor had killed him. Gray's body was completely still. Conor felt part of himself slipping away.

Gray. My friend. Please.

Conor heard yelling. Human yelling. He buried his face in Gray's broad back.

My friend. I am sorry. I cannot do this without you.

He felt a hand on his shoulder. And with it a burst of the purest love and thankfulness and comfort. It was so strong it staggered him.

WAR

"Conor," Telikonta said softly, "they are running away."

The black dome had become a ceiling, a low disc that stretched to the horizon. It had come down to what looked like twice the height of the Eliti spears. It was dark now, and only the light of the Eliti glow globes lit the square. It was an awesome, ominous sight, powerful and incomprehensible.

"They are running, Conor, Lord of the Hound."

Conor looked up at her, tears flowing down his face, overcome with sadness and relief. They had won, but the cost was almost too much to bear. Gray, his truest and most loyal friend...

You're welcome.

Gray!

Yes.

You are alive!

Evidently.

You, you did it. The hunters are running away.

Gray opened one golden eye. Conor watched as it focused, first on his face and then the sky. Conor felt genuine affection for a moment and then curiosity.

What is that?

Your smoke, your thing. It changed and grew and now it's... that.

Hmm.

It scared the shit out of the hunters. They ran.

You said that.

Yeah.

Doesn't it scare the shit out of you too?

WAR

Well, you were lying there and I was…

Conor was unable to continue. His emotions were bubbling over and he stuttered, his words caught in his throat.

Alright. No need to get like that.

Gray rose to his feet and shook himself. He wobbled and almost fell. Conor reached down and steadied him, kneeling in front of him, hands on either side of his face.

You okay?

Gray coughed harshly, two or three times. His eyes watered but he was firm on his feet.

I'm getting there.

Conor stood up and together they walked with Telikonta to her entourage. Their expressions were a strange mixture of thankfulness, awe, and fear. They clutched their thick capes around them; the black ceiling was forcing the temperature down.

Telikonta was very much in charge and she spoke to them. "Thank you, Conor and the Hound Gray. You have saved us."

"My lady," was all Conor could think of to say as he bowed.

They stood for a moment. Every eye in the square was on them. It was eerily quiet. Conor took a deep breath and when he blew it out, a cloud of steam formed.

"Perhaps we should form up?" Telikonta said. "And move north?"

It was almost an order and almost a suggestion. If Conor and Gray weren't in command, it was only because they hadn't chosen to be.

WAR

"Yes, of course. We need to concentrate our forces…" Conor trailed off as he had already had this conversation with Telikonta. "In case the hunters…"

"Right, I'll get the men moving." Telikonta waved at her officers and one came up close to her. "Will you be marching with us, Conor and the Hound?" She smiled at Gray.

"No, my lady," Conor said. "We'll go ahead. Take as much time as you need. We know what you and your men have been through."

She stood up straighter and looked Conor in the eye. "We'll be right behind you."

He nodded and smiled faintly. "Until then."

CH 13
A MIGHTY FEAT

Conor and Gray ran up the road again, away from the Eliti, under a flat dark cloud that covered the entire sky. It unnerved them to see the damage to the crumbling road and feel it move under their feet.

After running for only a few moments, Gray asked, *Should we stay on the road?*

Depends on where the hunters went. You alright?

Or if they went there together. And yes. I think so.

Did you see where they...?

Nope. And I didn't ask. Didn't think of it. Till now.

Me neither. Not too smart.

No.

That admission surprised Gray. And pleased him. Conor's strength of purpose and conviction had made him increasingly difficult to deal with. It had turned him into someone Gray felt he did not really know. Now Gray felt like the old Conor was returning and he was glad of it.

At least you didn't say something about it "not making a difference" and we need to "kill them all anyway."

A MIGHTY FEAT

I wasn't always like that.
You weren't always such a dick about it, no.
They ran on.
Faster on the road, Gray said. *Safer on the path.*
Road, then. Until we see something we don't like.

The air was cold and the dark ceiling was close above them. The tall trees lining the road disappeared into it. It was impossible to know if they were cut off or if they pushed through. The colours of the world were flattened into shades of grey and dark brown. Somehow, enough light was getting through for them to see where they were going but what Gray had brought into the world showed no sign of dissipating the way it had every other time he had coughed and hacked out the black smoke that acted like a living thing.

Is it solid, you think?
It seems to be. I have no idea, though.
Is it getting lower to you?

Conor craned his neck and looked up at the featureless sky as they ran.

I can't tell, so that means probably not.
Agreed.
I don't know if I feel better about that, or worse.
Scaring the hunters off, good. Everything else, bad.
Yes. It is spreading, though. Can you see an end to it?

Both of them peered down the road, unnaturally flat in its entire length. The people who had built it ages ago had abilities far beyond those of the Southlanders, the Chan, or the Eliti. It was arrow straight where they were so they could see to the horizon. Neither saw any light escaping the darkness ahead of them.

No. You?

No.

They heard the hunters twice. They slowed as the sounds came out of the forests that lined the road, flat and thin in the still, cold air. But they did not see them.

They stopped when they caught up to Baragara and his men. They stepped onto the road ahead of them. Many made signs across their chest and all stayed a respectful distance from them both.

"Baragara."

"Conor. Where are the hunters?"

"They ran. We were fighting in the battle; the Eliti were losing." Conor looked back. Then he pointed at the sky. "Gray brought this. The hunters ran. We don't know where."

Baragara grimaced. "Not north. We haven't seen them on the road."

The two groups stood and looked at each other. The D'ael were acting nervous, shifting weapons from hand to hand, looking down at the ground or up into the sky. Some looked frightened and were trying hard not to show it.

Conor knew they were all thinking the same thing: *And he will cover the world in darkness.*

Gray did not like the stares or the muttering. *Let's keep going. We need to get to the Chan. Tell them to hurry up.*

Right. And try to explain what happened to the sky.

A MIGHTY FEAT

Conor walked up to Baragara and put a hand on his shoulder. He wanted to reassure him. Instead, it became suddenly clear how much bigger Conor had become. Baragara's eyes widened, he looked at the huge hand and he stepped back.

Conor spoke softly. "We are going to meet the Chan. Will you stay? Watch for the hunters and Telikonta?"

Baragara gulped and nodded, looking almost like a child beside Conor. Arguing with him seemed ridiculous.

Conor and Gray hurried away. It was getting darker and colder. The night would be so black that travel without a torch would be impossible. They hadn't gone very far when they had to stop. There were no matches in the borrowed clothing and the wood in the forests was either wet or frozen in any case, so they simply sat down on the road. Conor pulled his cape around them both and they waited for what light the dawn would bring. Or, even better, the glow of the orange fires of the Chan coming toward them.

It was only when they shifted positions that Conor felt faint wisps of cold. Gray didn't. He was built for this kind of weather and his body heat and the thick Eliti cloak kept Conor warm, if a bit uncomfortable. Sleep, however, did not come to either of them.

The night passed slowly. Gray struggled to breathe if he lay on his side and Conor's new muscles cramped on and off. The horror of the battle and its emotional aftermath weighed on their minds. Both Conor and Gray were stunned by what they had seen and done. They could hardly believe it had been them. Conor's immense strength

A MIGHTY FEAT

and brutality and Gray's creation in the sky. And they were both very hungry. When the first inklings of dawn came, Gray roused himself to scout and hunt. The light that filtered through the dark grey barrier barely outlined the trees. The air was colder and completely still. They heard no sounds.

Maybe we should stick together today.
I'm hungry.
I know, but the hunters are out there somewhere...and the sky is....
Yeah.
I almost feel I'm going to bump my head.
Alright. Together. Let's go.

Gray's claws clicked and Conor's feet slapped lightly on the crumbling stones. They looked at each other often for reassurance, both realizing that they were in a world that was becoming unrecognizable and they had helped make it so. It was terrible, however inevitable it was.

When they saw the light of the Chan torches it was mid-morning, as far as they could tell. The distinctive orange flame flared in the gloom. There was no warm glow that preceded it. The light was just suddenly there. The Chan army moved in and out of the sharp shadows, their lumbering beasts like ghostly monsters.

That sky must be higher than it looks.
Yeah. Their heads don't seem that close to it.
Wait here?
Might be a bit risky to do anything else. I'll call out to them when they get close.

A MIGHTY FEAT

They waited. Gray was still. Conor shifted his weight back and forth, his breath showing in a cloud in front of them.

Is it colder?
Now that you ask, I think so.
And spring was coming.
Yes. It was.

Conor left unsaid the thought that it may never come again.

Even in the still air, the beasts smelled Conor and Gray before they could see him. The blood of the hunters on them spooked the huge animals. The Chan sent scouts ahead when they reared, huffed, stamped their feet and refused to move. Conor heard the crack of their whips and then saw small orange fires detach themselves from the black mass of men and wagons and bounce towards them. The torches slowed down a bowshot away. Light was not what it was before Gray changed the sky. Neither group could see each other well, even at close to midday.

"It' s Conor and Gray. We are coming towards you. Do not shoot."

His voice carried across the dead air, harsh and grating. The torches stopped abruptly.

Let's go.

Conor and Gray crossed the distance between them quickly. The Chan were in full battle armour. Only their pale blue eyes showed through their polished brown faceplates. One held a bow with an arrow already notched, one had an angular cutting sword and the other, the flaring orange torch and a long spear with a wicked-looking steel blade.

"It is good to see you, my friends," said Conor in Southlander.

The soldier with the torch answered, "You as well, Conor and the Torit. We are glad to have found you in this accursed place."

The soldiers turned around and one said to Conor, "Our commander will speak to you."

They marched back to their army with Conor and Gray close behind. The beasts at the head of the column were blinkered so heavily they could barely see. But Conor and Gray gave them a wide berth anyway. As they passed the marching army, it seemed to Conor that the soldiers were hunching their shoulders, feeling, like him, that the close, dark, blank uniformity of the sky was pressing down on them.

When they saw the banners of the Chan leaders and moved toward them, ranks of Chan soldiers stepped aside without complaint, eyes wide and fearful. Conor noticed Eliti spears rising above the ranks as well. Had Dareen had come too?

I would not have wanted to be in the camp on that hill when this sky came.

Right. I wonder…

All they had seen was flat ground. Would Gray's awful creation follow the contours of the Southlands or cut them off from any rise in elevation? Gettil came forward. Eromil was with him.

A MIGHTY FEAT

She grasped Conor's arm. "It is good to see you again, Conor!" Her eyes were bright but her face was even more pale than usual in the wan light.

Gettil spoke quickly. "You have seen the hunter army? You...?"

"Yes. They attacked the Eliti. Then they ran when Gray...when the sky came."

"Ran? Where?"

"We don't know. We came up the road to meet you and although we heard them once or twice, we did not see any."

The army rumbled past them. Soldiers passing looked at them expectantly, in search of a reason to be confident.

"Do we need to...?"

Dareen walked up and interrupted Gettil. "Conor and his Hound, Gray."

"My Lady Dareen," Conor bowed.

"Did you bring this?" she said, looking at Gray and waving at the sky without looking up. "Or is it the work of the Other?"

"Gray. We...it came from Gray. I ordered him to act. He had done it in the past when defeat seemed possible."

Dareen was shocked. "You have blocked out the sun before?" She said it directly to Gray.

"No," Conor said. "We have never seen this. Usually it dissipates quickly, usually it just..."

"You have covered the world in darkness," Dareen said.

Gray rolled his eyes.

"It is the end of days," Dareen said in a whisper.

A MIGHTY FEAT

Conor stepped away from Eromil and put his both hands on Dareen. She looked at him in horror. At his touch and at the world.

"No, Dareen. No. We are still breathing. It seems to be staying in place. We need to keep the army moving. We need to be ready to fight."

Her eyes lost focus and then regained it. She shrugged his hands off. "Yes. Yes, with what little strength we have, we will march."

Conor thought of something. "And Dvor? His people? What of those we found on the road?"

Dareen looked at him, her face bleak. "Dvor is at the rear of the column, with those he has left. The rest…"

Her hands covered her face. Then she looked up. "We were down in the Chan camp when the sky came down." She paused and frowned. "It spread so quickly, those caught at the top of the hill are lost to us."

"What? What happened?"

"It is a barrier, but it works in one direction only. It will accept you but once you are above it, you cannot return."

Conor looked at Gray. Beside him, Gettil waved a soldier over and told him something. He unslung his bow and fired an arrow straight into the sky. It disappeared into the blank grey roof over them and did not fall.

Well, that's something.

Dareen said, "Some men ran up the hill to be with their loved ones." A tear ran down her face. "Some just to grab some clothes or a weapon. They did not come back."

"All those people we met on the road—"

"They're gone."

A MIGHTY FEAT

Conor exhaled gently and caught himself before he sobbed.

Gray sidled up to him, touching his hip gently. *Either it will get worse, or it won't. Let's go down the road and join with Telikonta and her army. At least then if the hunters return, we will be better prepared.*

Right.

Dareen and Gettil were anxious to keep moving. Having a task made the unimaginable situation easier to accept. He understood that. *Don't look at the sky, forget about what you have seen on the hill, just keep the army moving. More people will be better than less; keep moving. The smell of the animals, the sounds of the marching men, the rumble in your belly or the soreness in your feet—anything is better than thinking about the dark sky pressing down on the world in the strangely still cold air.*

Baragara and his men came out of the forest to join them when they passed. Conor had another task for them. One he thought they would happily accept. He called out to them and they gathered around.

"Go northwest; meet the tribes. Tell them we are on the move."

Baragara glanced at his men and they nodded as one.

"Don't go up the hill. Don't cross the barrier in the sky. You will not return."

Baragara dipped his chin slightly and then signalled to his men. He took a last long look at Conor and Gray and then jogged off down the side of the road, his men following him in single file. They were soon lost in the dim half-light. The sounds of the marching army were deadened in the grey-brown miasma under the barrier.

A MIGHTY FEAT

That was what the Chan were calling it and the name stuck.

The Chan and Eliti armies met late in the day. Dareen and Telikonta acted as if they were long lost sisters. The actual armies stayed apart, eyeing each other nervously as their leadership met. Gettil congratulated Telikonta on her victory over the hunters.

She shrugged and said, "If Conor and the Hound Gray had not fought with us, if the sky had not been covered, we would all be dead. We owe our lives to them."

Gettil glanced at Conor and then said, "Still, your army stood and fought the hunters and the Chan Consolidation would be proud to fight beside you."

Telikonta flushed and then bowed her head. Her emotions were still close to the surface from the battle and the unexpected victory. When she looked up her eyes were shining with tears and she was unable to speak. Her officers crowded around her.

"What now?" was Dareen's response to the dramatic scene. "Will the barrier frighten them away? Will they be back? Do we look for them?"

No one knew the answers to her questions. One of the Chan wondered aloud if the plains west of them were higher than the Southlands. And if the entire army of the tribes might be caught above the barrier. Dareen assured them it was not so. The plains and the cities of the Empire were safely below it. Of the tribal mountain redoubts and the highlands of the far north, no one could say.

Gettil agreed. "Our maps say the same. If they left when we are told they did, they will come. But Dareen

A MIGHTY FEAT

brings up a good point. What now? If we are to wait for the hunters to gather again, we have food for half a moon, maybe a bit more. We need to reconnect our supply lines. Soon."

The fields and forests along the road had hardened in the cold the barrier had brought, and the countryside had been scoured by war long before the hunters had come. There would be little to forage.

"We must give the people time. The tribes are coming," Conor said. "We wait for two days; they will arrive before then. Then we go south. Gray and I saw where the hunters were gathered. That's where they'll be." Conor was not as sure as he sounded, but he didn't know what else to say.

Gettil held up two fingers. "Two days. Then we march south. Tribes or no."

Dareen folded her arms and looked at Telikonta, who nodded. "Agreed. Two days."

Once again, Conor and Gray wandered through the encampments of the armies of powerful empires. The nights were so black (despite the Eliti glow globes and Chan fires) that orders were given that no one was to move around after what light there was faded behind the barrier. The chance of a mistake by a sentry was too great.

They turned down food and drink a few times, but most of the men of both armies were too nervous and intimidated to offer. The Eliti were happy to see them but conversation was stilted. The sight of them was too much a reminder of how strange the world had become and how god-like they had been in the battle. They both felt it and did not stay at any fire long. The Chan had

A MIGHTY FEAT

heard the stories and saw how huge Gray was and Conor had become. They just nodded and Conor returned the gesture.

Conor did not notice, though Gray did, that all of the men, silent or not, were sorry to see them go.

In the afternoon of the second day, Conor and Gray were walking on the northern outskirts of the camp. That was where they expected to see the tribes first, and they wanted to talk to Dvor. They had not seen him since he went west with his men. After they had exchanged the formal greetings Dvor expected, they sat down by the fire on thick blankets.

"You brought this?" Dvor pointed to the sky.

Conor tilted his head towards Gray. "He did."

"Truly a mighty feat. A worthy weapon in the war against the Traitor. He cowers behind it."

Gray rolled his eyes. *Does he notice the world is freezing over?*

He's an optimist.

Conor changed the subject. "How many of your men got back, Dvor?"

"We lost six of my sister sons on the western plains. They did not return and we could not find them before we had to follow the Eliti south."

"I'm sorry."

"Yes. I grieve to think of them wandering in a foreign land, or staring with unseeing eyes into this dark sky."

Or worse.

He knows that.

The hunters may have caught them.

A MIGHTY FEAT

Yes.

But it's hard to make burning alive on the end of a spear sound heroic.

Maybe.

Conor had a thought. "Is it alright if we spend the night here with you, Dvor? We want to be the first to greet the tribes."

"If they come," Dvor said. "Do you believe they will come, Conor?"

Dvor's tone was doubtful. His lips were pressed together under his thick beard, his eyes questioning.

"I do," Conor said firmly.

Dvor nodded and almost smiled, obviously and immediately appeased by Conor's reply. "Then we will wait together. Sit at our fire and share our meat. You can tell us of your war against the Traitor and of the battle you fought with the Eliti."

Conor tried not to frown. "Share? Yes, but perhaps we can speak instead of your highlands, the beauty of your women, and the history of your people."

Dvor was puzzled. "The beauty of our women? Our women are warriors, Conor. They stay home in birthing years or you could see for yourself. They are strong and fierce." He shook his head. "Do you not want to tell the story of your victory? Of the hunters you killed?"

Conor ground his teeth. That was something he did not want to talk about—now, or maybe ever. He had almost lost Gray and that still pained him. But Dvor was Dvor, so he had to say something,

A MIGHTY FEAT

"First, your mountains, then your history and yes, even your women." Conor smiled a smile he did not feel. He clapped Dvor on the back. "Then, the battle."

"Agreed!"

This guy is an idiot. Are all Northerners like this?

Just sit by the fire and sleep. I'll do the listening.

You won't have to say a word. He'll go on all night.

I know. It's okay. Sleep.

As they ate, Dvor told a long version of the short story about how he and his men had wandered west aimlessly until they were found by the Eliti and brought back to the camp. Then he waxed poetic about his home in the highlands, not once voicing any worry over the barrier and what it had done to the people they had left on the hill. He hadn't wanted them around and now they were gone. He was being either inhumanly practical or incredibly callous.

Or willfully blind. What about his own people in the mountains?

Yes, yes. Go to sleep.

The men gathered closer to the fire as the night deepened into blackness. Conor noticed that Gray did, too.

It's warmer.

Right.

Dvor talked on and on about his illustrious family history and his many personal victories, and had just started on the women of the north when Dvak nudged him with his elbow. The men around the fire were asleep. Conor had been nodding on and off for a while, jerking slightly each time Dvor punctuated a sentence with a hard sound. Dvor had not noticed, or so it seemed. He

A MIGHTY FEAT

nodded to Dvak, smiled a little, settled into his furs and closed his eyes as well.

Not such a fool after all.

Conor blinked and looked around at the silent group of men, suddenly awake.

Gray?

How many men can sleep on a night like this? Yet Dvor's are. His words were a blanket of home and hearth. That was what they were thinking of when they fell asleep. Not this cold dark place. Dvor is not a fool at all.

No.

Conor rolled over on his side and went to sleep, but Gray had not been lulled by Dvor's florid recollections. He sat, his golden eyes open, and listened to the low murmur of thousands of restless men and women, and along with them, waited for the grey dawn to come.

CH 14
NISI

They were packing and preparing to move in the morning when the first members of the scout clans appeared. They were tall, lithe men and women with bows strung across their backs. They wore tight, brightly coloured leather pants and jackets and they ran as if they were born to it, which they were. They moved through the pickets like shadows.

Conor saw one and called out, "Hello! Hello! I'm Conor and this is my Hound, Gray. Have you come with the tribes?"

A pair of them veered towards him. Conor stayed close to the fire because even with the sun above the horizon, it was difficult to see.

One of them spoke. "Then it is true. You have survived."

"Yes. Do you bring news? Do they come?"

The scout who had spoken took a long drink from a bag of liquid that was hung alongside his quiver. The other waited, breathing quickly and evenly, hands on her hips.

NISI

"They come."

"How many?"

"All."

Conor felt a rush of relief and excitement. He didn't care what *all* meant. It was good news.

"Thank you," he said and he grabbed the scout's hand. "Thank you!"

The scout winced and then looked at Conor with alarm. Conor's hand had dwarfed his, enveloped it. His size was beginning to register. He took a step back.

The other scout said, "They will be here by midday."

"There are Eliti here. And Chan. They need to know. Will you come with me and tell them what you have told me?"

The other scout agreed quickly, glancing at her partner as she did. He shrugged.

"Come on, then," Conor said, and he scrambled through the crowd of Northerners, agile despite his bulk, running south towards the centre of the camp.

Dareen, Gettil, and Telikonta stood and listened to the scout. They thanked her for her news. Conor was satisfied. Finally, the people of the known world had gathered their forces together and would fight the Other, the Traitor, the hunters, or whatever else showed up. Together.

It was agreed that the unified force would move south to find and crush the hunter infestation Conor and Gray had seen on the road. There were also settlements and castles further south, so the chances of being able to forage or trade for food was better as well. And the Chan would be that much closer to their home on the other side of the Near Sea.

Conor and Gray walked back to their tent after the meeting.

What if they are not there?

I don't know why they wouldn't be.

Well, the sky…

Yeah. But there are thousands of them in the Southlands, we know that. We just don't know exactly where.

And you figure, if we gather a force large enough to perhaps defeat them, they will show up?

It put them here to kill us. It told me that. If they can, they will.

Alright. Where are they?

Conor did not reply because he did not know. What if they had already gone south and were burning and killing in smaller groups or even as individuals? Killing them one by one would be an almost impossible task.

Maybe that's why the barrier is there. If we can't win, it will fall. If the hunters destroy what makes this world livable for us, the Lords of Power will bring it down. The Other will not win, even if we can't defeat him.

Awfully bloody minded of them. Not sure I follow. Kill us all, so we can't die?

I know. But don't forget that for the Eliti, death and war are not the end for us. Maybe it matters who does it and how death comes.

Oh.

Yeah, I don't really want to think too much about that.

No.

NISI

Maybe it will speak to me. Tell me how it's going to make us suffer. It has in the past.
Do something irritating. You're good at that.
Maybe the barrier is keeping it out, like Dvor says.
Who knows?

When the tribes came, they were like a flood that wouldn't end. They didn't march in columns or ranks. They didn't march at all. First, more scouts ran up, breathing hard, dark eyes flat and expressionless, just nodding at Conor's greetings. Then the assault tribes came, heavyset men and women in coloured armour, faded in the grey light. Long swords in scabbards, full face masks, fierce and strange. There were masses of them, moving deliberately, close together but not as organized as the Chan or Eliti.

Like a pack of wolves. Jammed together.

They kept coming, more and more, then archers, thousands of them, longbows across their backs. Then D'ael, by the hundreds, in different mottled tunics, heavily bearded and hulking.

Any sign of leadership? Anyone look like they want to speak to us?
Should we go look?
There are so many.
I know. It's beautiful. Let's just start walking.

Conor and Gray plunged into the swollen crowds of men and women. Conor saw surprised and shocked faces but no one rushed to them like the Eliti had. They heard only muted cries of "The Lord and his Hound."

They knew we were here. Waiting for them.

NISI

After a while, Conor began noticing families. Children. Dogs and beasts of burden pulling wagons stacked with belongings and supplies. Crowds of them, young and old, all walking steadily southwards.

Are you seeing this?

Yeah.

All means all.

Yeah.

I wonder how many were caught above the barrier? In their mountain redoubts.

Maybe they saw it coming and got out.

Maybe.

Conor looked at the dirty, tired masses around him. His presence had not inspired excitement. The people gave Conor and Gray room when they noticed them, but it seemed that hope had left these people despite their belief in the mythical powers of the Lord of the Hound.

"Conor!"

Someone had called his name with a woman's voice. He turned to his right and saw her. His heart leaped in his chest. It was Nisi! Nisandi neh Tormusula, Dareen's oldest daughter. Dareen had sent for her and the tribes had brought her to him. Her guards were trying to push their way to him without being too rough.

And there she is.

Nisi ran up to him, her eyes shining.

"Conor."

She put her hands on his arms and nestled up to him. She looked up, he bent down. The strength of the feelings he had for her surprised him. Their eyes met. She was like

NISI

sunshine coming through the clouds. She did not fear him like the Eliti soldiers did; she was not wary like the Chan leaders. She did not see him as inferior as Dareen had done, worship him like Arusin, or like the D'ael, regard him as a dangerous and powerful stranger. No one had looked at him like she was now since she had left him that early morning in the Empire so many moons ago. All of a sudden he realized how much those peculiar looks had eaten away at him and at the same time distanced him from everyone else he knew. It was as if he wasn't human, not one of them. She was just ecstatic to be near him and he felt pure happiness.

"Nisi, Nisi, it is so good to see you. Safe."

She hugged him fiercely, her arms as far around him as they could reach. He felt full and almost in tears. His arms went around her. He was careful not to squeeze too hard.

"How did you—"

She leaned back to look at him, perhaps realizing how much bigger he had become. "Our Mother sent for me. Us. All my sisters are here somewhere."

Nisi waved at the crowd around them.

"The tribes caught up to us on the plains. We had no choice really. They…we got swept up." The people walked by them, stepping aside almost politely. "By the tribes."

"And now you are here."

"We are."

Again, Nisi's eyes were shining and he was speechless. But her face, despite her happiness and obvious feelings for him, was as tired and dirty as the others. The barrier loomed above and the piercing cold surrounded them.

NISI

His fullness was suddenly an ache in his heart, for her. He held her close again for a long moment. Then he held her at arm's length.

"Nisi, who leads here? We need to speak to them."

"Leads?" Her eyes lost focus, then she recovered. She had been lost in her emotions as well.

"Yes. There is a council. They are at the rear with the oldest and the youngest. It is their way."

"Thank you, Lady Nisandi." Conor smiled at her. "Your mother awaits you. Find her and I will find you before darkness falls."

"Conor."

She bowed her head and then turned her back to him. Her hand lingered on his forearm. She looked away and then leaped back into his arms and kissed him. Her lips were full and soft. Her grip was strong but she kissed him with affection and care. He kissed her back for a timeless moment. Then she released him and he set her down. She disappeared into the living river of people, her guards trying to catch up.

Conor stood there, watching. Gray waited.

Let's go.

Right.

Conor followed Gray as they worked their way towards the council. They flew no flags and wore no crowns. And they walked amongst their people. Conor and Gray passed by them twice in the streams of men and women moving by them. It was the D'ael that gave them away. A number of them surrounded the council in a casual circle of menace, mixed in with the others.

There was, Conor noticed when they got close enough, the slightest difference in the separation between the ten or twelve men and women and the rest of the tribe.

There they are.
You think so?
Yeah, look at the D'ael. That's them.
Let's go introduce ourselves.

Conor stepped in front of the group, Gray by his side. He had just started to speak to the two D'ael who appeared in front of them when he heard the distinctive warbling of the hunters. It was coming from the north, the rear of the massive flood of people. The D'aels' heads snapped up and around.

The sounds grew louder. The hunters were back and they were attacking. Their ululations, hoots, and cries were suddenly echoed by screams and shouts of the tribes.

"What the fuck?" The D'ael looked at Conor, wild-eyed.

"It's the hunters. Monsters the Other brought into the world. Get the young ones and the old away. Then send everyone you can."

Conor drew his sword. Every member of the council had drawn as well. The D'ael he had spoken to threw up his right hand and made a series of quick gestures. They were repeated throughout the crowd around them. D'ael surrounded the council while others grabbed children and shepherded the old away from the chaos. The rest of them streamed through the fleeing civilians, heads up, calling for the others to flee, their long knives flashing out as they ran towards the hunters.

NISI

Conor saw white sparks flying in the grey sky. The burning spears of the hunters flared blue flame. People were burning, again. His rage rose up. A door slammed shut in his mind. The affection he felt for Nisi disappeared as suddenly as it had come. He would break them all. He would smash them.

Gray flinched at the violence of the change. He planted himself in front of Conor.

Conor! You need to get to the leaders. Tell them what is happening here. You must go.

No. Conor shook his head and tried to step around Gray. *I won't run away. I—*

At least tell the tribal council. They aren't far. At least speak to them, Conor.

Conor's mind returned for a moment. *Alright. Alright.* He knelt down and put his hands on Gray's broad shoulders. *They'll need you. The D'ael. I'll come as soon as I can.*

Right.

Conor went one way, Gray the other, both into the now heaving and panicked crowds of people. And above them, the barrier that was the sky began to turn, massive, slow, and inexorable.

CH 15
THE FALL

Conor and Gray did not know then that the hunters had attacked everywhere. No help was going to come from the Eliti or the Chan armies, because they were under assault as well. Conor spoke to one of the council while she was being bundled away. She listened intently, her dark eyes showing that she could barely comprehend what he was saying. But he said it, told her what the hunters would do and how he would react to them. He was in a rush to get back to the battle at the rear of the column. Back to Gray.

As Conor suggested, the council ordered their warriors to the outside of the column to protect those who could not fight. Soon they were in close combat with the hunters. The faster, taller, stronger hunters. The armoured warriors were speared like fish swimming in a shallow river. It was almost mass murder and the horrific gobbling and hooting of the hunters sounded triumphant. The tribes' massed archers were more effective. They rained arrows down on the enemy who were coming at them in a mass of arms, legs, and spears. They were like huge insects, a jagged, disjointed juggernaut of death and confusion. But gathered together they were a target, so the archers shot every arrow they had into the closely packed tubular bodies.

While he forced his way through the tribes towards the battle lines, Conor thought of Nisi, her tired face and her passion for life. She had come so far, she was so brave, and she was so precious to him. She was the symbol of what he was defending and the thought that she might die on a hunter's spear grew until it was almost a separate living thing inside his mind. He bellowed in rage.

"NO."

This one thundering word was so loud that heads turned and eyes widened at the sound, even in the chaos of battle. It was the voice he had used in the Chan tent. The one Dareen had spoken of by the fire. It was the voice of someone no longer just a man. It should have frightened them but the men and women who heard it took heart, and echoed it, less loudly but no less fierce.

"NO."

We will not let these hunters kill our children.

"NO."

We will not run.

"NO."

They will not have our world.

"NO."

Conor crashed into a group of hunters who were hacking the limbs off a fallen warrior. They went down in a heap. Conor felt the hard, gritty surfaces of their bodies against the skin of his arms and back. He rolled off,

THE FALL

gained his feet and then grabbed a limb with his left hand. Spinning, he threw the hunter out over the battlefield. He stomped his foot into the eyes of another, feeling a pop and a crunch underneath his boot. He ducked a spear and hacked off an arm, then a leg, and cut another hunter in two with a backhand blow. Then he was in a clearing, the savaged body of the warrior on the ground in front of him, steam rising from the blood pooling out of her. Her eyes were lifeless beneath her mask.

"NO."

Again, the primal sound burst from him and he sensed more warriors rushing to his side.

Behind you, coming up on your right.

Gray!

Conor felt a bump on his hip. Conor put his hand into Gray's thick black fur. Like the battle with Telikonta's army, the hunters were giving them a wide berth, but they were attacking everywhere else.

We need lances here. Something to keep them away.

The assault tribes like fighting in close. The hunters are too strong for that.

The archers are doing good work.

Yes, but once the hunters close…

Conor looked at Gray in desperation, his rage and frustration fountaining inside him.

We can't be everywhere.

But we can be right here.

Gray pointed his snout in the direction of a horrible melee involving a large group of D'ael and several hunters. The hunters were darting forward and pulling

THE FALL

the tribesmen out of their ragged formation by their arms or legs and then skewering them like pieces of meat on their long spears. The D'ael were hacking at them vainly as they were picked out one by one.

"NO," Conor roared as he plunged into the hunters, Gray by his side. His sword was out and back, he started to swing, a shadow flashed over them, and the barrier crashed down.

CH 16
WORLD OF STONE

When Conor woke he was lying on the ground, Gray beside him. He was immediately alert. Gray shuddered and then leaped to his feet at the same time Conor did. He growled, low and menacing. Conor's hand went out to reassure him. He did not know what to say. Or think.

Around them, the battle was frozen in time. Hunters held warriors at arm's length. The steady light from their spears outlined their black eyes and the tortured grimaces of their victims. Conor gingerly touched the arm of a warrior. It was hard. He pushed against it lightly, then with more force. It was as if it was set in stone. The battle was over.

The air was colder. Conor could feel it bite on his skin. Wan light was coming from somewhere. It was diffuse and weak but they could see.

Well, this is horrible.

Conor was still incandescent with rage at the hunters. He had to stop himself from kicking one of them. But another part of him, the human part, was stunned. The Lords of Power had acted. The world had been covered in darkness. Gray had done it after all—and Conor had ordered him to. It was all over. He stumbled over a body, solid as rock on the ground.

What is happening?
It has already happened.
Gray, we lost. It's over.
But the hunters didn't...
Gray couldn't say more. Words failed him.
What do we do now?
Let's look around.

They spent the rest of the day wandering through the battlefield tableau, looking at scenes of bravery, sadness, fear, and sickening gore. People at their best and worst, frozen in an awful instant. The carnage was spread over a huge area. The hunters had come from every direction, and there were more than Conor could have possibly imagined. A door to another world had been left open and a nightmare had come in.

Conor sidled by a running D'ael, hair flying, knives out, balanced on one foot, and he saw Nisi standing beside her mother, Dareen. They were talking to each other when the barrier fell. Their expressions were intense, but not afraid. Conor was glad of that. His heart nearly stopped seeing her and Dareen held in the grey light like statues. Fear on her face may have broken him. He lingered for a moment. Gray stopped beside him.

I can't believe this.
Gray hung his head and said nothing.
We were both just weapons all along.
Not just. We tried.

WORLD OF STONE

But we were only two. It wasn't enough. We weren't enough. Not yet, anyway.

There was a moment of silence between them and then Conor asked, *What?*

Gray looked at Conor, his golden eyes shining. *Think about it. We are still here. Alive somehow. Why?*

Conor was lost in his bitterness. *Maybe it's because the Other is intent on torturing us, letting us wander in this frozen horror until we starve to death.*

But we did this. Not the Other. This is a darkness called down by the Lord of Power and his Hound Gray.

I made you do it.

Whatever. But perhaps there is another chapter. Another part of the struggle we have to fight.

Conor's chin went to his chest. The rage and defiance in him wanted so much for that to be true. That the fight was not over, that they had not lost. But he was in despair. Everywhere he looked he felt the pain and terror of the battle stopped in time.

Then where is it?

A spasm of guilt coursed through him and Conor shuddered. *I could have died so many times. Why am I still alive?*

Good question.

I wish I had died. Better not to have ever seen this.

But you are not dead. And you have seen it. We have breath. We live. We cannot give up.

Conor turned and stomped away, giving in to his anger, kicking a hunter as he passed it. Gray followed him at a distance. They walked through the battle again, past the men and women warriors of the tribes, the

WORLD OF STONE

Eliti formations and the Chan war wagons packed with archers, their arrows still flying towards the enemy. Beasts reared and Hirashu leaped, baring teeth and claws as they did. Several were attached to the bodies of the hunters, black blood bubbling up from their powerful jaws. Gray could feel Conor's anger and frustration wheeling into sadness and despair and back again. But as they moved off the road to circle the battle Gray realized that the grass underneath their feet, although frozen, was not set in stone like the hunters or the people. It crunched and bent like grass in an ordinary winter. Gray felt a slight breeze ruffling his fur. Something he had not sensed since he had brought the barrier into the world days ago. He hurried up to share this knowledge with Conor but saw him looking down at his feet as he did.

You noticed too?
Yeah.
Maybe just the battle is frozen in time.
I think there's a stream not too far off the road, east of here. Let's go take a look and see if it's running.

Conor agreed. To Gray, anything was better than giving in to hopelessness and sorrow. And if Conor wanted to see this creek right now, then it was a good idea.

It didn't take them long to find it. The water bubbled and coursed through rocks and weeds the way it should. Conor knelt down beside it, took a deep breath, and then put his hands in. It was achingly cold. But it was clear and while he was looking down, a fish, small and dark, flashed by his fingers. There was life in this place, in this world.

WORLD OF STONE

Still. He had done this in another stream, in another place long ago. And the same things he had felt then were true now. This world with its overwhelming disappointments and small pleasures was worth fighting for. He felt the beginnings of hope. He stood up. He felt his heart beating and air in his chest—just as when the Other had shown him the void. He knew that his purpose had not changed, even if the place he was in had.

Now, if we can just find someone, or something, to fight.

Conor looked up at the uniformly grey sky and then at Gray.

Let's go look.

Conor stood, rubbed his face with his wet hands and then shook them. *Where?*

Not here. Gray wanted Conor away from the awful battle. It was too painful a reminder of their failure. The haunting gray faces were too familiar and too close. He wanted away from it as well. At least for a time. There might be game to be hunted. They had to eat. And the Southlands was as good a place as any to look for some hint of what to do next.

Alright. But I have to do something first.

Gray followed Conor as he twisted and turned through the still figures. He knew where Conor was going. When he got there, Gray saw him cut a strip off his Eliti cloak and tie it around Nisi's right wrist. He looked at her briefly and then walked over to the closest hunter and punched it as hard as he could. There was a loud crack. He punched it again. A crunch. He whipped out his sword and swung it hard. A piece of the hunter broke off. Then he was a whirlwind of blows, smashing the hunter, arms and legs flying, the body breaking into many pieces. He stopped when it had disintegrated entirely. He was breathing heavily. He stepped over the rubble and walked towards Gray, massaging his knuckles.

Finished?

Yes. Conor shrugged. *Good to know I have something we can do if we can't find something to fight against.*

It would take a long time to destroy them all.

Yes. Worth doing though, and we may have the time. Conor took a deep breath and blew it out. *I need to run.*

I'll tell you when I get tired.

CH 17
DEATH OR WORSE

They went south, running until the weak light faded into blackness. Conor could have kept going but Gray was exhausted. He eventually just slowed to a halt without saying a word. The landscape they passed was unchanged. Brown and dirty white fields, abandoned houses and farms. They saw no people. It was very cold. They camped right on the road, sheltering under Conor's cloak again. They both slept.

When he woke, Conor pulled off the cloak slowly, using the cold, trying to clear his mind. He opened his eyes and saw the dark grey sky. His heart fell as he remembered. He closed them again, just for a moment, and then stood up. There was a man sitting on the road not too far from them. They hadn't seen him the night before. He could have been there; the nights were so dark. But Gray would have smelled him. Conor shook his head to clear the sleep from it. The man looked familiar, but Conor could not place him. He sat and looked at them, just out of sword range. He waved. Conor jumped up and drew his weapon.

Gray growled and tensed to leap.

DEATH OR WORSE

"Good morning," the man said. "Sort of."

"What...who are you?" Conor pointed his sword at the sitting figure.

"Conor, I'm hurt that you don't remember."

His voice and face were familiar. Yet...

"Is this another dream? Are you the—"

The man ran his hand over his clean-shaven face. His hair was short and white, his eyes hard and dark brown.

"No. Not a dream. A nightmare for you, perhaps. Am I right?"

"Thesi!"

Dareen's guards had killed him a few weeks ago—the holy man she had hired to make him aware of his place in Eliton mythology. He had sold Conor their holy book on the road to the capital of the Empire so long ago. Conor's sword wavered and then he pulled it back. This man was dead. Conor started towards him.

"Please, Conor. Let me explain." Thesi cringed, his hands over his head, exaggerating his fear, smiling while he did.

Conor stopped, stunned. Seeing a dead man alive had, despite everything else they had witnessed, shocked him.

"You—you are him. It. The Other. The Traitor. Itax."

"So many names here." Thesi looked pleased. "Well, yes and no. I am different but the same…"

Gray's eyes were full of hate. Conor was angry and confused.

"Look, when I got here the door had already been opened. You know the one I am talking about." Thesi smiled. "The, uh...what do you call them?"

DEATH OR WORSE

"The hunters?"

"Yes, the uh…Hunters. They were here before I was. But the only way you could have ever dealt with them was if you, Conor, were able to unite the known world. Which I found out you were again trying to do. So I took on the guise of a holy man who worked for the most influential Mother in the Empire."

"Dareen," Conor said in a whisper.

"Dareen, yes. I gave her very persuasive and very bad advice." Thesi shook his head and chuckled. "Oh, those Mothers. Their followers went at each other like crows on a carcass. It all came apart. The cities burned, the tribes ran wild in the countryside, food stopped coming in. Incredible, really."

"You died once," Conor stepped closer, sword arm still ready. "Maybe you can again."

"Oh, yes. This body can be killed. We have learned what happens when we are one that can't be." He wagged his finger at Conor. "You remember that, don't you?"

Conor hesitated. What was he talking about?

"But I have answers, Conor. The armies of the Empire were weakened. I made sure this world would never be able to defeat the…what did you call them? Right, hunters, sorry. But despite my best efforts Dareen heard about you, still fighting on here in the Southlands. So she came to find you."

"That's not what she said."

"Yes, well, she wouldn't, would she? Very proud, the Mothers."

"Unlucky for you that she did. You died."

DEATH OR WORSE

"And now," Thesi said, his arms wide, "I'm back."

Kill him. Now.

I have questions. I'll listen. If we don't like what we hear, I will kill him.

Or I can.

"How did you come to be here?"

Conor lowered his sword but he did not put it in its scabbard. Gray did not move. His eyes were locked on Thesi.

"First, a question. I'm wondering what you think of all this." Thesi waved at the cold grey world around them, a hint of smile on his lips.

"Why…what do I think? I think it's your fault."

Thesi raised his eyebrows and tilted his head towards Gray. "Not his?"

"You opened the door between worlds; you brought the hunters."

"Oh, I didn't do that."

"No? No? Then who did?"

"One of us, I admit. A previous iteration. One of those not of the…uh…this physical plane, for lack of a better term. They are powerful and unpredictable. Earthquakes. Storms. Lightning. Fires. Opening doors from odd places in the universe. They are unstable here, and don't last long. But they can make quite a mess."

"A mess? Those people who died…" Conor seemed to grow with his anger. His sword came up again. Gray bared his fangs and inched forward.

Thesi stepped back, his hands out. "Yes. Admittedly, there was death. But weren't almost all of them soldiers

DEATH OR WORSE

about to war on each other anyway? How many would have died in battle? Or in the next one? More? Less?"

Conor waved his sword at Thesi like a pointer in a classroom full of children. "Battles brought on by the war against the Believer. You! The only reason the Chan and the Eliti were in the Southlands to begin with."

Thesi smiled again. "Yes, the Believer. Another iteration. Not my doing. Although its path was instructional, it was mad. And it solidified resistance by being mad. Too greedy. Too impatient. I was given a different path. The inside man." Thesi smirked. "However, the Believer was smart enough to try and smoke you out. It had a notion that an opponent might arise, someone who could stop it. So it tried to stop you before you got too strong. Its Bonded abandoned their children. You were one of those left behind, were you not, Conor?"

He was unable to speak. He was ten when his parents had left him. Conor was stunned.

"But it underestimated you and your Hound, here. You persevered, the two of you." Thesi winked at Gray. "Your strength of purpose is impressive." Thesi made a fist and shook it at Conor theatrically. "And this body they gave you. Stronger and faster than any man. You are the lucky one!"

Conor felt an uncontrollable spurt of anger. He punched Thesi in the face with the pommel of his sword. It happened so quickly that Thesi did not have time to move. He went down in a heap. There was a moment of silence.

Did you kill it?

DEATH OR WORSE

Conor peered at Thesi until he saw his chest rise slightly up and then sink down.
I don't think so. He's breathing.
Too bad. What the fuck is going on?
I don't know.
Other iterations? What does that mean?
The Other shows up in many forms, or so the Northerners said. Conor moved away from Thesi and started walking in a circle as they talked.
And we have to kill them all. Remember that, Conor.
Then there's no end to this. Conor kept talking and walking. *We're here because it is, so the war goes on.*
It's not going on right now.
If there is something after this horror, then, alright. But if there isn't, what's the difference? Conor rubbed the knuckles on his right hand again. They both looked at the now-stirring form on the road in front of them.
Are we going to keep listening to him?
Yes, but only if he answers my questions.
Conor pulled Thesi to his feet. His nose was pushed to one side and he was bleeding profusely. His eyes were half closed and he snorted a couple of times.
Conor shook him.
Thesi's eyes opened and he smiled.
Before he could say anything else, Conor said. "Listen to me, you shit. If you don't answer my next question, I'll have to wait for the next version to show up."
Thesi grinned even wider. His mouth was full of blood. It leaked from the corner of his mouth in fat drops.
"Fire away."

DEATH OR WORSE

"What the fuck are you doing here? Why aren't you dead?"

"Me? Dead?"

Conor shook him again, this time harder. Thesi's hands came up. Blood spattered on Conor's shirt.

"You know what I can do. Tell us!"

Thesi's hands came down. He was smiling again, but this time it was a smile Conor almost recognized as madness. It was a smile of abandon and of malice. Thesi's face had changed.

Gray saw it too. *Now I might believe him. He may be another version. He may be...*

"I will always appear in this creation, Conor. I'm here to help the world fall. Into chaos. Into despair. Into its natural state of decay. It will happen eventually—it always does, in all of them. I'm one of those who helps to make it happen...quicker."

"The Other." Conor said it reflexively, a curse.

Thesi shrugged, "Guilty. Look, Conor, everyone dies. Everything does. I just want…"

"Shut up." Conor shook him and then pulled him closer until his feet were right off the ground. "Shut up, you bastard."

But Thesi didn't. His eyes narrowed. "Did the last one show you the void, Conor? The nothingness that is most of this, uh...place? Did it? And how did that go?"

It had. Somehow Conor had been thrown into the vastness between the stars by the Other. He had seen and felt its cold and ancient indifference. It had been meant to drive him mad. It had only hardened his resolve to defend life in this world.

Conor held Thesi at arm's length. "Oh yes, I've seen it, felt it. Can you feel this?"

Conor drew his left hand back in a fist and then faked a punch at Thesi, who closed his eyes and cringed. Conor put his hand on his shoulder and squeezed gently instead.

"This is just as real."

Thesi opened one eye and then the other. Then he chuckled softly. "A hero with a heart. The worst kind."

Conor put Thesi down and took his hands away. He didn't regret the blow but he recognized the hypocrisy.

Thesi spit out a mouthful of blood. He smiled redly. "You know that you will be dust before too long. As will all of this." He waved at the grey world around him. "What's the point? That's my question."

"You are full of shit. Traitor. Liar." Conor spat the words out. "You don't want to speed the process of decay and destruction. You need it. You need the death and the hatred and chaos. It feeds you somehow."

Thesi's grin grew wider and wider. It looked as if his jaw had unhinged. Conor took a step back, eyes wide.

"That is a bonus," he said. "To be sure."

Conor reached for his sword again.

Gray advanced. *Wait. Not yet. We need to know more about him. It.*

Conor took his hand away from his sword hilt. He took a deep breath and then asked something that had been weighing on his mind for a long time.

DEATH OR WORSE

"The Believer consumed the souls of those who Bonded with him. Or so it was said. The Other said something similar to me. That he would be waiting for me on the Outside."

Thesi grinned wider. "He did, did he?" He laughed, harsh and deep. It was an inhuman sound. "There are many worlds, Conor. Many kinds of life, and many creations. This is only one. Most of them contain the life we enabled. We will have our due."

"You? Created?"

"Yes, yes—well, we helped. But it was so long ago." He dragged out the word *long*. "And isn't it obvious that life is an absurdity? Especially when it is an unravelling random event, like in this dreadful place. It always ends in disorder, decay, and death. It must. But when it starts to think—oh, when it *thinks*, that is even worse." Thesi shook his head. "Then, sometimes, it's like you, Conor and his Hound. Playing your parts in this charade, using the right lines so that it will all make sense to the players."

He smiled the horrible too-wide smile again. "And they say *I* am mad."

Conor insisted, "You didn't answer the question. Do you eat souls?"

Thesi shrugged. "There is a taste that life possesses. An awareness that lasts after what you call death. I don't need it, but it is, like the chaos, a reward for my labours—"

Conor grabbed the front of Thesi's shirt and pulled him close again. He slapped Thesi in the face. Hard. His head rocked back and blood sprayed out in a red arc.

DEATH OR WORSE

"Do you like this part of the story, Thesi? I can write more." Conor hit him again, this time with the back of his hand, a cracking blow. "Do you want another reward?"

Thesi's head lolled and his eyes fluttered.

"Did you forget who you are talking to?" Conor snarled. "I am Conor, Lord of the Hound Gray, and you will get nothing else from this place. And whatever form you take, we will be waiting for you. Those were people. And they died in fear and in pain because of you."

Thesi opened his eyes a bit. Conor let go and he slumped to the ground. He wasn't smiling anymore.

"I am aware of what waits for me, and for everything in this ridiculous place." The words bubbled from his bloody mouth.

"Yes," Conor said, "but for you, it could be quicker."

Thesi wiped his face and then looked at his hand in disgust. "I can rebuild this body, Conor. That will not be difficult for me."

Conor had a thought.

Gray heard it. *No.*

"What if you couldn't?"

Thesi scoffed. "I can."

"I could kill you," Conor said slowly, his thought formalizing as he did, "and chop the body up in tiny pieces. Scatter them all over the Southlands. Or I could burn you to dust."

Thesi raised his eyebrows.

"This world has changed, Thesi. Every person is frozen solid. There is nowhere for you to go."

Conor, no.

DEATH OR WORSE

Conor looked at Gray, who looked at Thesi.

"The barrier didn't freeze you. But you can't kill or hurt me or Gray, or you already would have. You know, I think I might actually be able to kill you. Or the version of you that exists here and now. And keep you dead. There is no human suffering for you to feed from now, no pointless deaths to keep you strong."

Thesi grimaced.

Conor kept on, his mind racing. "I mean, you had your chance to jump to a different body, or take a different form. That's gone. The barrier prevents it, obviously. Now, it's just you and me and Gray."

Thesi shrugged. "Killing me doesn't change anything. This world you and your dog have made will stay this way, covered in darkness. And if you do find a way to end my life, another one of me will come."

Conor shrugged. "Oh, eventually, maybe. And so what? We will kill that one too. It's a stalemate, you prick. Admit it."

Thesi said nothing at first, then almost petulantly, "I think I could put this body back together. I could."

Conor folded his arms across his chest. Gray sat down.

"Why?'" Conor asked bluntly. "What is there for you here?"

The two looked at each in the almost darkness. Gray wheezed slightly in the background, still suffering the effects of coughing up the barrier. Conor was strangely calm. The worst had happened. The world had ended. Yet he was confronting the author of it all. The Other was right here in front of him, bleeding from its nose and mouth from his hand. Perhaps the satisfaction of being the cause of that was enough to put aside the awful reality of the world, just for this moment. That, and his growing sense that there might be a way out.

Kill it.

"Conor, I think you misunderstand me—and yourself, for that matter."

Thesi's nose was swelling up.

"Really?"

"Yes. You see, I'm here to do what I was put here to do. I'm one of very, very many, and despite our differences," Thesi gestured at his ordinary human body, "we all have to do it. It is who we are and what we are, so talking to us or asking us *why* we do it is quite senseless. Our minds were made up long ages ago."

Conor said nothing.

"Oh yes, and yours was, too, if I understand how this works like I believe I do."

"You don't understand us at all."

"No?" Thesi had a feigned look of shock on his bloody face.

"I chose," Conor said. "I chose to fight because you offer nothing. I fight for the chance for life to exist and struggle and maybe make something better out of itself."

Thesi frowned. "From that limited perspective, I can see your point." Then he grinned the too-wide grin. "But that's not my view at all. To me, you're a rat in a cage in a burning barn. And now, look what you've done." Thesi waved at the grey landscape around them.

DEATH OR WORSE

Conor felt a flush of anger but it faded quickly. "Yet this new world doesn't work for you either, does it, Thesi?"

"No, not really. But I might get used to it. It's pretty terrible. Not much life here anymore. A lot like it's going to be in a few millenia anyway." He tried the horrible smile again but it wasn't quite as convincing.

Conor corrected him. "Human life, you mean. The streams run, the fish swim, and the deer run."

Thesi looked annoyed. "Nothing I can do there. Not my area…and with no sunlight and this cold…"

"So," Conor interrupted him, "why don't we make a deal?"

Conor, no.

Thesi narrowed his eyes. "Go on."

Conor walked away from their conversation and looked up into the dark sky.

Gray repeated, *Don't, Conor. No.*

Conor turned to Thesi, ignoring Gray. "If we keep killing you, maybe you come back, maybe we can keep you dead or maybe, one day, you don't come back at all. Some other version will pop up, I'm sure, but it won't be *you*. It fits, doesn't it? First the Believer, then the Other, then you, Thesi, and then something else. Different and the same. But you, the one that is here now, you are gone. Forever. We keep fighting the endless war, but not against you. You no longer exist."

Thesi said nothing, but he looked hard at Conor and Gray both, his eyes cold and his mouth in a thin line.

Conor finished his thought. His profane thought. "Or, you agree to help us get rid of the hunters, and to stay where we can keep an eye on you if and when things go back to the way they were."

Thesi smiled a little. "Conor, I am surprised. Despite everything I have said and done, everything that all of us have done to this world and its people, you want to make a deal? You've played your final card and now you want to renegotiate the terms? Not very heroic."

No. Conor, what are you thinking?

I'm thinking that maybe the barrier will disappear if we smash the hunters and he promises to behave.

It won't. Behave.

Maybe. But at least this gives us a chance. What kind of victory is this, Gray? It is worse than death. We have already lost if we don't do something.

You do know how terrible an idea this is? Even if it works, what happens if it betrays us and we lose next time? I mean really lose. And the barrier doesn't fall or the world burns or our souls get eaten. Maybe we have done the best we can.

But there has to be a next time. The myths of Eliton and the northern stories tell of the endless war and the Other and the Traitor returning countless times in different forms. They have to have been defeated—or even bargained with—before we came along. Here, and on other worlds. We have to try.

Kill it.

No. Please listen, Conor pleaded with Gray. *You told me I needed to be more than a weapon and I'm trying to find a way to the next time.*

Gray looked at Thesi. He stood there, bloodied and smiling.

DEATH OR WORSE

I have done all I can do. I have covered the world in darkness. I say we should let it be. Wait.

"A fascinating conversation," Thesi said. "I think your dog has a point—"

Gray leaped upon Thesi, knocking him flat on his back on the ground. He flipped him over, put his massive jaws around his head, gave a sharp twist, and broke Thesi's neck with an audible crack.

Conor stared in shock.

He's a monster, Conor. No one has ever heard our thoughts before. We have no idea what he can do. Leave it be.

Gray had never done that. Ended a disagreement his way, no discussion, no argument. It was like Conor's mind had been split in two. He looked on in silence as Gray walked away.

CH 18
ENDURE

Gray killed Thesi several times over the next few weeks. The Other would come back to life in Thesi's body after a few days and try to talk or run—or even fight. It was far stronger than a man but Gray was Gray and that was enough. Conor didn't help and Gray didn't ask him to. Conor felt Gray's conviction and he did not, could not, fight him to protect Thesi. Conor fumed while Gray killed Thesi over and over again.

Eventually, Conor told Gray that he had decided to walk back to the battle. He knew what he wanted—needed—to do if there was no war to fight. Gray followed him, Thesi's body hanging from his jaws. They did not speak other than about food. In their minds, they both had work to do. Once there, Conor looked for a war hammer. He found one on the belt of a tribal warrior. She was a large and muscular woman and it was too big for her, but it looked like a toy in his hand. He hefted it easily. Now he had a tool and he started to use it, smashing the hunters into pieces, one by one. He eventually amassed an arsenal of hammers so that when he broke one he did not have to go and look among the frozen hunters and their prey. Gray hunted when he could and watched Thesi with his golden eyes when he wasn't. Despite their nearness, the two of them drifted apart like slow boats on a wide river.

Conor tried not to think of the sick monotony of his enormous task. He tried not to imagine the colours and sounds of life before the sky fell. He just hit the rock-like bodies of the hunters until his hands bled and the hammer cracked. Then he found another and went back to work.

When he lifted his head and wiped the sweat out of his eyes, he would have to see the grey-brown world, still and cold, littered with the piles of hunter bodies he had built. And the tortured and twisted bodies of the people they had killed or were killing when the barrier slammed down. He told himself he had lost the war. Gray would not listen to him and he was paying the price.

Pitch black nights turned into dim, cold days. And day after day, week after week, moon after moon, Conor broke the hunters with his hammers and Gray maintained his vigil. Conor's arms hardened until they were like the rock bodies he smashed. His huge hands were gnarled and callused. His back broadened and his feet clenched the earth with every blow. His hair grew long and wild, and he tied it back with a leather strap like the one he'd tied to Nisi's wrist. He spoke no words and as he smashed the hunters, his mind wandered into the blank spaces near madness.

One morning, long after he had killed Thesi for the first time, Gray was gone. Thesi's body lay by the smouldering fire. There was enough food and he hadn't told Conor he was going hunting. Conor reached out for him and felt nothing. Conor's heart was as dark and hard as the bodies of his friends. He thought about going to look for Gray but he had no idea where to begin. After he ate, he picked up his hammer, looked at it, and then dropped it. It hit the frozen ground with a flat thump. He could not work.

He spent the rest of the day wandering through the frozen battlefield. He had avoided seeing Nisi and Dareen (and anyone else he knew) as much as he could. But today, he sought out familiar faces. He saw some of them—Eromil, Arusin, Gettil—gathered together in the centre of the battle, desperate, frantic, fearful and the nearness of the hunters to some of them drove him to tears. Then, as he moved to the front lines, he saw Dvor impaled on a spear, his hands clutching at it, and Dvak beside him on the ground, his face a rictus of horror as he watched his son die. Conor knew that Dvak could not see, but the image of the death being prolonged in front of him for so many dark days was heart-rending. No sculptor had ever created such a powerful illusion; this was real. Grief overtook Conor and he knelt by the scene for a long time. Eventually he moved on, his mind moving from stoic acceptance to deep despair between one moment and the next.

Late that night he sat by the fire. Thesi had not moved. He was dead, for now.

Gray has to know that I will offer the deal again if it returns before he does, Conor thought. Something has changed him. Or maybe he has to see for himself if he has truly done it. Covered the entire world and ended the war forever.

Conor had no knowledge of mythology, other than what he had learned about other civilizations and their stories. The Southlanders scoffed at the religious and he had been one of them. But how else to give meaning to this terrible scene? This half-life of cold and stillness. It was a living nightmare. A disaster of mythical scope. Yet what holy book would tell of what they had seen and done? Andaine and Tingish long ago and now Dareen, Baragara, Gettil, Dvor, Nisi, and of course, Gray. All of them. So much sacrifice. So much death. And his journey had taken him to this barren awful place, alone. He looked at the flames and remembered without hope.

Early in the morning a few days later, Thesi awoke. Eyes bulging, he jumped up and turned his head quickly in all directions. He backed away from the fire, hands out. "Where is he?"

Conor looked slowly up from his breakfast. "Gone."

"Gone?"

"Yes."

Thesi stopped moving and looked directly at Conor. "Gone where?"

Conor shrugged.

"How long?"

Conor shrugged again and held up three fingers and then four.

"You are still here."

"What?"

Thesi frowned and said, "Nothing. Any more of that?" He pointed at the bowl of cornmeal Conor was eating.

Conor nodded at the black pot hung over the fire.

Thesi helped himself and then sat down. "So, having fun?" He smiled a mad smile.

Conor looked at him from under his dark brows. He stared at him for a long while.

Thesi turned around slowly, moving as if he was oil instead of flesh. He smiled again, his teeth white and long and suddenly shaped into sharp points. He straightened his arms, palms up, fingers slightly curled, nails black and long. Thesi looked at his hands, one then the other, as they kept extending away from him, too far for a normal man.

"I'm different this time…" he crooned. "I feel like…I could…murder the world." Thesi's dark eyes flared open. "Oh, I wish that dog was here."

Conor got up. He carefully put his bowl and spoon down, his eyes never leaving Thesi. He wasn't armed, his swords were behind him, sheathed beside his blankets. He cursed his carelessness silently.

"He's not. But I am. And think, Thesi. My offer stands."

Thesi grinned, "I don't think so. This new…frame seems so much better. Which is good because I just have to kill something."

Conor felt the familiar implacable rage rising, pushing aside the reasonable voice inside him. "You are done killing."

ENDURE

"I don't know, Conor," the words came out of the wide, strange mouth in a mocking tone. "I'm feeling strong, and the only blood flowing around here is in you. I can smell it. And this time..."

Conor leaped over the fire, barrelling into Thesi and driving him backward. But Thesi turned and shifted Conor's weight off as they fell. Conor hit the ground with a thump and Thesi was astride him, an elbow pressing on his throat, black eyes staring into his, saliva dripping on Conor's face. Thesi raised his right hand, finger splayed wide for a raking strike. But Conor had been in many of these struggles. He whipped his right hand around Thesi's head and as he pulled it down, he head butted him, feeling the cartilage and teeth crunch under his forehead. The pressure on his throat lifted and turning his shoulder into Thesi, he scrambled out from underneath him. Thesi stayed down, hands to his face, howling with pain and rage, a sound unlike anything Conor had ever heard. As he started to rise Conor kneed him in the face, snapping his head back. Conor was beyond anger, beyond feeling, he was a force of nature, a falling mountain, a tidal wave. He pistoned punch after punch into the mess that was Thesi's face. But somehow Thesi spun down and away, twisting his elongated body in a way no human could.

They faced each other. Thesi laughed, spraying blood and spit as he did.

Conor's hands clenched and unclenched. "I'm still here," he said. "Waiting for you to kill me."

"I have a better idea." Thesi said as he turned and ran into the frozen battlefield.

ENDURE

Conor felt a spurt of alarm. If Thesi broke one of the frozen people like he had the hunters, that person would be truly dead, lost forever. He followed Thesi as he flitted through the stone forest of people, sudden fear in his heart as he knew where the monster was going.

Thesi had his long arms over the shoulders of Nisi and Dareen when Conor caught up to him. Blood flowed down his body black in the grey half-light. Conor could see his teeth red and white as he smiled at him. He shuddered in the cold as he saw the monster's fingers tap on the hard breasts of the women.

"Thesi, stop."

The monster's arms curled right around their necks as if he was part snake.

"Or what?"

"I'll…"

"Kill me? That's not much of a threat, I'm afraid. I'm actually looking forward to my next iteration, if it's anything like this."

Conor saw Thesi's arms moving around the women, taking more and more of their bodies in a grotesque embrace. His mind went back to another impossible situation long ago. That time he faced an Eliti officer and two Hirashu, one on a leash in each hand. That man, Embessilissi, was an arrogant prick. A faint echo of the thing in front of him but they both had made the same mistake.

In a blink Conor was at his throat, one hand around it and the other pulled back, his massive fist cocked. "You're going to die again, Thesi. And these women are stone. You aren't strong enough to break them."

This was a guess and Thesi called him on it. His arms flattened as they squeezed. Conor dared not look but he heard the rasping of skin and stone and his heart fluttered. There was a moment of strain on Thesi's face and Conor's heart almost stopped, and then Thesi's face fell.

"Well, shit."

Conor did not punch him. Like he had so many battles ago, he chose not to kill when he had the power to do so. He loosened his grip slightly.

"The deal?"

Thesi squinted at him yet he said nothing.

"There is nothing for you here Thesi, except a painful death. Gray has killed you many times. Now I will, if you choose it. You cannot defeat us if the Other with all his power could not."

Thesi bared his teeth and hissed at him, spraying spittle into his face. Conor turned away but did not let go.

"The deal?"

Thesi frowned, his face splitting into an inverted half- moon. "I really thought I could do it this time." He frowned even more, his serpentine mouth distorting his face into a terrible caricature. "But you have a point. The others failed and I might be smarter, but I'm not stronger. Obviously." Thesi sighed, "If I agree, I don't want to see you be a hero, or the dog either. if it all comes back. You can't …run things."

Conor thought for a moment. He was tired. Fatigued was a better word, he thought. He always believed he had a duty to fight as did Gray. But if them not being in the middle of every conflict between the Empire and the Chan and the Southlands was part of the deal that saved the world, he could live with that.

"Alright. I'll back away and let somebody else do it. Unless you fuck it up. Then it's off, and I will come for you."

Thesi nodded and his frown faded.

Conor nodded back. There was an awkward moment of silence. " So, can you…change back or do I have to smash your… and then you…?"

Thesi said nothing but as Conor watched, his arms retracted silently. His face rearranged itself and he got noticeably shorter. He showed Conor his hands, normal fingernails, and smiled without pointed teeth.

"Alright?

"Alright."

They walked back to the camp and ate in silence. Conor looked at his bowl and the fire.

"I don't know how many times I would have come back. And I don't know if I would have wanted to, if this is all I can come back to." Thesi waved his arm at the world.

Conor said nothing.

"And dying isn't a lot of fun," Thesi continued, speaking quickly. "Even for me. It hurts every time. And as I said, I never really know if it's the last time or not. It's quite frightening, really."

Conor grimaced, and when he spoke, his voice was hoarse and strained. "Do you hear what you're saying?

ENDURE

You know that we die only once and that we know that. How many have you killed? How many died in fear and pain? Do you expect me to feel sorry for you?"

Thesi was silent for a moment. "No. Just explaining myself. To myself, I think."

Conor put down his bowl and lifted the black pot off the fire. He got up and wiped his hands on his pants. "Something tells me nothing will happen until all the hunters are destroyed."

Thesi made a face and snorted. "Something tells you?"

Conor looked at Thesi, his face blank and his dark eyes intense. "It doesn't matter if it's true. It's what I can do and what I will do."

Conor walked over to the low forest of hammer handles sticking up from the ground near him. He grabbed a long one and threw it over his shoulder.

"You," he said, pointing at Thesi, "are going to help me."

"Now wait a minute," Thesi stuttered. "I don't think…"

Conor turned to face him. "If you won't, I will smash your head in with this." He hefted the huge hammer as if it was a reed. "And then we will see if the next one of you thinks differently."

Thesi threw his hands up in surrender, half mocking, half seriously. "No, no need. A deal is a deal." He walked over and took a much smaller hammer in both hands and lifted it up. It pulled him over to one side; he staggered but caught himself. "Let's get to work," he chirped.

ENDURE

Conor ignored him and walked towards the frozen tableau that loomed in front of them.

Together, Conor and Thesi, Lord and Other, broke the bodies of the hunters. Conor was an inexorable force, as hard and as strong as the sky that had fallen on them. From dim morning to dark night, his hammer fell rhythmically. He stopped only to eat and sleep. Thesi was forced to accept what Conor had: bleeding hands, screaming muscles, sleepless nights suffering the effects of the day. But he learned to endure the pain like all thinking life does when it has no choice.

Conor did not care about Thesi's pain. He only required him to work and Thesi had been killed enough times. He knew what he had to do.

Late one afternoon, endless days after they had begun, there were no more. Conor and Thesi had broken every hunter into at least three pieces, the standard Conor had set. He had not been counting down, intentionally. He had simply moved from one hunter to the next. If it had been hoisting an Eliti or Chan warrior on a spear, Conor held the victim carefully while Thesi hammered the hunter apart. Then Conor would gently set the warrior or soldier or child on the ground, their grey wounds open, broken pieces of spears inside them. Now, he looked blankly around for more to break but there were none.

Thesi had been counting. He had even commented to Conor that morning that their task was nearly complete, but Conor was still surprised. He lowered his hammer and surveyed the scene. All he could see were statues of Eliti, Chan, the tribes, and the beasts, forever frozen in their

ENDURE

frantic battle against an enemy that no longer existed. It looked even more bizarre than it did before he began.

"Feel better?" Thesi asked.

Conor hesitated. "No. I should…but no."

"Yes, you should. It's quite a feat. I'm sure it will find its way into one of your stories. So lordly, so mythical, so heroic."

Conor shook his head. "Not if they find out that you helped. Who you are. What I agreed to."

"No," Thesi said. "Well, I won't tell if you won't."

Conor surveyed the battle scene. Thesi dropped his hammer.

"So, now we wait for Gray?"

"Yes."

"Is he…?"

"Looking around to see if he actually did it? Covered the entire world in darkness? I think so. And perhaps when he returns he will see our only chance is…"

"To make a deal. With me?"

Conor was irritated by Thesi's interruptions but they didn't talk much so he let it go.

"Yes."

"What if he tries to kill me?" Thesi bluntly put into words what Conor had been wondering.

Conor looked at Thesi intently, for the first time in many days. His mind was usually elsewhere or barely present during the long bleak days of breaking apart the hunters and stacking their bodies in the cold grey light under the barrier.

"I'll try to talk him out of it."

"But you won't stop him?"

Conor shook his head.

"Perhaps I should run, then. One night after you are asleep."

Conor shook his head again with a humourless grin. "He'd find you."

Thesi grinned back. "Probably." Then he looked around. "This is a horrible place."

Conor squinted at him and said nothing.

"Cold. Dark. Boring."

Conor nodded in agreement.

"Who would have thought that we could make it worse than it was. But we did."

Conor was not sure if Thesi was actually taking responsibility, or just playing for sympathy. He didn't trust him yet, so he assumed the latter.

"Right."

They didn't speak for a while. They walked away from the battlefield and Conor built a fire. They ate in silence.

Thesi was still careful to put himself on the other side of the flames before he spoke, "So, what makes you think that if we have agreed to a truce and Gray agrees not to murder me, and now that we have broken the hunters apart, this all will end and the world as we used to know it will begin again?"

Conor blinked a few times and rubbed his face with his hands. Then he held them out to the fire, warming them. "I'm not sure. But the process seems almost mechanical, from a distance. The Believer rose up, we were there to fight him. The Other brought the hunters, the barrier came. You undermined the Eliti and weakened the Empire. We were going to lose the final battle, it fell. If we reverse that, maybe, I don't know, the process will work in the opposite way."

"You don't *know* that, though," Thesi said.

"No. I don't. But even you are a part of it. Killed? Reborn. Defeated? New iteration. But never quite strong enough to defeat us." Conor looked up from the flames. "Do you have any choice in the matter? Did I? My anger was uncontrollable at times. Made me into something hard. Inhuman almost. I couldn't control it. Do you feel anything when you are dead? Are you asked if you want to come back?"

Thesi sat for a moment, uncharacteristically puzzled. "I'm not being consulted, if that is what you are asking."

"Right. And we knew what we had to do." Conor settled back and looked back at the fire. "And now we wait for Gray."

"And hope he's seen enough to change his mind."

"Yes."

Thesi nodded and leaned back. "I'm glad we are not working tomorrow."

Conor couldn't help but roll his eyes.

Thesi scrambled up. "I wonder if there is any wine in the supply train. I can't believe I didn't think of it till now." Thesi took a burning stick from the fire to light his way and wandered off towards the battlefield.

CH 19
LIGHT

Conor didn't join him. Enjoyment of any kind seemed wrong—blasphemous, even—in this world. Since the barrier fell he had eaten and drank only to fuel himself for the task of destroying the hunters. Conor had never been a drinker and wine did not appeal to him now even though that task was done.

Thesi found some wine, the biting yellow kind the Eliti loved. Conor refused it when offered. Thesi grimaced with every swallow, but that didn't stop him. They sat in the cold black night while Thesi drank and Conor brooded, missing Gray with a sudden rush of feeling. Their break had wounded him; he felt as if he was only now letting himself realize how deeply. He looked at Thesi, who was admiring the wine in the bottle, outlined against the flames. If Thesi wasn't able to truly commit to a truce, Conor thought, the barrier would not lift. He won't be able to lie his way out of this. Whether Gray agrees to let him live or not.

"So Conor," Thesi slurred slightly, "you spend your life fighting to save your world and you won't fight Gray to save me? Save the world?"

LIGHT

Conor nodded slowly without looking up.

"That's friendship," Thesi raised the bottle in salute, "not even to save the world."

Conor stood up. "You would not understand. How could you? If we break our bond, then…" he thought for a moment. Why wouldn't he? Shouldn't he consider it, if it gave them all a second chance? But Conor knew he could not. There was something so fundamental to their connection that if he severed it by killing his companion, he would condemn this world to perpetual darkness. The lords, even if he was one, would not allow that to be rewarded. That story of Conor killing his Hound, Gray, would never be written because there would be no one to write it.

"It is you who must decide, Thesi. Not me. Then we will have a chance."

Thesi stood up as well, a little unsteady. "I have. I think. Because this is fucking terrible." He held up the wine bottle and snickered. Then he fell into a sitting position with a thump, rolled over and went to sleep.

The next morning Conor woke very early. Thesi was snoring. The morning was cold and dim, the kind of light he had become used to. He stayed underneath the warmth of his cloak and looked around. He saw nothing new. Conor thought that he might build a house of some kind if they were going to be here a while, waiting. Might as well be more comfortable. He dozed off as he was gathering materials in his mind. He dreamed he was still smashing the frozen hunters, when one of the liquid black eyes swivelled towards him.

LIGHT

He woke with a start. "Damn!"

Conor shrugged off his cloak and stood up, windmilling his arms and stomping his feet to get some feeling in them and forget the awful vision in his mind. He glanced up at the sky and thought it might rain. Then he bent down to tie up his boots. He stayed bent over after he had finished tying them.

Rain? Here? Why had he thought that? He sniffed the air. It did smell of rain. He remembered that smell. A promise of…spring. He dared not look up. Was he imagining it? Were there clouds? Or was the awful barrier still there to crush his spirit entirely?

He was awake, he knew that. His back muscles were complaining so he straightened up. Conor tilted his head slightly, almost afraid to look. It was still there, solid and low. His heart fell but then he noticed that it was not a uniform blank grey. There were darker patches. And it was lighter everywhere else. It is brighter this morning, Conor thought, it really is. He looked over at the battlefield. He could see the statues that were people more clearly. It wasn't like before the barrier came, but it was lighter. He walked over to the closest warrior and touched her. She was still cold and hard. He tried a few others and it was the same. Disappointed, he walked back to the barely smoking fire.

He added a log and poked and prodded the embers. Things were changing. He felt more clear-headed than he had for as long as he could remember. He pushed aside his feelings for Gray and went to the stream to drink and wash his face. He would start something today. A home

LIGHT

of some kind. But not until he had seen one of those small fish. He knelt and waited. There, one was flitting along the shadows near the bank. Satisfied, he rose up. Shadows? Here? He raised his head and looked at the sky. There was no blazing sun, and he could see dark streaks, but it was even lighter. Now, if it would only warm up.

Conor kicked Thesi's feet when he got back to the fire. Thesi just groaned and rolled over. Conor left him. He ate and then went to find an axe. He kept his head down on the battlefield. He didn't want to see anyone he knew today. He could not allow himself to get ahead of what was possible.

He spent the day working. It was, he realized early on, the first time in a very long time that he was doing something other than breaking the hunters, running away from or towards mortal danger, arguing over the existence of life on this world, or fighting and killing to save it. It made Conor feel something approaching good. Had he started to hope again? Not just for a chance at defeating the Other, but for a chance at life without war and impending disaster? Wouldn't it be something, he thought, to have only the usual human failings of deceit, arrogance, and stupidity to worry about?

If only Gray would return.

When the light started to fade he had only the beginnings of a frame. Gray would scoff at what he had done, Conor thought, and ask why he didn't walk down the road and use a building made by someone who knew what they were doing.

LIGHT

For many days, Conor worked and worried about Gray. He didn't mind that Thesi drank too much and spent most of his time reading the books he found in Eliti packs. They were, Thesi said, often books about the Southlands.

"This guy was a student, Conor. Mathematics! He brought his school books to war. Imagine that!"

Thesi seemed genuinely impressed, or else incredulous at this man's naivete. Thesi's mockery sometimes took a fine edge. Conor wasn't sure in this case, but he didn't really care. Thesi wasn't trying to get away or kill him. The barrier was thinning and lifting a little more each day. And after dinner every night, Conor would stand just inside the circle of warmth the fire gave them and look for Gray down the road.

LIGHT

of some kind. But not until he had seen one of those small fish. He knelt and waited. There, one was flitting along the shadows near the bank. Satisfied, he rose up. Shadows? Here? He raised his head and looked at the sky. There was no blazing sun, and he could see dark streaks, but it was even lighter. Now, if it would only warm up.

Conor kicked Thesi's feet when he got back to the fire. Thesi just groaned and rolled over. Conor left him. He ate and then went to find an axe. He kept his head down on the battlefield. He didn't want to see anyone he knew today. He could not allow himself to get ahead of what was possible.

He spent the day working. It was, he realized early on, the first time in a very long time that he was doing something other than breaking the hunters, running away from or towards mortal danger, arguing over the existence of life on this world, or fighting and killing to save it. It made Conor feel something approaching good. Had he started to hope again? Not just for a chance at defeating the Other, but for a chance at life without war and impending disaster? Wouldn't it be something, he thought, to have only the usual human failings of deceit, arrogance, and stupidity to worry about?

If only Gray would return.

When the light started to fade he had only the beginnings of a frame. Gray would scoff at what he had done, Conor thought, and ask why he didn't walk down the road and use a building made by someone who knew what they were doing.

LIGHT

For many days, Conor worked and worried about Gray. He didn't mind that Thesi drank too much and spent most of his time reading the books he found in Eliti packs. They were, Thesi said, often books about the Southlands.

"This guy was a student, Conor. Mathematics! He brought his school books to war. Imagine that!"

Thesi seemed genuinely impressed, or else incredulous at this man's naivete. Thesi's mockery sometimes took a fine edge. Conor wasn't sure in this case, but he didn't really care. Thesi wasn't trying to get away or kill him. The barrier was thinning and lifting a little more each day. And after dinner every night, Conor would stand just inside the circle of warmth the fire gave them and look for Gray down the road.

CH 20
BAD DEAL

He had four walls up and a door cut out when Gray walked back into camp. Conor felt his presence before he arrived, but he had just said hello and tried not to show his excitement. Gray was relaxed. He had encountered no danger. His black coat of fur was glossy but had not grown over the burns made by the hunters' spears. His golden eyes were clear, but tired. They were relieved to be back in each other's presence again.

Nice place.
Thank you.
Where are you going to put the servant's quarters?
Very funny.

Thesi stood up when he saw Gray. He held the books to his chest. His eyes were wide and he glanced back and forth at Conor and then at Gray.

I notice you haven't killed it yet.
And you didn't while I was gone.
It got close.
I'll bet.

Conor waited. Thesi waited.

BAD DEAL

Nod if you can hear us, Thesi.
Thesi nodded.
Gray looked at Conor. *I don't like that much.*
I won't listen.
I don't believe you.
Probably smart. Thesi couldn't help himself; he grinned after he said it.
Gray growled deep in his throat. *I don't want you in my mind. Speak out loud or I will kill...*
Agreed. We must hear your voice, Thesi. But remember, Gray, he can't lie his way out of this. Somehow, the Lords will know. This won't end till he commits to a truce, a permanent truce.
How permanent? And when we die? We won't live forever, Conor. Will it?
Conor turned to Thesi. *Will you?*
Thesi was dumbstruck. "I have no idea."
Conor—
Gray, we are deciding how to stop an endless war. You and I must acknowledge that this is not a victory, and Thesi must agree that being alive is better than being dead. I think other than that, guarantees of the kind you are looking for are impossible, for all us.
Gray sat, his eyes fixed on Thesi.
Is it everywhere, Gray? The cold, the sky, the people held like statues?
Yes. As far as I walked, it was the same. All the people are like...that. Gray nodded at the tableau behind them.
And if the barrier was to stay, the winter would not end, and all life would disappear in time.
Yes.
Have you noticed the changes in the sky?

BAD DEAL

Hard not to.

Is it a sign for us? To keep going, keep trying to come to an agreement?

I'm pretty sure it started to change the moment I decided to turn around and start walking back here.

Conor grinned. *I thought it was when we finished destroying the hunters.*

Either way.

Thesi interrupted. "What about the people? Why aren't they coming back?"

Conor had tried not to think about that. Every morning he went to the edge of the battle and touched what used to be the warm skin of a tribal warrior. And every morning it was cold and hard.

"Well, we decide. We all agree, and then they will." He tried to smile but he could not. He hoped. That was all he had. "They have to come back."

Gray looked at Thesi. *They haven't. Maybe it's not telling us the truth. Maybe it's going to start the whole thing over as soon as we...*

"Maybe you're not!" Thesi shouted, pointing at Gray. "Maybe you are going to kill me as soon as they return. Maybe the Lords don't trust you!"

I'm here, aren't I? And you're still alive. Gray's fur was standing on end and his ears were flat against his head. His fangs were showing and his growl was a low rumble.

Conor stepped between them. *This is getting us nowhere. Gray, do we agree that this,* Conor waved his hands in the air, *is worse than the possibility of life with Thesi in the world?*

Yes.

BAD DEAL

And Thesi, do you agree that being alive in a world you can't consume or destroy is better than being killed over and over again by one of us in this place?

Conor and Gray stared at him, waiting.

"Yes! You convinced me, alright? Watching you destroy yourselves slowly on your own in the old world is much better than being murdered for the rest of time—or until I'm truly dead—in this one."

Conor looked at Gray.

We must step aside when the world returns. I will not be a ruler in the Southlands, or anywhere else.

Suits me. If it behaves, I will.

Alright then. Alright.

Conor's hands were down by his sides. His face was calm, if his mind was not. "Then we wait. But first, Thesi, when they do come back, I assume you will regain more of your powers?"

Thesi swallowed hard. "Well, yes, I guess."

"You can't be him when they come back. Thesi's dead. Dareen and her men watched him die."

"Oh, I can fix that," Thesi said with a smile. "No problem."

Conor pointed a finger at him. "You will change form and you will do it in front of me as soon as they return. You will not run or steal another's body."

"Alright."

"You will be a man. One man. Same height. Same physical attributes as this one."

Thesi frowned.

"You will stay in my or Gray's sight."

BAD DEAL

"Always?"

"Always."

"I'm to be a prisoner?"

"Until we get this figured out. Until we know more about everything."

"Okay…" Thesi said slowly.

"Just hang around. We'll find a way to make it make sense. It is the only way."

"Yeah," Thesi agreed. "I haven't been thinking that far ahead. I can make it so I'm familiar to the right people. That, I can do. I want all this to be over, too, you know."

There was nothing else to say. Conor and Gray looked at each other. Conor raised his eyebrows and tilted his head slightly, asking Gray silently if he acknowledged the deal, once and for all with no reservations. It was the kind of gesture only life long friends could make and understand how deep with meaning it was. Even those who shared their deepest thoughts. Gray dipped his head once sharply, and then they and Thesi spent the rest of the day being intentionally too absorbed in what they were doing to notice what the others were about.

CH 21
A BETTER STRANGE

The next morning the barrier had lifted even higher, although angry black streaks could now be seen. It was misty and cool. The moisture felt good on Conor's face and he saw it as another good sign. He went to check on the Eliti soldiers closest to them. There was no change. He sighed, trudged back to the fire, and prepared breakfast. He ate, left some for Thesi, and began working on his new home as he couldn't think of anything else to do. Gray watched, shaking his head more than a few times as Conor fumbled to complete a task he had only seen others do. Thesi woke later, as usual, and wandered the battlefield looking for more books, after replacing the ones he had read, at Conor's insistence.

It got dark early and the temperature started dropping as soon as the light faded. They had gathered around the fire when they heard a clattering sound coming from the battlefield. Thesi jumped, Conor looked up, and Gray swung his head towards the sound.

"What the fuck was that?"

A BETTER STRANGE

They all looked over. Even in the fading light something was different, they just weren't sure what. At first.

Then Conor said, "The arrows. The arrows and the spears are down."

The barrier had stopped the arrows and the spears in their flight, held in the air as impossibly solid as a fly in amber. Now they lay on the ground.

"It's happening!"

Before any of them could move, more things fell. This time it was bodies, the ones that had been held at extraordinary angles, or in mid-stride or leap. They thumped to the ground in a staccato series of sounds like the beating of an old drum. Conor ran over to the once-suspended battle. It was now a strange jumble of bodies, piled on one on top of the other in some places, arms and legs jutting awkwardly in the air. Conor touched one and it was still stiff and cold. Life had not returned to them yet.

Gray and Thesi joined him.

"Quick, help me."

Conor began to shift them off one another, carefully lifting them to open ground.

This is fucking strange.

But better strange, not worse strange. Conor kept working as they spoke. *Better strange.*

Thesi was moving gingerly through the bodies. He hadn't touched one yet.

"I'll give you that. Your Lords have cornered the market on strange."

Conor started to lecture him but then he said, "Just shut up and help."

A BETTER STRANGE

Thesi rolled the twisted body of a tribal warrior off another with an extended toe. "There."

They worked as long as they could see. Conor kept thinking that the people were going to spring to life at any moment, but they did not. The nights were still pitch black and very cold, and the battlefield was vast, so they decided to stop and wait for morning to continue.

Conor could not sleep. He wanted to carry Nisi over to the fire but he felt like it would be wrong somehow in a way he did not understand. She was still as hard as a statue. It was too painful to look at her, and he might have to touch her in a crude way to move her. And then he would have to lay her on the ground, hands out, looking at someone who wasn't there. No, he would wait. He closed his eyes and tried to think of something other than the image of Nisi's blank eyes staring at the black sky.

Conor woke when he heard a thin keening. It was a plaintive cry of need and discomfort. He rolled over and looked at Gray. His head was up and facing the battlefield.

That's a baby crying.

What?

A baby. A baby is awake.

Conor got to his feet. His head cleared quickly. The tribes had bro=ught their families. It was still dark, but the fire had burnt down to embers. The sound continued. It pulled at him. He wanted to console the little one, alone and afraid in the darkness.

They are coming back. The people are returning.

It sounds like it.

A BETTER STRANGE

Conor started towards the battlefield, feeling his way in the pitch black. Gray was at his heel then ahead of him.

Put your hand on my back; I can see better than you.

He did, stepping carefully when he saw shapes looming ahead of them in the darkness.

Not long till morning. Do you want to wait?

No. Let's try and find the little one, anyway. Then we'll see.

The crying continued, growing louder as Gray led Conor towards the source. And then there it was, on the ground. It had rolled away from a woman who lay beside it, her arms curled around the little body that wasn't there anymore. Conor scooped it up and folded the blankets it was wrapped in around it as best he could. It was a girl. He had never held a baby before. She was ridiculously small in his huge hands. Conor held her like she was made of eggshell. But she immediately stopped crying, and that was something. Conor smiled at her.

Hello, little one. Welcome back.

Others are moving. I can see ...

Then they heard more crying, shouts, and groans. It was happening all at once. The people who had been held suspended in time had been released. Above them the stars suddenly shone bright, and low on the horizon the pale moon appeared. It was hard to see but not impossible, as before. Night was night again.

He knelt down in front of Gray, his free hand in his thick fur, their eyes locked.

It has happened. Thank you, Gray, my friend. They have returned.

A BETTER STRANGE

There was a moment of communion between them. An acknowledgment of their bond and what they had accomplished together. It passed and Conor stood up.

We have to find Nisi, Dareen, and Telikonta. Tell them what happened, we need them to calm the people down.

The woman at his feet gasped and reached for him. Conor knelt and gave her baby back to her.

"It's alright," h e said to her in Eliti. "It's going to be alright. You're safe." He patted her on the arm while she looked at him in fear. "You're safe. They are gone."

She smiled hesitantly and then Conor stood and said to Gray, *Help me get to Nisi. Please.*

They worked their way through struggling crowds of people. They heard orders being shouted in Chan and Eliti, the screams of the wounded, and calls of men looking for their women and women looking for their men. Some sat numbly beside those who had not woken, their torn bodies spilling blood in red-black spurts. Some were still lying on the cold earth, faces blank, unable to understand what had happened.

Conor started shouting out, "It's alright. The barrier has lifted; the hunters are gone. It's alright!"

All he got were frightened looks and people scrambling away from him and Gray.

You are quite a sight, you know that, right?

Conor stopped. *What?*

The hair. The muscles. Your size.

I can't do anything about that now. Just get me to Nisi. We have to get some order here or someone is going to get killed.

A BETTER STRANGE

The Chan had begun to relight their torches, and scattered Eliti glow globes gave off stuttering white light. Conor could see well enough that he began to walk faster. He pushed his way through a Chan column, the soldiers stepping aside, their faces fearful. Two huge war beasts of the Chan trumpeted their unease to his left and then he saw her, her left hand clutching her right wrist, where he had tied a strip of leather from his cloak.

Conor turned to Gray. *Find Thesi and watch him.*
Right.

Then he shouted, "Nisi!" long before she could see him. She looked around. He called again, "Nisi!" and then they saw each other.

She was as confused and afraid as most of the people who had seen him that night, huge and hairy, but when she recognized him her eyes widened. "Conor!" And she ran up, put her hands on his forearms and looked up at him. Their eyes met and he was happy as he had ever been.

"What is happening? Where are the hunters? And the sky is...back. How?"

"It's a long story, but the hunters are gone. You must get Dareen and Telikonta to use their power to help people through this night. The only danger left is that someone might start a war by mistake."

"How do you know they are gone? Could they not return, should we not..."

"I broke them all, Nisi. They were...uh...frozen along with you. It has been many moons for Gray and me since

A BETTER STRANGE

you...were aware. We smashed them all. You are safe, believe me."

She was confused by his brief tale. "What?"

He repeated only the last two words, slowly and firmly, "Believe me."

She nodded and smiled briefly. "Okay Conor. Come on."

CH 22
THE STORY

"The world ended, and you brought it back by making a deal with the Other?"

Dareen and Nisi were sitting across from Conor in similar long dark dresses edged in white fur. A large fire roared between them. The day had dawned warmer but as the sun set it had cooled again. The shock of dealing with the aftermath of the return had stunned them all, so it had been agreed that everyone would look after their own until the leaders could meet the next day. After the chaos of three large armies finding out in the dark that the war was suddenly over and they were safe in what for them was still the middle of the battle, and then dealing with the hundreds of wounded and killed, Conor had insisted that Dareen and Nisi hear their story in full before he shared it with Telikonta, the Chan, the tribes, and what was left of the Northerners.

"Well, it didn't call itself that, but yes. It was here with us and we…made a deal."

Dareen nodded her head slightly, saying nothing, her face expressionless.

THE STORY

"And we broke the hunters. That needed to be done."

"We saw that this morning. There were so many. How long did it …"

Conor put his hands over his eyes as his chin lowered to his chest, "A very long time."

"I am sorry," Dareen said.

After a moment of silence Nisi asked, "So, Gray brought the darkness, and while we slept for many moons…we were frozen, you say?"

Conor dropped his hands and looked up, his face bleak, remembering. "Yes. As hard and as cold as a marble statue. Everyone."

"With no sun, moon, or stars?"

"No. The barrier came down and…it was a grey, dead world."

"Everywhere?"

"Well, as far as we went. Gray wandered far to the south and the west and he saw only the same."

"And only you, Gray, and this thing, were left, and you…" She was thinking of the hunters.

Conor shrugged. "We had to." Then he asked, "Did you feel anything, Nisi? Lady Dareen? Did you have any sense of time passing?"

Nisi shook her head. "No. We were trying to get our guards to form up on us when there was a flash of darkness. And then I was standing beside my mother in what has suddenly become the middle of the night."

"I had time to think the end had come, and then Nisi was there and the hunters were not," Dareen added.

THE STORY

Conor smiled a little. "I am glad you did not see what the world became when the barrier fell."

"Yes," Nisi said.

There was a moment of quiet when all they heard were the crackle of flames and the murmur of thousands talking around fires just like they were. Nisi leaned forward and after looking at her mother for permission asked, "What were the terms of this deal, and where is the Other now?"

"It's in our tent. Gray is with it. It has promised not to go anywhere or do anything. And the agreement was basically, we let it live, it behaves."

Both Nisi and Dareen looked confused.

Dareen spoke first. "You could have killed it and you didn't?"

"It's more complicated than that. It will come back if we kill it. Gray killed it many times while you were…" Conor ran his hands through his hair and then rubbed his face. "Gone. And it always came back. And it changes when we kill it, or at least, it can change. From the Believer, to the Other, and then to this thing in the shape of a man. We feared something worse was to come. We came to believe this was the one to make an arrangement with. It wasn't a fanatic; it didn't shake the earth or open the door for the hunters to come into our world. It was evil, yes. But… the only way to get the barrier to lift, for life to return was to agree to end the war without victory for either side. At least for now." Conor did not mention his promise to stay out of human affairs.

Nisi and Dareen exchanged a glance.

Dareen spoke. "And you believe it?"

THE STORY

"You are here, so yes."

"And you say you will watch it always? Make sure it doesn't...?"

"Yes. Gray and I."

Nisi leaned back and studied Conor.

"I do not believe you can tell the Chan or the tribes—or anyone—about this deal you have made. They would want to kill it, and maybe both of you. They will not trust you or something or someone that has shown itself to be so powerful and dangerous."

Dareen nodded. "I agree. This secret must be kept. And you cannot possibly watch over this thing, day and night for the rest of your life, even with Gray beside you. And if what you say is true, it must not be left alone, ever."

Conor looked away from them and into the night, lit by the fires of the Chan and the tribes and the Northerners and the pale white of the Eliti globes. He even saw stars in the blue-black sky.

"We will try. We must." He faced the two women again. "And if I agree to keep silent about the deal, you will say nothing? You will protect me and my secret?"

Dareen smiled half a smile. "Do not forget what I told you, Conor. It is what I believe. You are the incarnation of a god. I will do what I can if it is your will. But let us do one thing for you. Let us take it back to the Empire."

"What?" Conor shifted upright in his chair.

"If it has agreed to behave, we do not need your strength to control it. And what better place for it to be? We have resources that you do not. We have family and followers who will act for us without question. We will

THE STORY

know what it is and even if we do not tell anyone, our feelings of suspicion will be enough to inspire those who guard it."

Conor thought for a long moment. He had not considered a life without that responsibility. He did not know how to respond.

"I don't know, my lady. This is our burden. We …"

"You could stay with us," Nisi said. "In the Empire. With it. As long as you like. Until you are sure."

That offer intrigued him. It would fit what he had agreed to with Thesi. He could be close to Nisi and he could watch Thesi, with help. He wouldn't have to sleep in the wild under a cloak, hunt for his dinner, wash in a stream or eat cornmeal every morning. He wouldn't have to worry about the Chan or the tribes or finding work in the Southlands. He could rest and just *be*.

"Let me think about it," Conor said. "And I'll have to speak with Gray."

Dareen nodded and Nisi smiled at him, her eyes shining in the firelight. Conor smiled back at her. The way she looked at him was intoxicating. He knew it was partly because it had been so long but he didn't care. He reveled in the feeling until Dareen cleared her throat.

"So, it's agreed? You will speak only of the destruction of the hunters tomorrow? And the…uh…thing…will come with you to Eliton when it's time to leave?"

"Yes," Conor said. "Agreed, as long as Gray consents."

Nisi added, "And perhaps tell a story about you and Gray confronting the Other while we slept, and killing it?"

"We did that. It didn't stay dead."

THE STORY

"Yes, but in this version, it does."

"Right," Conor said. "Of course. Probably a good idea. Ties things up nicely. I'll give Gray most of the credit, that might head off some hard questions."

Dareen put her hand on Nisi's arm, obviously pleased with her eldest daughter's suggestion. She stood up. "We will sleep now and in the morning we will be surprised and respectful and appropriately in awe of what the Lord and his Hound have done for us." She bowed to Conor slightly. "Nisi, come."

"Yes, M other."

Conor stood up as well and bowed deeply. Nisi skipped around the fire and kissed him when he arose. It was quick, but affectionate. Their eyes met for an instant, and his heart jumped at the thought that she felt the same way about him as he felt about her. Then she turned and hurried to follow her mother, who had already walked away into the dark.

CH 23
FALSE FAREWELLS

Gray was awake when Conor returned to their tent. He did not argue against taking Thesi to Eliton, which surprised Conor. Gray had been to the Empire in the past and had not liked it. But now Conor noticed a deep tiredness in his loyal friend. Coughing out the barrier had nearly killed him. Gray had just searched the Southlands alone for many days looking for signs of life. His fur, however thick and shiny, was crisscrossed by scars. His teeth were chipped. One of his huge fangs was broken nearly in half. He had been through so much, Conor realized, and Gray liked the idea of having many eyes on their prisoner, which would lighten his load, though he wouldn't concede to that at first.

I might just eat and sleep outside Thesi's door for a full moon. Then we'll see.

Yes. But in the Empire, you won't have to.

Perhaps, but I'm tired, Conor. I'm going to rest for a few hours.

No problem. I'll stay up.

Conor sat in front of a small fire and rehearsed what he was going to say to the leaders of the other nations. He wasn't going to add much to the story of what happened after the barrier fell. The Other would be made to seem bigger and more threatening than he actually was, but he would still be a man constrained by the barrier from being anything more. And that's all. Conor knew he was a bad liar and that it was easier to fool someone when the lie had elements of truth. Still, he wasn't looking forward to the deception.

As the morning broke clear and calm, a squad of six Eliti soldiers marched up to Conor's fire. He looked at them in surprise.

"Good morning."

"Good morning, Lord. Lady Dareen has ordered us to stand guard."

Conor just stared and said nothing.

The officer said hesitantly, "For you. Here."

Gray broke into his thoughts. *It's for Thesi. So we can go to the meeting.*

Right.

"Thanks…?"

"Shalka. First Spear"

"Shalka. Thanks."

Conor ducked back into the tent. Gray was on his feet. Thesi was still rolled up in his blanket. He had chosen to take a tall, young, ridiculously attractive male form. He had black hair and brown eyes. He wouldn't stand out in the Empire, if that is where they ended up. They were calling him Rilni. Conor nudged him lightly.

"Stay put. We'll be back for you later."

Rilni just mumbled.

FALSE FAREWELLS

"And there's a guard outside. Dareen and Nisi know the truth and they sent us some help."

Rilni had been asleep last night when they came back from their story-telling. A hand came out of the blankets and waved him away.

I don't know how I feel about this. Leaving it here.

Yeah, the first time is going to be tough.

And it's happening much quicker than I could have imagined.

Yeah.

Are you sure you need me there? I could stay...

Yes. The people need to see the hero. And it will be our last meeting for a while.

Maybe...hopefully forever.

Right. Let's go do it.

With Gray by his side, Conor told the tale he had agreed to tell to the gathered leadership in a massive tent. Gettil, Eromil, the rest of the Chan, and the tribal leaders watched impassively. Nisi and Dareen smiled faintly and nodded appreciatively at the right moments. Telikonta looked surprisingly happy, her hands resting on her protruding belly. The Eliti officers and what was left of the Northerners gripped their swords and leaned forward when he spoke of Gray killing the Other in the bleak dead world after the barrier fell. He left out his fight with the snake like Thesi and his promise not to use his power and become the Lord of all people.

Some of the Eliti exclaimed, "The Lord and his Hound!"

Conor felt little of his previous hard conviction. He was lying to them. He had been convinced and understood the rightness of it, but it still felt wrong. And he was tired as well. He had run so far, given so many speeches and fought so many battles, trying to defeat the enemy or inspire others to join him and Gray in their fight. He had made his promise. There was nothing left to do, and he knew it. And the long days in the grey world that had ended without the triumph he had been born to win had worn on him more than he had admitted to himself.

There were speeches made, some of which concerned him and Gray, about how much everyone owed to them. He was embarrassed but tried not to show it. They had won a victory, but a limited one. Their overriding mission to completely defeat or kill the Other or the Traitor or Thesi had not been achieved and he had to act like it had. But he and Gray had given them all another chance and the world was breathing again. He concentrated on that truth and tried to look proud of the lies he had told.

When they started discussing the terms of disengagement for the three armies in the Southlands, Eliti, Chan, and tribal, his mind wandered. He couldn't care anymore. Then the refugees from the Southlands showed up outside the tent demanding to know what was going on, and he volunteered to go out and speak to them. The falling barrier had frozen them up on the hill encampment, evidently. They had suffered the same fate as everyone else, just earlier. Conor filled them in. Some wanted to shake Conor's hand or kiss him. Gray was too imposing to be petted and Conor waved the most persistent ones off as best he could. They looked at him and Gray in awe and fear.

FALSE FAREWELLS

I never want to see that look again.
Neither do I. But we will.

That night, there were three huge celebrations and two small ones. There were places of honor for Conor and Gray at every table. The Eliti had their wine, the Chan had dark beer in huge kegs, and the tribes had fragrant hot drinks that did the trick for them. All of them shared what they had with the ragged Southlanders and the small remnant of Northerners. Most of them had died in the initial part of the attack as they had been near the rear of the column and had rushed at the hunters without hesitation. It was just Dvak and eight others now.

The Eliti army that Lady Telikonta had brought to the Southlands went at it harder than the rest. The survivors had fought the hunters twice and they were celebrating being alive as much as the victory over their mythological enemy. It was among those happy people that Conor felt the most uncomfortable. His sheer size was a daunting obstacle to normal conversation everywhere he went, but many of the Eliti had heard the old stories as children and then witnessed him and Gray fight the hunters and cover the world in darkness, just like the old myths prophesied. They were gods to them and any attempt at small talk or camaraderie faltered under the adoring or intimidated gaze of the soldiers.

Conor and Gray ended up standing with Nisi and Dareen, watching as soldiers reeled noisily around them. Telikonta had taken to her bed; she was very near to giving birth.

FALSE FAREWELLS

Dareen said, "Tomorrow, you and Gray will escort us back to the Empire where you can be properly recognized."

Conor grimaced. "I cannot express strongly enough how much I hate that idea. Not the escorting," he added, "the recognizing."

Dareen shrugged. "It is the price you must pay for our help. There is no way to smuggle you and Gray and that thing into the Empire. And if you come, the people will want to see you. Best let them and then get on with your life."

Nisi turned to him. "We have large estates in the countryside. Once the...formalities are over, we will take you there. We have a promise of peace from the tribes. You and Gray can rest and..." Her voice trailed off.

"I apologize, my lady," Conor said as he bowed slightly. "It is hard for me to show gratitude for the great service you have promised us. We are very tired of all of this. But we do thank you, Lady Dareen and Nisi. Now, we have other people to see."

Conor backed away, and Gray followed him.

"In the morning, then." Dareen smiled a little, Nisi beamed.

"In the morning."

Conor went to say goodbye to Gettil and Eromil next. The Chan were moving out early the next day and their celebration was somewhat muted by their preparations. Soldiers came and went from long tables spread with food and drink. They eyed the wild revelry of the Eliti warily, which made sense to Conor after having fought an all-out war of attrition with them not long ago. The Chan

FALSE FAREWELLS

army had suffered grievous losses under the nightmarish attacks of the Other and had chased a battle with the hunters for weeks only to have it end not long after it began. Their men were ready to leave this strange place and head south to the Consolidation. Their myths told them that the homeland was safe from war and they were anxious to get back.

They found Gettil and Eromil in the command tent. The Chan were a disciplined army in the field and, like their soldiers, they were both in part armour. Orange fires in tall braziers threw stark shadows and burned hot. The tent was very warm. After a mug of Chan beer and a quick toast to the fallen, Eromil started to thank Conor but he cut her off—firm, but friendly.

"You more than returned anything you got from me, Eromil, war wife of the god Shenzi."

She persisted. "You saved my life and I gave you my sword and—" She started to unsheath her blade.

Conor gently put his hand on hers. "And it is yours again, Eromil. Go back to the homeland with your people, where war cannot follow."

She bowed to him. Her pale blue eyes filled with tears as she stepped away.

Gettil came forward. "Know that you are welcome in the Consolidation, Conor and the Torit," Gettil said as he presented Conor with a short black dagger. His bow was brief and shallow. "Show this at the border and I will send Eromil to escort you. It would be our honour to show you our homeland."

"Thank you, Gettil. Safe travels, and I hope we meet again someday."

"I hope so as well, Conor," said Gettil. "But it will be in the Consolidation. I will never again come to the Southlands. It is a cursed place." Gettil spat out the last sentence.

Conor raised an eyebrow but said nothing. First Eromil, now Gettil. The Chan did not usually show emotion, but Conor understood.

Perhaps it is.
Yeah.

Conor bowed to them both and pushed his way out of the tent. The air outside was refreshingly cool and mist was falling again. He took a deep breath. Conor felt a bit better about the deal at that moment. All those people—Eliti and Chan—now had a chance to make a life for themselves.

They may fuck it up, but maybe not.
Right. To the tribes and then bed?
Don't forget the Northerners. Poor bastards.
Right.

The Clans were eating and drinking separately yet together. The leaders moved between the groups, talking and laughing and calling out clan members for recognition and gentle ridicule. Some looked up as Conor and Gray approached, then others noticed them. Soon, conversation came to a stop. Baragara came wobbling up beside them. He was a big man, like all the Dae'l, but he looked small and frail beside Conor. He was relaxed and intoxicated enough not to be in awe. He slapped Conor on the back.

FALSE FAREWELLS

"Big man!"

"Baragara. We came to say farewell."

"Right. Making the rounds, are we?" Baragara's voice had been thickened by the hot brew.

"Yes. To say goodbye," Conor raised his voice and spoke to all who could hear, "and thank you to the tribes. We owe them a great debt."

Baragara wagged a finger in Conor's face and said loudly, "Oh, we've seen you fight, Conor and the Hound, Gray. We know what you did." He waved at the watching crowd. "And even then, most of us thought the end of days was here. And they were—and then they weren't!"

He ended his sentence with a smile and spread his arms wide. That made some of the people around them laugh; even Conor grinned. The awed silence was broken. People went back to their food and drink. Men and women from the different clans came up and talked to them. The clothes they wore were loose and brightly coloured. Shirts and wide pants were in reds, yellows, and blues, faded and dirty from their long journey to the Southlands. Heavily muscled assault clan members, stocky archers, long-limbed scouts and then even their children thanked them, shook Conor's hand in double-handed grips, asked about Gray or just stood near. Baragara's familiarity helped, and the tribes had never been as intimidated by Conor as the Eliti. And he knew the tribes didn't have much use for hierarchy. In their understanding of Eliti mythology, Conor and the Hound were just man and beast, despite their power and responsibilities.

FALSE FAREWELLS

More and more people came to meet them. Conor nodded, smiled, thanked them back one by one—and almost forgot that he was a liar. Gray sat beside him and was admired from a respectful distance. Once in a while a bold or curious child would come near and stare, but never touch him, which he didn't mind.

Conor learned that the tribes were going to stay in the Southlands for a few weeks until the weather turned warmer and the paths to the west firmed up and were easier to walk. Then they would go back home, an agreement with the Empire in hand to let them pass into their forest and highland fortresses. It seemed everyone was tired of war and anxious to use the second chance they had been given. When Conor and Gray left them, explaining they had more people to see, it was without fanfare, and the tribes were singing of those they had lost in the war of the Lord and his Hound. It was low and melodic, sad, and yet strong.

When they reached the Southlanders they found out that many of them had left already to the encampment on the hill. There was shelter there, and food the Eliti and Chan had left in their dash to the battle with the hunters. What was happening around their small fires felt to Conor more like a wake than a celebration. His exploits were well known in the Southlands but this group of people were utterly broken by what had happened to them and their home. The coming and fall of the barrier was just the latest calamity. Even after their rescue they knew they were weak, scattered, and leaderless. On top of the depredations of the armies of the Believer, the

FALSE FAREWELLS

Other, and the hunters, the size and strength of the Chan, Eliti and tribal armies that were still here reminded them of this fact. As Conor walked among them the thing he heard them say most often was that they only hoped that they had homes to go to.

Perhaps we should stay and help them. They need it.

I understand that. But we must deal with Thesi and live up to our end of the bargain. It is our duty and the Empire is where we can do it best.

Conor nodded, his face grim. *Yeah. The Southlands must get along without us. Maybe some of the asshole lords or the patrons will be around to provide order.*

Maybe.

Neither of them voiced what they were thinking. They were tired of being looked to as saviours. The war was over. Let someone else take charge and shoulder the responsibility. None of the Southlanders noticed when they stole away after only a few minutes.

The last of the Northerners were sitting around a huge roaring fire. They were quietly talking to each other. Dvak and his black-leather-clad brothers rose to greet them.

"Conor and the Hound! Welcome." Dvak said, his arms held open. "Sit with us and tell us again of your mighty victory over the Traitor, Itax the demon."

Conor stifled a frown and Gray bumped his hip.

Maybe these guys have earned the truth.

No, Conor. No. Just tell the story and let them be as happy as they can be.

The faces of the hard men looking at him showed the devastation they felt. Most of their brothers had fallen in the first seconds of the battle, foolishly and bravely attacking the hunters. Their leader, Dvor, had been brutally killed. The images of his death would never leave them. His voice was what they needed and they would never hear it again. Conor didn't want to tell the lie, but if anyone had earned it, these men had.

"Of course, Dvak. We would be honoured."

He told them again of Gray and his imaginary deadly struggle with the Traitor. They toasted the victory with beer the Chan had given them. Conor drank deeply, honouring the sacrifices these men had made and the losses they had suffered. They were now so few.

"Will you start home tomorrow, Dvak?"

Dvak looked into the fire and then stirred the embers with a long stick. Heat flared and he leaned back, turning his head away. "I do not know. Itax is defeated, yes, but Dvor is gone and we have lost so many of our brothers. I am not sure of what kind of welcome we would get."

"You must be a hard people not to understand what has happened here," Conor said. They must know what you risked and what you have given."

"The elders expect much, it is true. Our women warriors will want to know where their husbands, sons, uncles, and brothers are. And why we walk the Earth and they do not."

Conor was immediately angry. "Tell them to find me, Conor, Lord of the Hound, and I will explain it."

Dvak turned to Conor. "If you came with us…"

FALSE FAREWELLS

"I'm sorry, Dvak. We cannot." Conor deflated just as quickly. "We have made promises to Lady Dareen and Nisi."

Dvak nodded imperceptibly. His bearded chin barely moved. "I understand. Perhaps someday you will come north. See our homes and tell the story of your victory."

"We will, Dvak. That is a promise. And we are proud to have fought beside you." Conor stood. Dvak and his brothers did as well.

He smiled but his eyes did not. "And that must be enough. We thank you, Conor and Gray." He held out his hand and Conor shook it. "It will be our privilege to spread the tale of your glory throughout the northern territories. And, because of you and Gray, we will be able to see our families again and perhaps they will allow us back into their lives."

"I hope so, my friend Dvak."

Conor could not think of anything more to say, so they walked away into the darkness.

Not a lot better than nothing for those guys.
Tough crowd up north, I guess. Let's get some sleep.

CH 24
LEAVING

Thesi—*Rilni*, Conor silently corrected himself—was up when they returned, sitting outside their tent, drinking wine. The six Eliti guards were different than the ones who had been there when they left but they were all watching him as intently as the first group.

Conor tried to dismiss them. "Thanks men, we appreciate your help, but we have it from here."

The soldiers regripped their spears, shuffled their feet and looked at each other, but did not move. Deciding whether to contradict a god or disobey their Mother was a difficult choice.

Finally, one of them spoke. "We have orders to stay until we are relieved, Lord Conor. Direct from Lady Dareen."

Gray rolled his eyes, pushed past Rilni, and went into the tent.

Conor pondered a response and then just said, "Alright. I'll leave you to it."

LEAVING

Conor heard a collective sigh of relief. They looked at Rilni even harder, who ignored them and kept taking long swallows from a large bottle.

Conor leaned towards him as he went in the tent and spoke in a low voice. "We start a lengthy walk tomorrow. We won't be slowing for you. Remember that."

"Yes, yes," Rilni said. "I'm aware. I'll be ready."

Conor left him by the fire and lay down beside Gray inside. For the first time in a very long time they had no responsibilities to take up in the morning. They both slept a deep and dreamless sleep.

The sounds of the moving armies woke them. They had said their farewells so they just stood in the morning haze while they ate and watched with Rilni's escort as the Chan and Eliti forces moved out. The soldiers in both armies were boisterous. They were going home. The sounds they made were so different from what Conor and Gray had heard from the same formations when they were moving towards the battle with the hunters. There were creaks of leather and wood, the snap of whips and shouted orders, and above all, the thud of marching feet—but these sounds had lost their foreboding power combined with the laughter and easy chatter of soldiers on the march in good weather in peacetime.

Like a great snake uncoiling, the Chan marched south down the road. The Eliti formed into their massive blocks of spearmen and moved cross-country, west, towards the plains that separated the Southlands from the Empire. It got quieter quickly. The sun shone stronger and it was almost warm.

LEAVING

Men came to pack their tent. Conor gestured to Rilni and Gray to come in before they did.

"So what are we going to tell whoever asks about you?" Conor said to Rilni.

"Don't worry about it. They won't."

"What do you mean? Why not?"

Rilni shook his head. "I mean I'm not completely helpless anymore. As far as anyone around here is concerned, I'm someone they know from back home. I'm Rilni, a clerk, a scribe in the service of Lady Dareen who has been tasked with writing down the history of the war of the Lord and his Hound." He winked at them. "Straight from the horse's mouth. That's why I'm staying with you. And they believe I've been with her all along."

"You can…?"

"Yes. I can put memories of me into their minds. It's better this way, isn't it?"

Rilni looked at Conor and then at Gray and then grinned. "No uncomfortable questions for you and I've got a job I only have to pretend to do."

Conor rubbed his face with his hands. "Alright, but no fucking around with Dareen or Nisi. They must know who you are. At all times."

"Right. I'll let you do the fucking around...with Nisi." Rilni giggled as he said this.

"Careful, Thesi," Conor said, his fists clenched, eyes narrowing. "Careful."

"It's Rilni now. You had better remember that. And alright. I was just—"

LEAVING

"Well, don't. You could slip and fall and end up with a broken nose."

Rilni rolled his eyes. "As if I couldn't fix that."

"But you won't, because you are Rilni now, remember? A very pretty young man who is more used to libraries and sitting rooms than marches and war. If your body gets a mark, it will stay."

Rilni eyed Conor warily. "So it's going to be like that, is it? A punch in the face if I say the wrong thing?"

Conor shrugged. "Not necessarily. I will treat you like the man you are supposed to be. And you will do the same for me. No more and no less. Other men will have to watch what they say about Nisi and Dareen around me. So will you."

"Alright, Conor," Rilni said, his hands up in mock surrender. "So, do I have to act tired on this trip?"

Conor grimaced. "Just shut up and pack."

The sun shone between fast-moving clouds as they got underway. It was almost warm, and very windy. They were to move in the van of Telikonta's force, independent of them but close enough to be protected if need be. Conor could not see what or who could threaten them but he wasn't in charge, so he went along without question. Dareen and Nisi rode in comfort in a wide enclosed coach set on springs and pulled by muscular black horses. Telikonta had a spare and she had lent it to them. Conor was offered a horse but after having a look at it, he decided he would walk. It was just too small. Gray trotted beside him. Rilni had batted his brown eyes at the older men

LEAVING

until one smiled back and he cadged a ride on the soldiers' supply cart.

Conor wasn't pleased but Gray reminded him, *It could have done that differently. Used its...power. It's better this way.*

Yeah. I guess.

Dareen's people are watching it. No matter what it does. It knows that.

Yeah.

Conor knew that many days of walking were ahead of them and that the sooner he relaxed into the semi-conscious state of just being, without expectation or anticipation, the better it would be for him. So he looked at his feet and concentrated on putting one down and then the other.

Once they got through the thin forests that edged the Southlands, the march to the Empire was easier, although walking in the muddy path made by the army in front of them made life difficult at times. Once on the plains, Dareen ordered her little force to veer slightly to one side so they didn't have to fight through the churned up ground left by Telikonta's soldiers.

The weather stayed fair. There was rain and wind on some days but the temperature was mild and to Conor and Gray it was an almost idyllic journey. They weren't desperately running into or away from deadly danger, or living in the dreadful grey-brown world after the barrier had fallen. The sky, whether blue or covered in clouds, was the right distance above them, and the rich black soil below was growing softer by the day. They were well fed, warm, dry most of the time, and out of harm's way.

LEAVING

Rilni rode with one man and then another. No one seemed to mind when he went from cart to cart. Conor assumed that Rilni made it so. He pretended to write their story as he sat. Conor watched him as he crossed his arms, acting as if he was deep in thought and then with his chin in one hand, he would scribble nonsense in a leather notebook. Rilni obviously thought it was an enjoyable part to play so far. Dareen's guards were always around him, but they were not a large group so it did not look odd. Conor was glad they were there.

Some days, Nisi walked with him. On other days it was Dareen. One was full of excitement and hope for the Empire, the other was apprehensive. Conor asked questions about the Empire, its people, and its workings, and just listened. This allowed him to learn more and to not talk about himself. Nisi was young and eager to explain her country and articulate her vision for it and did not notice his silences. Dareen replied only in generalities. They both knew Conor was not interested in a public role and she did not press him on his plans for the future.

One morning they found themselves winding through the gates, a series of crumbling walls that passed for the eastern boundary of the Empire.

Gray and Conor spoke as they did.

Not far to the Eliti roads.

When I put one foot on that brick, I'll believe we have truly left the Southlands behind.

I would imagine Dareen's people will meet her there and we'll get reinforced.

I hope so.

LEAVING

They walked for a few moments, looking up at the red brick walls that led to openings and then other red brick walls. They relied on the fact that someone up front knew which paths to take.

Are they going to honour us, like they said?

Yes. A parade through the capital, I believe.

Gray scoffed like only he could. It was a harsh guttural sound. Conor heard and felt the distaste Gray had for human sentiment.

I feel the same way. But we owe it to her. To them.

Gray did not reply, at first. Then he said, *Well, we are the Lord and the Hound. And we did save the world.*

Sort of.

Right. Sort of.

EPILOGUE

From his vantage point on the roof of the villa Conor could see woods, fields, and in the distance, the white peaks of the eastern mountains. It was early evening. It was calm and the heat of the day was dissipating. He often came up to watch the sun go down behind the trees. The table beside him had books and writing materials. He had remembered his ignorance about literally everything outside of the Southlands and how stupid it made him feel when he encountered the Chan, the Northerners, and even the Eliti. He was taking the time to learn about the world.

He walked away from the edge and looked down on the broad courtyard below. Dareen's guards had set up rings and were sparring in all three fighting disciplines, as they did every night. Conor watched. None of them were any good, but like most Eliti men, they loved the fights and were going at each other enthusiastically. They also knew he was paying attention, which only added to the intensity. Maybe I'll go down there one evening, Conor thought. Give them a few pointers. But not today.

One of the Eliti was tall and dark and reminded him of Rilni. They had left him in the capital with Dareen

EPILOGUE

and Nisi. He had asked to stay after the parade and the ceremonies which kept them there for over a moon. Gray had slept outside its door the entire time and there had been no incidents, whatever those were supposed to look like. After speaking with Dareen, Conor had agreed. Gray wasn't happy about it, but Dareen had forty men watching it in shifts. They didn't know why, but they were their Mother's men and they didn't need to know to be convinced of the necessity. Gray eventually gave in and together they travelled to the villa he was in now, deep in the countryside of the Eliton Empire. Rilni had waved goodbye with a silly grin on his handsome face. Conor could not fully trust him, but he gritted his teeth and walked away. He had to.

Nisi was coming to visit tomorrow or the next day. They had resumed their relationship, with Dareen's blessing. She was obviously hoping for a child out of the arrangement so they could start to judge whether or not Nisi was going to be an influential Mother in the Empire. Conor did not know what to think about being looked at like a stud horse, but he was deeply attached to Nisi and her presence and her touch were treasures to him. A child would be life-affirming for him and pragmatic from Nisi and Dareen's perspective, Conor thought. And having the Lord of the Hound as the father would only help Nisi.

Conor saw Gray returning from the scouting trip he made every day at this time. His path across the field from the woodlands was a dark furrow. There was no need for his patrol— the tribes and the Empire had agreed to a truce and peace talks— but Gray was a predator and

EPILOGUE

securing the place he was going to sleep was as natural as waking.

Conor took a deep breath and looked at the setting sun. It was an orange streak, flaring its light from behind white-blue clouds. The colours around him stood out, dark and light greens of the fields and forests and the deepening shades of blue in the sky above him. He could feel his heart beating and the warm air on his skin. Life in this world could be good, Conor thought. If Rilni plays his part, we have given them a chance.

Am I interrupting something poetic?
No. Not really.
You coming down to eat?
Yeah. I'll be there in a moment.

Conor took one last look, gathered up his books and notes and went down the stairs to eat and talk with his friend, Gray.

THE END

ABOUT THE AUTHOR

PF Legge is an over educated father, grandfather, husband, retired teacher, football coach and author. He was born in Toronto and has lived in southwestern Ontario his entire life, the last 45 years in London. He is the author of four

About the Author

other books; Almost a Myth, Slaughter by Strange Means, Better Strange and The Fire: Tales from the Southlands.
   http://www.pflegge.com
   http://www.@pflegge
   http://www.facebook.com/PFLegge
   http://www.instagram.com/pflegge3

ALSO BY PETER LEGGE

Almost a Myth

Conor is a law keeper, fighter and warrior. Gray is his Hound. Linked by a bond of mind and mission, they walk together through a world of political weakness and religious terror.

Their fractured land is threatened by The Believer, a figure from nightmares who lives in the minds of his followers, the Bonded. He desires to unite the Southlands by conquest and subjugation.

Conor and Gray, along with Lady Andaine, a fierce noblewoman, will gather an army to fight for the freedom of their homeland. And they will come to understand that their powerful link is part of a larger war for life itself

Also by Peter Legge

Slaughter by Strange Means

Conor led the army that won the war against the Bonded. Prophecies seemed fulfilled and peace at hand. Yet the conflict brought hungry empires and forces far worse than those of men into the southlands. And victory had not prevented Conor from being imprisoned and his homeland ravaged and occupied.

Alone and grieving, Conor faces new threats and the emergence of an ancient enemy as he fights his way across a chaotic landscape to find his friend and ally, the Hound Gray. In the Empire of the Eliton Conor must prove his worth in ritual combat and persuade the powerful Mothers to join his quest. Once together again, Conor and Gray must strive to save their home and their world.

Also by Peter Legge

The Fire: Tales from the Southlands

A carefully crafted book of short stories based in the same world as the the realistic and gritty fantasy novels 'Almost a Myth' and 'Slaughter by Strange Means'.

A soldier running from a burning city, a woman dreaming of a peaceful life past, a warrior on a deadly mission, a lawman investigating a murder with no killer: all these tales are set in a familiar yet distant world in turmoil.

Also by Peter Legge

Try and Other Stories

Try and Other Stories is a collection of science fiction and fantasy short stories set in familiar yet subtly different settings where the humanity of the characters and their thoughts, hopes and dreams remains the focus.

A frustrated soldier deprived of technology by alien tourists who want to hunt their exotic prey without interruption. An aging courier in a desperate encounter in a land controlled by jealous nobles. A street dealer squeezed between powerful drug lords and a surveillance state. A young cavalry officer fighting an enemy he does not understand. Two brothers squabbling while the destruction of all life on earth approaches.

Written in clean, clear prose these stories open windows to other worlds while providing insight into ours.

Made in the USA
Columbia, SC
29 January 2021